THE
SHOP
GIRLS
of LARK LANE

PAM HOWES

Bookouture

Published by Bookouture in 2018

An imprint of StoryFire Ltd.

Carmelite House
50 Victoria Embankment
London EC4Y 0DZ

www.bookouture.com

ISBN: 978-1-78681-471-5
eBook ISBN: 978-1-78681-470-8

Dedicated to the memory of the wonderful band of Liverpool musicians who are sadly no longer with us, including John Lennon, George Harrison and Billy Fury. Your music lives on in our hearts forever.

Chapter One

August 1945

Alice Lomax dashed a hand across her sweaty brow, and wrestled the final sheet out of the old washing machine and into a sink of cold water for rinsing, before feeding it through the mangle. She cranked the handle round and round, catching the drips in a bucket underneath. It had been a good idea of her husband Terry's to fix her mam's old mangle, as wringing out the wet sheets and towels by hand had been hard work, but the strength it took to turn the wheel on the contraption meant she'd have arm muscles to equal any of the fellas who worked down the docks at this rate. One day, when Terry managed to find a new job, they'd hopefully be able to buy another machine with one of those electric wringers on top that were all the rage now. Anything for an easier life. To make matters worse, she'd got her four-year-old daughter hanging around her legs again, wiping her sticky fingers on her skirt. There was never a minute's peace at the weekend.

'Cathy, if you've finished your toast and jam, go and find Daddy please, love. Tell him to wipe your face and hands in the bathroom. Let me get this lot out of the way and then we'll all go down to the park. You can have a go on the swings, and if you're a good girl he might buy you a cornet from the ice-cream man.' Alice hoped she sounded persuasive enough.

Cathy pulled a face as Terry came up behind Alice, slipped his arms around her waist and dropped a kiss on top of her head.

'Leave my mammy alone,' she shrieked, stamping her feet.

'Now stop being rude to your daddy,' Alice ordered, dropping the sheet into a basket on the floor with the rest of the washing. 'Say you're sorry. Look, Daddy is sad,' she cajoled as Terry did a pretend pout. 'Give him a big love better.'

'No!' Cathy folded her arms across her chest and stuck out her bottom lip in a pout that equalled her father's. She stomped out of the kitchen and into the back sitting room.

'I'm sorry, love,' Alice said to Terry, seeing his dark brown eyes cloud with hurt. Eyes just like their daughter's, and they both had the same thick, dark brown hair too. Peas in a pod, as everyone said. 'It'll take time. She's so used to being with just me and Brian or your mum. I'm sure you're not the only daddy to come home from the front line whose kiddies don't want to know. One day it'll click, and you and Cathy will be the best of friends, you'll see.'

Terry nodded and picked up the kettle, but not before Alice had seen him blink away tears.

'I do hope so,' he said quietly, filling the kettle at the sink and putting it on the gas hob. 'I've waited a long time to be with her.' He sighed. 'I'll make us a brew while you hang that lot out.'

'That'll be lovely.' She felt sorry for Terry. He was trying his best with Cathy, but the stubborn little madam was unbending.

Alice picked up the basket of washing and carried it into the small back garden, where the remains of a home-made wooden coop stood. It had housed her young brother Brian's two chickens during the war, when everyone was encouraged to be self-sufficient: to dig for victory by growing vegetables, and keep fowl for eggs, if they had the space. The elderly chickens had since been returned to the farm they came from and the coop would be chopped up and used as firewood when the winter months arrived.

Alice took a sheet from the basket, ready to hang. She didn't normally do the washing on a Sunday, but tomorrow she was going back to work at Lewis's store after a couple of weeks off with Terry, following his demobilisation. She'd used up all her annual holidays now, but it had been good to spend the time with him, getting to know one another again and adjusting to being a family. Prior to that, all they'd had was a one-night honeymoon in 1940, following a hasty marriage, before he was sent overseas with his troop. That one night together had resulted in the conception of Cathy, who Terry had only met for the first time in June.

Alice finished pegging the sheets and towels onto the washing line and pushed a wooden prop underneath to prevent them dragging on the small lawn. She chewed her lip as she wondered how best to help her little daughter and Terry to bond. The constant tantrums were wearing for them all. Later today they would be going to Terry's mother's place. Hopefully Granny Lomax would have a few suggestions as to what to do. She'd always looked after Cathy while Alice worked and she knew her granddaughter inside out. A nice walk in the park first and then a tasty Sunday dinner would finish the day off perfectly, Alice thought. Her brother Brian, who she'd brought up following the death of their parents, was out for the day with his pals but would be joining them for his meal later.

'Tea's brewed,' Terry shouted from the kitchen. 'Shall I bring it out and we can sit on your dad's bench and drink it?' He carried two mugs outside and Alice joined him on the old bench her dad had made, which sat under a shady apple tree.

She took a welcome sip and sighed. 'That's a good brew, just how I like it, sweet and not too strong.'

Terry nodded. He looked worried. 'Do you think she'll be okay with me tomorrow?'

Alice shrugged. 'I hope so. Until you start work again, we might as well as try. Oh, I know your mum will still offer to look after her, but it'll be best if we persevere and get her used to being with you. I think if I'm out of the way, she's got no choice but to let you do things for her. She's probably feeling a bit jealous because she's not getting all my attention right now. If it gets really bad and you find you can't cope then you'll have to walk her round to your mother's. But we won't know until we give it a try, will we?'

She leant her head against him and breathed in his scent. He'd used her Camay soap to wash with. It reminded her of the shower they'd shared on honeymoon, when he'd lathered her from top to toe in Camay bubbles and then made love to her while they were still in the shower. Mixed with the smell of his Old Spice shaving stick, it made her tummy flutter with longing. Her Terry; how dearly she loved him. She'd missed him more than she'd thought possible and it was good to have him home. Much as she loved Cathy and Brian, she wished with all her heart that she and Terry could have some time alone, even just for half a day. But it was unlikely to happen; no one had offered to look after the kids yet, so they'd just have to get on with it.

*

'There's your friend Sadie,' Terry said to Alice, pointing to a young woman clutching the hand of a small boy who seemed to be arguing with her. They were queuing at the ice-cream seller and the little boy was dancing impatiently from foot to foot as he tried to loosen her grip.

Alice called out and Sadie Romano turned and waved, a look of relief crossing her face.

'Thank God for that,' she said as they reached her side. 'He's being a right little pest today.' Sadie let go of his hand. 'Now see, Gianni, here's Cathy. I bet her daddy will know how to sail a boat better than Mammy will.' She held out a canvas bag with a large sailboat inside. 'There's also a sort of stick thingy in there with a hook on the end so you can pull the boat back in to shore,' she said to Terry. 'My brother bought it for him and was going to come with us today, but he's not feeling too good, so it's down to me. Gianni's upset because Uncle Harry promised to be here and also because I won't let him go near the lake on his own. He's so giddy; he's bound to fall in.'

Terry nodded solemnly. He bent down to speak to Gianni. 'Let's have our ice-creams and then we'll go to the boating lake and see what we can do. This is a job for men, wouldn't you say so?'

Gianni smiled, his big brown eyes lighting up. 'Can Cathy sail the boat with us?'

'If she wants to,' Terry said, looking at his daughter, who was holding onto Alice's hand. 'Want to sail Gianni's boat with us, Cathy? After we've had our ice-creams, of course.'

Cathy shot him a look from under her heavy fringe and gave him a half-smile and a slight nod. He smiled back and took his place in the queue. It was a small acknowledgement from her, but better than nothing.

'Shall we go and sit on that bench, Sadie?' Alice suggested. 'Terry will get our order. Wafers for us two and cornets for the kids,' she instructed Terry and led the way to a bench near the Palm House. Sefton Park was busy with families out for a stroll and the brass band was warming up on the bandstand ready for their afternoon session.

'Isn't it nice to see things getting back to a bit of normality?' Alice said. 'It's good to have all the children back with their families and people not looking as anxious, waiting for the air raid sirens to go off at any minute.'

'Yes,' Sadie agreed. 'And not having to cart flipping gas mask boxes everywhere as well makes life much easier. How's her ladyship getting on with Terry?' She nodded in the direction of Cathy, who was running around following Gianni as he played his favourite aeroplane dive-bombing game.

Alice puffed out her cheeks. 'We're still not making much headway, but I'm back in work with you tomorrow, so he's going to try and manage on his own with her. His mother will be in if it all goes pear-shaped, so he can whizz her round to hers. Hopefully he'll be working himself soon and then she'll be back with Granny Lomax as usual until she starts school in January. He's got a couple of late afternoon interviews booked in for next week to fit in with when I finish work, so with a bit of luck he might get a job soon. But we both think that him seeing to Cathy on his own for a few days while he's still at home may help them bond a bit better.'

'I'm sure it won't take long. He's very patient. Gianni loves Terry. It will all be fine. Here he comes with our wafers.'

Terry had given the kids their cornets and was making his way across to them. Gianni and Cathy had flopped onto the grass nearby and Terry sat down next to Alice on the bench.

'That's them two sorted while we enjoy these,' he said, handing Alice and Sadie their wafers, raspberry syrup dripping from the squares of greaseproof paper wrapped around them. 'Beautiful day, isn't it?' He looked up at the clear blue sky and smiled. 'You've no idea how good it is to see skies that aren't full of aircraft, and smoke and flames from planes that have been hit, and not knowing which ones have gone down. Ours or theirs.'

Alice smiled wistfully. 'We had our fair share of that here as well. Okay, we could dive down the nearest shelter while you boys had to be on your guard out in the open, but you can see for yourself the mess Liverpool is in. We got absolutely hammered.'

Terry nodded his agreement. 'I was shocked when we came out of Lime Street station on demob day and saw the state of some of the buildings nearby. It'll take years to rebuild, but we'll get there. We've a lifetime in front of us to get the place back on its feet again, and the workforce to do it now the boys are home. Oh, I know a lot of you women won't agree with that as we're slowly taking over your jobs again.'

'Hey, I don't mind in the least,' Alice said. 'I'd rather be selling knitting wool at Lewis's any day than making aircraft wings at Rootes. And I'm sure half the female workforce will probably agree with me now they're back in their usual jobs. And a lot want to spend time just being mothers again now their children are back home after being evacuated.'

'You know what we could all do with,' Sadie said, and licked the drips from her wafer.

'No, what?' Terry asked.

'A good night out at the Legion. What about next Saturday? We could rally the usual gang. Your old workmates, Alice; my friend Jenny; and we could ask Millie to sing.'

'Sounds like a great idea to me,' Terry said. 'I fancy a good night out. A few pints and getting together with old pals would be really nice. But you're back in work at the Legion next Saturday, aren't you, queen?' he directed at Alice, who worked part time at Aigburth British Legion as well as at Lewis's store.

Alice nodded. 'Yes, I'm due back in again next weekend, but I get regular breaks so can join you all when I'm having ten minutes. I think it's a good idea to have a bit of a reunion.'

'We'll ask my mum if she'll let Cathy stay over and Brian as well, maybe,' Terry suggested, nudging Alice slightly. 'Gives us the chance to have a bit of time to ourselves later, eh, gel?'

Alice blushed and smiled as he raised an eyebrow.

Sadie laughed. 'Have you two not had a minute to yourselves since Terry got home?'

'You guessed it,' Terry said. 'I suspect my mother thinks we're enjoying playing happy families after so long apart, but it would be nice to get a bit of time without the kids.'

'I'm sure it would. Is Millie home next weekend?' Sadie asked. Millie was Alice's best friend and former co-worker at Rootes, until she'd left to become a singer. 'I know that her and Jimmy take turns at staying at his mam's in Blackpool and at her mam's here.'

'She's in Blackpool this weekend and then back on Monday to help her mam with the hairdressing salon,' Alice said. 'Although her mam said she's shutting down now the war's over. Millie's dad said he wants his front room back now he's not out every night with the ARP. He was complaining about being invaded with gossiping women last time I went round to have my hair trimmed.'

Terry laughed. Millie's mam ran a front room parlour and he didn't blame Millie's dad one bit for wanting his privacy back.

'You can pop round in the week and invite her and Jimmy then,' he said. 'I'll nip in the Legion one night as well and tell Jack and Arnold to expect a party and to make sure the pianist is there to accompany Millie.'

'She'll love that,' Alice said. 'She's not done any singing for weeks. She misses the band as well. The war ending has brought such a big change for us all really. Millie was used to trekking up and down the country and entertaining the troops after she left Rootes. She said she was really bored recently.'

Sadie nodded as Terry got to his feet and picked up the bag containing the boat.

'Right, I'll go and do *my* bit of entertaining now. See if I can coax a smile from my daughter again. See you in a bit,' he said, making his way over to Cathy and Gianni, who were shrieking with excitement as he walked towards them.

'Have fun,' Sadie called. 'I've been thinking, you know,' she continued in a lower voice to Alice. 'Millie could do with looking for a proper job until her and Jimmy get married. I wonder if they'll settle here or Blackpool?'

Alice shaded her eyes as she watched Terry reach out for Cathy's hand. The little girl ignored him and ran on ahead towards the boating lake with Gianni.

'I don't think they've decided yet,' she said. 'But you know what a little home-bird Millie is; can't see her going too far from Liverpool. Maybe she could enquire at Lewis's and see if there are any jobs available with us. Have you heard any word from Luca since the war finished? I wondered if they'd got back safely to Italy.'

Luca was Sadie's estranged Italian husband and the father of Gianni. His family fairground had reportedly returned to Italy a couple of years ago when the government started rounding up Italian immigrants as prisoners of war.

Sadie shook her head. 'Not a dickey bird. I would imagine they'll let things settle before they get back on the road again. I'd like to know that he's okay, but that's all. I don't want him to come looking for us and if he does he's not taking Gianni. I'll do my best to be out of town if they show up in Liverpool. I just can't go back to that dangerous lifestyle. All those shady characters that come and go when the fair sets up and dismantles, and the packs of dogs roaming around. Never knowing whether I'm coming or going with all the moving around. I can't deal with all that again.'

Alice nodded. 'Don't blame you. You and Gianni are nicely settled back home anyway. He's enjoying school and you love your job.'

Sadie smiled. 'I do. But I'd love to work in a library eventually, so I'm going to start looking around when things settle down a bit more. I might not be qualified enough, but I won't know if I don't ask. Shall we walk over to the boating lake and take a peep, see if Cathy's talking to Terry yet?'

'Okay,' Alice said. 'But if she is, I don't want her to catch sight of me or she'll come running over and spoil the moment. Let's walk the long way round past the bandstand. It'll give them a bit longer. We can wave at Millie's dad if he's playing with the band this afternoon.'

Chapter Two

'Why don't you just bring her over here?' Granny Lomax suggested when Alice answered her query about Terry and Cathy. Alice had told her that things were still a bit iffy. They were in the kitchen washing up after dinner with the door closed so that Cathy, who was out in the garden playing with her ball, couldn't just walk in on them. Terry was sitting on the patio smoking a ciggie, watching as she threw the ball up into the air and tried to catch it. Young Brian was reading the Sunday papers in the lounge after clearing the table for them.

'It's very kind of you, but we don't want to do that,' Alice said. 'She needs to learn that she can't have things all her own way. Terry is trying really hard and today at the park she seemed more relaxed with him, although she wouldn't hold his hand on the way here. But it's a start.'

'Well, you know where I am if he needs me. Ah, son,' she said as he came inside. 'I was just saying to Alice that you can bring Cathy here tomorrow if she's being awkward.'

'Thanks, Mum, I'll bear it in mind. Er, I was wondering. Could she stay next Saturday night while we have a bit of a catch-up with old friends at the Legion? And perhaps Brian could stay as well?'

'I don't see why not.' Granny Lomax wiped the last plate and hung the tea towel up to dry. 'Brian will have to use a sleeping bag on the sofa as my spare beds are at your place now, but Cathy can share with me.'

'Brian won't mind that. Thanks, Mum.' Terry caught Alice's eye and winked. 'Alice is working, but she gets breaks so will join us when she can and we'll get time to have a dance, won't we, gel?'

'All being well.' Alice smiled. A nice night, a dance and a bit of time to themselves, something to really look forward to.

*

On Monday morning Alice dashed out of the house leaving her daughter screaming blue murder in Terry's strong arms. She waved at them from the corner and hurried to meet Sadie at the tram stop, Cathy's cries still ringing in her ears. She smoothed her dark brown hair down; she hadn't even had time to fashion it into her usual work style of a neat French pleat today. The tram was just coming into view as she puffed up to Sadie, and it pulled up beside them with a squeal of brakes.

'Right, let's go and see what delights await us today in haber-dashery,' Sadie said with a grin as they jumped on board. She led the way up the stairs. 'Not as crowded up here,' she said as they took seats near the back of the tram. 'How did it go?'

'I'm surprised you couldn't hear her screams from Aigburth Road,' Alice said. 'God help Terry. She's had her breakfast but I told him to make some toast and jam for her and her dollies as soon as he can. His mum's agreed to have her Saturday night so he can come to the Legion.'

'Oh, that's good. Jenny's coming over tonight,' Sadie said. 'I'll invite her along.'

'And I'll pop in and see Millie on the way home from work,' Alice said. 'It will give Terry and Cathy a bit longer.'

They travelled in companionable silence until the conductor called out, 'Ranelagh Street.'

'Here we go,' Alice said, jumping up and following the rush of passengers down the stairs. They hurried up to the second floor of the Watson Building, the only part of Lewis's that was still trading, amongst the noise and mess of the regeneration of the rest. People said it would take years before it was completed, but at least Alice and Sadie still had jobs while work went on around them.

The haberdashery department close to the top of the stairs was always busy. Wool was their biggest customer demand, as people bought it to knit new garments as well as darn and repair old ones. Rationing remained in force on many items and the make-do-and-mend attitude had been adopted by most Liverpool women. Clothing coupons were still in use, but a lot of ladies came to buy threads and trims to adapt garments picked up second-hand, mainly from Paddy's Market. Alice and Sadie did their best to make the counter and surrounding area as attractive as they could, displaying their wares in glass-topped and glass-fronted cabinets. Keeping the dust down was a particular problem; with demolition and rebuilding work going on left, right and centre, it was a never-ending task. The store had taken several direct hits during the Blitz. To have even one small part of it still standing was a miracle in itself.

Alice ran a cloth over the ever-dusty glass counters as Sadie looked through a fresh batch of Simplicity sewing patterns that had just arrived. She pulled one out of the box to show to Alice. 'This dress is lovely. Nice neckline too. It would suit you, Alice.'

Alice looked at the sketch of the full-skirted dress with its button-through front, and stylish sweetheart neckline. She smiled. 'Very nice, but I couldn't even afford the buttons right now, never mind the fabric to make it. One day, maybe.'

'You'll be fine once Terry gets fixed up with a job again. Won't be long now.'

Alice sighed. 'Let's hope not.' She brushed some white lint that had come off the duster and attached itself to the full skirt of her dark blue uniform dress, and adjusted her name badge pinned just below the neat white collar. At least she didn't need to worry about clothes for work as the Legion also provided her with a uniform: a nice fitted black skirt and white top. It was things to go out in that she struggled to afford. But as long as she could dress Cathy nicely and keep Brian smart in his school uniform, they'd manage for now. Terry had his navy pinstripe demob suit to wear for his interviews and his mother had bought him a white shirt and navy tie recently, so he'd do. She became aware of Sadie waving something at her and looked up from her daydreams.

'What?'

'Name tape,' Sadie said, holding up a roll of white cotton tape. 'I bought some of this for Gianni's clothes when he started school and so far he hasn't lost anything. You just write their name on with a special pen and the ink doesn't wash off. They have the pens in the stationery department. I know it's a while off yet, but you should get some in ready for when Cathy starts school after Christmas.'

Alice nodded. 'I think I've still got some left from when I labelled Brian's uniform when he started grammar school, but put me a yard to one side in case I need it. I know it goes quickly once the uniforms start to come in stock.'

*

Alice's feet were killing her by the time she'd got off the tram and walked to Millie's house. Millie lived on Bickerton Street, just off Lark Lane and adjacent to Lucerne Street where Alice lived. Standing all day in her black patent high heels was perhaps not the best way to treat her feet, but Alice couldn't afford to buy any new shoes right now and her only other pair were her white peep-toe summer sandals, which just wouldn't look right with her smart uniform. Still, having achy feet was better than the bad shoulders and neck she used to get on the production bench at Rootes, riveting the wings for the Halifax bombers. She knocked on the front door and when it opened blonde-haired Millie flung her arms around her in a welcoming hug.

'Come on in, we've just brewed up.' She held the door wide, beaming.

'You look happy. Are you just pleased to see me or have you won the pools?' Alice teased, stepping into the narrow hallway and following Millie into the back sitting room, where Mr Markham, Millie's dad, was reading his paper. She could smell perming solution and hear the soft murmur of female voices behind the closed front parlour door, and guessed that Millie's mam was seeing to a client.

'How do, chuck,' Millie's dad greeted her. 'Come and sit yourself down.' He gestured to a chair the other side of the hearth from where he was seated. 'Wife's busy in there.' He inclined his head to the adjoining wall and raised his eyebrows. 'God knows why women want that muck on their hair. Stinks of rotten eggs if you ask me.' He shook his head as Millie handed him a mug of tea and gave one to Alice.

'Does pong a bit. But if they get the desired effect then I suppose it's worth it,' Millie said, winking at Alice, who grinned. 'Have a slice of cake while we've got some left.' She held the plate out and Alice helped herself to a piece of Victoria sponge.

'Thank you. What a nice treat.'

'So to what do we owe this pleasure on a Monday afternoon?' Millie asked. 'Thought you'd be dashing home to see how Terry got on with Cathy.'

'Well I am, sort of, but I thought I'd give them a bit longer and come and catch up with you. And to ask if you'd like to join us on Saturday night at the Legion, maybe sing a couple of songs.'

Millie's blue eyes twinkled. 'Terry beat you to it. Asked me to come along, I mean. He was in the bakery when I popped in to get the cake. Getting a meat pie for his dinner and a jam tart for Cathy. We had a cuppa in the café.'

'Did they seem okay?' Alice asked, holding her breath.

'Absolutely fine. Best of friends. She was dragging him off for sweeties when we left.'

'Phew. Well that's good to know. But he can't give in to her with sweeties all the time. We've no spare money for treats – and I'd left something in for their dinner.'

'It's only the first day, so give him his due for trying. I'm sure he was doing what he thought was right. A few sweeties won't hurt, even if they're bribery ones.'

Alice took a sip of tea. 'I suppose so. So she wasn't crying or anything?'

'Nope. Looked happy as Larry as she pulled him into the newsagents.'

Alice laughed. 'Crafty little monkey.' She finished her tea and cake and got to her feet. 'Right, I'd better go and see how he's doing. So we'll see you on Saturday night then?'

'You will. Jimmy's over here this weekend. We'll look forward to it. Good luck to Terry with his interviews this week as well. He was telling me about them. Fingers crossed.'

'Thanks.' Alice said her goodbyes and dashed home. She let herself into an unusually quiet house and walked to the back sitting room, where father and daughter were fast asleep in the armchair, Cathy curled up on Terry's knee. Brian was home and at the table quietly reading the *Boy's Own* comic. He smiled and put his finger to his lips.

Alice shook her head and whispered, 'She won't sleep tonight now.'

'She might,' Brian whispered back. 'They've been to the park and he said she'd run him ragged. A quick nap now before tea won't hurt her. What *is* for tea, Alice?' He grinned, his blue eyes hopeful. 'I'm starving.'

'You always are.' Alice laughed. 'Anyway it's egg and chips as usual on a Monday night. I'll just get changed out of my uniform and make a start.'

*

Alice curled up next to Terry, relishing the peace and quiet as they relaxed in the front room and listened to the wireless.

'You did really well today, love,' Alice said. 'I hope she's as good for you tomorrow.' Cathy was now in bed, a little later than usual, but Brian had been right, she'd been tired again after tea. Following a quick bath, she'd gone out like a light. Brian was upstairs finishing his homework before getting into bed.

'She wasn't too bad at all considering the racket she made as you left this morning,' said Terry. 'Bet the neighbours thought she was being murdered.'

Alice laughed. 'Why don't you come down on the tram tomorrow and meet me from work? Just for a little ride out. You could take her to see if there are any big ships in down the docks first. She could at least look at the ferries if there's nothing else. Bet she'd love that. The only boats she's ever seen are the ones on Seffy Park boating lake.'

Terry rooted in his trouser pocket. He pulled out a squashed packet of Woodbines and sighed as he retrieved a slightly bent-looking ciggie.

'Last one,' he said, looking at it sadly, 'so best make the most of it. Let's hope I get one or other of those jobs this week. I'd love to go back and finish my engineering apprenticeship, but we need a proper wage coming in for a year or two to get us on our feet so I'll take anything within reason. But yeah, we'll come and meet you from work; it'll be a change for her. Pity we've no spare money to take her out for tea to Lyons's. Mum used to take me after school and they always had chocolate cake. One day though, eh?'

Alice nodded. 'The Tate and Lyle's job sounds okay, doesn't it? Foreman position should earn you a decent wage.'

'Probably the better of the two,' Terry said, getting up to reach for a box of Swan Vestas off the mantelpiece. He lit his ciggie and took a long drag, his eyes closed with pleasure as he exhaled slowly. 'I'll have half now and save the rest for tomorrow,' he said.

'I'll go and see if Brian's finished his homework and then I'll make us a brew,' Alice said. 'Fancy a slice of toast? I'm sure Brian will want one when the smell reaches his nose.'

'Go on then. Put a scrape of jam on it. Let's live dangerously.'

*

Cathy didn't like the noise and smells down at the docks. She whimpered and pulled on Terry's hand.

'Okay, gel; let's go up and meet Mammy from work, eh? Bit noisy, isn't it?' He hoisted her onto his shoulders and set off. He felt shocked at the sorry state of everywhere they passed. Down near the Dock Road and the immediate areas it was like one huge demolition site. Row upon row of bombed-out terraced houses and tenement buildings, like blackened teeth in a gaping mouth, no roofs or windows. Gangs of workmen were in the throes of pulling them down and clearing the land of rubble, ready for the rebuilding of new homes and flats as promised by the local authority. Terry and Cathy hurried past boarded-up shops, schools, churches and pubs, all gone or nearly gone.

What a mess. Apart from Lime Street and his own home, this was the first time Terry had ventured further than the Lark Lane area since his demob. He couldn't begin to imagine how terrifying it must have been for the wives and vulnerable children left at home. How terrifying it must have been for Alice, Cathy and Brian. It made him realise how lucky he was to still have a wife and child to come home to. Alice hadn't told him too much bad news in her letters as she'd always tried to keep things cheerful, and had written mainly about Cathy and how she was growing up into a proper little girl. She'd really gone through the mill, giving birth to Cathy in a shelter during the middle of an air raid and surrounded by her workmates. It had been no picnic.

He'd make it up to her though, as soon as he could. He'd work hard and show her how grateful he was that she'd held the fort so well, in spite of her losing her mam and her older brother Rodney while Terry was away. She and Brian had inherited the family home and Alice had made it nice for them all the best she could with the little money she had. And hopefully, once they'd got a few bob behind them, they could think about extending the family. Have another baby together that he could be there for, to see it grow up, and to support Alice right from the start. A little brother or sister for Cathy.

*

Alice put the finishing touches to the cottage pie she was making. She popped it into the oven to brown the mashed potato topping, and turned the light up under a pan of sliced carrots. Brian had taken Cathy down to the bakers for a loaf, and Alice was waiting on tenterhooks for Terry to return home from today's interview. She went into the back sitting room to set the dining table under the window. As she laid out knives and forks she thought about Terry's disappointed face when he'd come back yesterday. That job interview hadn't gone well. Unbeknown to him when he'd applied for the job, it involved driving a van, and Terry didn't drive, although it was something he planned to learn to do when he could afford it. He'd told her there were ten other people being interviewed so he'd come straight home; there was no point in hanging about, as someone who could drive would be given the job no doubt. Today he'd gone to the Tate and Lyle's refinery on Love Lane in Vauxhall, to interview for the foreman job.

The front door flew open and Cathy rushed in followed by Brian and Terry. 'We found Daddy,' Cathy shrieked excitedly. 'He came home on a tram.'

Alice smiled and looked at Terry, who was beaming. 'Did you…?' She hardly dared to say it.

'I did, gel.' Terry grabbed hold of her and dropped a kiss on her lips. 'And I start on Monday. So I'm afraid my days of being chief baby-minder are over.'

Alice laughed and hugged him. 'Oh, I'm so glad.'

'Can Granny mind me again?' Cathy asked, jigging from foot to foot.

'Yes, love,' Alice said, feeling relief wash over her at the thought of another wage coming in at last.

'Oh goody. Daddy can't make cakes. Granny can.'

Terry laughed. 'I don't measure up, do I? But I think me and Cathy are on the way to becoming good pals, even though I can't make a cake.'

Cathy nodded. 'Read me a story after tea then,' she demanded, thrusting a book at him. 'I like this one. Three little pigs.'

Terry laughed and gave her a cuddle. 'Bit of a trek on the tram to Love Lane though,' he said to Alice. 'I need to get my motorbike roadworthy again. I'll take a look at it on Sunday when we go to my mum's. See what needs doing.'

Brian's face lit up. 'Can I help you with it? I love motorbikes. Our Alice hates them. She wouldn't even let me sit on it while you were away.'

'I know she does, lad, and so does my mum, but until we can afford a car it's better than nothing. And yes, you can help me.'

Alice chewed her lip. The thought of Terry riding that flipping bike filled her with dread, but he was right. It was a fair trek across to Love Lane, so needs must.

'I'll go and dish up while one of you takes Cathy up to the bathroom to wash her hands.' She smiled, putting the thoughts of the bike out of her mind for now. No point in worrying before she needed to. 'Good job it's payday tomorrow. You can have a pint or two to celebrate on Saturday night.'

*

Alice woke from a deep sleep and lay listening to the muffled sounds of crying. Cathy? She rolled onto her back and reached her arm out to Terry's side. But he wasn't there. She sat up and switched on the bedside lamp. Terry was on the floor curled into a semi-foetal position, his pillow wrapped around his head, sobbing. As she slid out of bed he began to scream and thrash around, his arms flailing above his head. She hurried around to his side and dropped down beside him. She couldn't remember if you were not supposed to wake someone from a nightmare, or was it sleepwalking? Alice sat by the side of the bed and rubbed his back gently, making soothing noises to him. After a few seconds that seemed like hours he woke up and stared at her, panting, terror in his eyes.

'Terry,' she whispered. 'It's okay, darling. It's me, Alice. You've had a bad dream. Let's get you back into bed, come on.' She helped him to his feet and he clung onto her.

'I thought I was back in France,' he whispered. 'I thought they were going to kill me.'

'You're safe,' she said, as he lay beside her. She cuddled him close.

'It must have been my walk through the bombed-out city that triggered the nightmare,' he said. He took a slow deep breath, sweat still shining on his forehead. 'I'm lucky to still have you and our baby.'

Alice smiled and kissed him. 'And I'm lucky to still have you,' she said, hoping the nightmare was a one-off and wouldn't happen again. He'd seemed genuinely terrified and he was still shaking as she held him close.

*

Alice looked across the crowded concert room at the Legion and smiled as she saw Terry talking animatedly to Jack Dawson, the barman, who had gone out to collect empties. She pulled a pint for the customer standing at the bar in front of her and poured a gin and tonic for his wife.

'Put the change in your tips, chuck,' the man said and picked up his drinks.

'Thank you,' she called after him and dropped the few pennies into the pint pot where she and Jack pooled their tips. It was mounting up quickly tonight. They were really busy and, in spite of hardship, most customers had been telling them to keep the change. There'd be a few extra shillings to take home with her wages later to eke out next week's housekeeping money. She might even be able to treat Terry to a packet of Woodbines as a surprise to last him until his first pay packet.

Jack put the empties onto the bar and Alice took them to the sink to wash while he collected more.

'You okay, gel?' he asked as he limped back towards her, his hands full. Jack had lost half his right foot in a shooting accident before the war got started properly. He'd been medically discharged from his soldiering duties and had thrown himself into helping at the Legion and raising money for injured soldiers by organising shows and raffles. 'I'll just finish collecting pots and then you can take a break with your hubby and mates. Great to see everyone enjoying themselves again, isn't it? Good to have you back working again as well. I've missed you.'

Alice smiled. 'Aw, thank you, Jack. I've missed you too. It's nice to be back at work. I'll pour myself a sherry ready to take across for my break.'

'Pour me a scotch while you're at it. Make it a double. Back in a minute.'

Alice poured the drinks and waited for Jack's return. He liked his whisky, did Jack – a bit too much, some said. But Alice knew he drank to mask the nerve pain in his injured foot at times and tonight, with the steward and his wife being away for the weekend, they were extra busy and he might be feeling the pain more.

*

Terry smiled and moved over to make room for Alice as she joined the noisy table. She dropped a kiss on his lips and sat down beside him, raising her glass to everyone.

'This was a good idea of Sadie's,' she said. 'Lovely to see my old workmates again.'

'Nice that you've all kept in touch,' Terry said.

'Well, Freddie and Marlene, along with Millie, are Cathy's god-parents, as you know, so we'll always be in touch with them. Talking of Millie, she and Jimmy should be here soon too. They're a bit late. Jimmy must have got delayed on his travels from Blackpool.'

The doors flew open as she spoke and Millie and Jimmy hurried inside. Jimmy went to the bar and Millie looked over as Freddie shouted to her. She waved and came over to the table, giving hugs and kisses all round.

'Lovely to see you all again,' she said. 'I'm so excited about tonight. A bit nervous as well, because I haven't sung for a while.'

'I'm looking forward to hearing you sing,' Terry said. 'It's a first for me.'

'Oh, you're in for a treat,' Freddie said. 'She's got the voice of an angel, has our Millie.'

'I'll have a quick drink first to calm my nerves,' Millie said, grinning at Freddie. 'Then I'll go and see Jack and the pianist to ask what time they want me to start.'

*

Jack introduced Millie and she began her first spot with 'That Old Black Magic'. She was soon into the flow, flinging back her head, long blonde hair swishing around her face and shoulders. The claps and cheers and shouts for more echoed around the room. Next came 'Swingin' on a Star', followed by Billie Holiday's wistful 'I'll be Seeing You'.

Alice felt a mix of pride and emotion. Pride at seeing her lovely friend giving her all, and emotion, because the song reminded her of being without Terry for all those years. He tapped her hand and nodded to the dance floor. She got to her feet and he took her in his arms. They swayed together, eyes closed, lost in the music. Her head on his chest, Alice breathed in the scent of him. She felt a tremor go through her and was so glad they'd have the house to themselves when they got home.

As the audience rose to its feet and applauded, Millie took a bow and blew kisses, telling them she'd be back later to do an Andrews Sisters spot with her best friend Alice. Cheers and whistles followed and Alice smiled. They'd always finished Millie's second spot with a duet or two. She walked with Terry back to his seat and then hurried behind the bar, where Jack raised an eyebrow at her flushed cheeks.

'On a promise then, is he?' he said, smirking.

'Jack, don't be so smutty. That's the first dance we've had for over five years.'

'Only teasing, queen,' he said, pulling a pint and banging it onto the bar. 'Here, take him that, from me. Right, who's next?' he called, turning his back on Alice.

Alice hurried over and gave the pint to Terry, who raised it in Jack's direction. 'Thanks, mate,' he mouthed as Jack nodded.

Following a mad rush at the bar while everyone got a refill, Jack nipped to the stage and announced Millie's second spot. She beckoned to Alice, who looked at Jack.

'Can I? It can be my second break.'

'Yeah, go on. The bar's quiet for now.'

Millie began to sing 'Don't Fence Me In' with Alice harmonising with her. They bowed to the applause and wolf-whistles and grinned at each other. Alice looked across at Terry and Jimmy, who were staring open-mouthed at the pair as they sang 'Rum and Coca-Cola' and couples got up to dance. She smiled at Sadie, who was dancing with Freddie, Alice's foreman from Rootes. More people took to the floor as they sang 'Don't Sit Under the Apple Tree' and then finished with 'Boogie Woogie Bugle Boy'. And in spite of not having a band to back them, Alice felt they'd carried it all off well with the piano man's help. She looked over at Jack, who was looking at his watch, an impatient expression on his face.

'I'd better go back to the bar while you finish off,' she whispered to Millie. 'I'll see you later.'

Jack announced last orders just before Millie began her final songs and Alice didn't have time to think as she pulled pint after pint and poured sherry and gin for the ladies.

'I gather you enjoyed that?' Jack said as a lull descended.

'I loved it,' Alice enthused.

'Hmm.' Jack nodded. 'Can't say as I'd be happy if fellas were wolf-whistling at *my* woman. Surprised Terry puts up with it.'

Alice stared at him and shook her head. 'Terry doesn't mind. He's not the jealous type. Thank goodness.'

Jack shook his head and pushed past her to go and collect empties. Alice wondered what had made him say something like that, but was too busy to let it bother her for long. She just wanted to get cleared up as quickly as they could so she could get off home with Terry, to their much needed night alone.

Chapter Three

December 1945

Leaving Terry snoring gently, Alice slipped out of bed, pulled on her dressing gown, slid her feet into fluffy slippers and crept down the stairs into the back sitting room. Shivering, she banked up the cinders in the fire grate with a shovel of nutty slack from the brass coal scuttle, threw on a firelighter and some twists of newspaper and ignited the lot with a match. Once the flames were roaring up the chimney, she drew back the curtains and grimaced at the dull grey sky that looked heavy with rain, or maybe even snow. It was certainly cold enough for it, as her mam would have said. In the kitchen she put the kettle on the hob and spooned tea leaves into the old brown pot that had been in use since Alice was born. Yawning, she stretched her arms above her head. Just over one week to go to Christmas and she was so looking forward to it this year.

It would be the first Christmas of six without the war and the first as a proper family, but sadly, the second without her lovely mam. As she rinsed two mugs at the sink, Alice thought back to Mam's final Christmas in the convalescent home. She'd passed away not long after.

While the kettle boiled she went to pull back the curtains in the front room, smiling as she sniffed the pine-scented air. They'd decorated the best room with a real tree this year, complete with lights and baubles, and had hung crepe paper streamers on the walls and ceiling. Now the blackout linings were down, the criss-cross tape removed from all windows, and with the curtains remaining open until late at night, it was a joy to see all the pretty trees twinkling in the windows on Lucerne Street after such a long time of nothing but total blackness.

The festive air continued in the shops on Lark Lane. Although there were still shortages and rationing on many goods, things were easing slightly and people were looking relaxed again. The family had been invited to Terry's mother's for Christmas dinner and Alice was looking forward to it. Granny Lomax's farmer friend had promised her a turkey this year. Terry had originally invited his mother here, but she was having none of it, and to keep the peace, Alice had persuaded him to go along with her plans. Granny had come to them last year while Terry was still away on the front, and insisted it was her turn to host this time. Brian wasn't bothered either way, as long as he was fed and watered, and Cathy was always happy to spend time with her granny.

Back in the kitchen Alice brewed the tea and poured it into the two mugs. She popped the cosy on the pot and carried the mugs carefully up the stairs. Cathy and Brian were still sleeping, but Terry was awake, lying with his hands under his head on the pillow. He smiled, brown eyes twinkling, as she placed the mugs down on the bedside table.

'Come on, get in quick,' he said, throwing back the covers on Alice's side of the bed for her to climb in beside him. She snuggled close and he kissed her, running his hands through her long brown hair, fingers tangling in the waves. She loved these few precious minutes with him before the kids woke up. Now a daddy's girl, Cathy would be in soon with a book for Terry to read to her. She loved that he could do all the voices to the characters and he made her laugh.

Brian and Terry were getting along well and, with the exception of the motorbike issue, Alice was pleased that Terry had helped fill the gap that Rodney's death had left. Brian needed a big brother. He was desperate for a go on Terry's Harley-Davidson bike that he'd kept stored in his mother's garage during the war, but Alice had forbidden Brian to get on it.

Last night as they'd got ready for bed Terry had casually let it slip to Alice that Jack had offered his services when he was ready to work on the bike. Terry had been to the Legion for a couple of pints and he said they'd discussed getting together soon at his mother's house to take a good look at the Harley and see what work was required to get it back on the road. After standing unused for so long, the bike would need a complete overhaul and a good servicing before it was ready to ride again.

Now Terry was working again he'd been saving up for any parts the bike would need. He wanted to get it up and running as soon as possible so he could use it for his daily travel to Vauxhall instead of dashing out to jump on the overcrowded trams each day. Alice still wasn't happy about Terry riding his bike, but at least it meant he'd be home a bit earlier than he would using the trams.

Alice finished her tea and Terry took the empty mug from her and pulled her into his arms. The door opened and their daughter ran into the room, giggling. She bounced onto the bed and squeezed in between them.

'Passion killer,' Terry said, tickling Cathy until she screamed for mercy. 'That's what you are, a right little passion killer.'

'Passion killer,' Cathy repeated, grinning. 'I want my toast and chucky egg now.'

'Oh you do, do you?' Terry said. 'Demanding little monkey, isn't she, Mammy?'

Alice raised an eyebrow. 'You've got your mother to thank for that. She's always given in to her every whim.' She lowered her voice. 'And be careful what you say to her, she tells Granny everything!'

'Does she indeed?' Terry grinned and slid out of bed. 'Mother was the same with me though, spoiled me rotten. But I've turned out all right, haven't I?'

'If you say so!' Alice teased. 'You'll do, I suppose. I'd better get up. No lie-in even on my day off with this one. And as soon as Brian gets scent of the toast he'll be up wanting breakfast too.'

Downstairs Alice put a saucepan of water on to boil for the eggs and sliced some bread. She turned on the grill and stood with her back to the sink while it heated up, deep in thought. On the surface of it Terry seemed fine, but sometimes at night he still had a recurring nightmare where he thrashed around in his sleep, crying out and howling for mercy. It made her blood run cold, imagining what he'd endured while abroad. When he awoke, sweat dripping from him, he refused to talk about the horrors that still haunted him. He'd told her he wanted to shut it all out of his mind now that he was home, but Alice knew it was impossible. What those poor men had gone through didn't bear thinking about. All she could do was support him and hold him until the terrors passed and he fell back to sleep.

Millie said Jimmy was the same and she hoped the nightmares would pass or become less frequent once they were married. Millie had accepted Jimmy's marriage proposal on the platform of Lime Street station on the day he and Terry were demobbed. They'd now set the date for Valentine's Day in February. Prior to their engagement they had only met once, on the day Alice married Terry; Millie and Jimmy had been their witnesses at the wedding ceremony. The pair had written to each other throughout the war and become close enough to fall in love. Alice smiled as her thoughts veered all over the place with happy memories. Their friends' wedding was something to really look forward to next year.

*

Alice groaned when Cathy was up at the crack of dawn on Christmas Day and rushed into their bedroom, dragging her sleepy parents down the stairs, whooping with delight at the sight of the gaily wrapped parcels under the tree. Cathy flopped down on the floor with a bulging stocking that she'd pulled off the end of her bed and proceeded to empty all the little things Alice had sought out, secretly wrapped and kept hidden away. Wax crayons, a colouring book, colourful ribbons and matching hair slides; a tangerine, an apple and a shiny half-crown tucked in the toe.

She shrieked excitedly and put everything carefully to one side while she unwrapped the parcels under the tree. A chubby teddy bear with a red bow around his neck from her godfather Freddie and his wife Rose; a knitted cardigan in a soft shade of pink from godmother Marlene; a dolly wearing a nurse's uniform from Millie and Jimmy (a timely reminder to Alice that Cathy might just decide to indulge her mother's dreams of becoming a nurse one day); a teddy bears' picnic jigsaw puzzle from Brian; and a beautiful red velvet party dress from Granny Lomax.

'What a lucky little girl you are,' Alice said.

'Now it's Mammy's turn,' Terry said, handing Alice a tiny red square box that he pulled from his dressing gown pocket.

'For me?' She opened it and gasped. Nestling inside on white satin was a ruby and diamond eternity ring. 'Oh, it's beautiful, Terry, thank you so much.'

Terry smiled and slid it onto her finger just above the wedding band he'd given her five years ago. 'You waited an eternity for me, or that's what it felt like, so it seemed appropriate to give it to you.' He kissed her and she flung her arms around his neck.

'Daddy's turn now.' Cathy pointed to a large parcel with Terry's name on it.

Alice handed it to him. 'Now, this doesn't mean I approve, because you know I don't, but if you're planning to ride the damn thing, I'd like to see you dressed properly to protect your body.'

Terry tore off the wrapping paper and looked at the brown leather jacket lying on his lap.

'Wow, Alice, a biking jacket; and a warm one at that.' He stroked the thick sheepskin lining. 'This will keep me snug as a bug. How on earth did you manage to get such a luxury? It must have cost you a fortune, love.'

'Lewis's staff discount comes in handy,' she said. 'And I've been saving my Legion tips for weeks. As soon as you mentioned doing the bike up I decided there and then on what I was getting you this year and I had it put away as it was the only one in the store.'

He laughed. 'Beats the usual socks and hankies into a cocked hat!'

'Ah, well,' she said, trying not to giggle, and handed him a parcel from his mother. They both burst out laughing at the contents of black socks and white, initialled hankies.

'Ah, here's our Brian. Come on and open your parcels, lad,' Terry said as Brian stumbled into the sitting room, brown hair standing on end and his old pyjamas at half-mast around his shins. 'Think we might have chosen the right thing for you, me laddo, eh, Alice?' He handed Brian a package that contained new navy and white striped pyjamas and a pair of tartan slippers. 'Just what you need, eh, mate?' he said as Brian nodded happily.

'I'll go and make a start on the bacon sarnies while you lot clear away the wrappings,' Alice said. 'Put them on the fire. I'll call you when breakfast is ready.'

*

Granny Lomax admired Alice's eternity ring but frowned when Terry modelled his new biking jacket.

'I hope this doesn't mean you're going to be tearing around on that contraption again, Terry Lomax. You know how much I hate you riding it. I'm surprised at you, Alice, for encouraging him.'

'I didn't. And he's going to ride it whether we like it or not,' Alice replied firmly. 'So it's better that he's warmly wrapped up when he goes out on it.'

'I suppose so.' Granny pursed her lips. 'And don't you go getting any ideas about having a go,' she said to Brian. 'You're too young. Now then, let's have a look at what Cathy has got in her bag. Oh, aren't you a lucky little girl. What are you?'

'A little passion killer,' Cathy replied with wide-eyed innocence as Alice blushed and shook her head in Terry's direction. 'That's what Daddy said. Didn't he, Mammy?'

*

After a turkey dinner complete with all the trimmings it was nice to relax and listen to the King giving a completely different type of speech than the ones he'd given over the last few years. Afterwards, Brian and Terry announced they were going outside to the garage to take a look at the Harley.

'Don't let Brian get on it,' Alice called after them.

'Nobody's getting on it,' Terry said. 'Well, apart from having a bit of a sit on it. We can't go anywhere. It's got no petrol for starters. I just want to have a look at the tyres and see if they're still usable. I'm going to start buying the things I need each week now, a bit at a time, and then we'll get it back on the road come spring. Jack's really good with bikes. Always the one to go to when something needed fixing. Can't imagine he's lost his skills, even if he doesn't ride one now. He's the only one of my old mates that can drive as well, so he knows what he's doing around engines. He should have been a mechanic instead of a barman. He was supposed to be working mainly on servicing tanks when he had the accident with the gun. Shame really. He's wasted pulling pints.'

'Well, it can't be helped, and he's a good barman,' Alice said in Jack's defence. 'He was telling me the other day that when Arnold retires soon he might consider applying for the steward's job at the Legion. But he needs to put money down, it's called a bond, except he's not got enough saved up yet. It's a shame, because it would give him a nice place to live as well if he could manage to get the money together. He'll lose his chance unless he can borrow it from somewhere.'

Terry nodded. 'Well if he can manage it, it sounds like a good plan, *if* he doesn't drink the bar dry while he's running it. He used to love a drop of the sauce and I doubt that'll have changed.'

'It hasn't,' Alice said. 'But I'm sure he'd love helping you with the bike.'

When Brian and Terry went outside, she did the washing up while Granny played with Cathy. Through the kitchen window she watched Brian sitting on the Harley, pretending to rev it up, his delighted grin splitting his face. Alice sighed. The wind was whipping his hair into his eyes as though he was riding along. She thought about Sadie and how she'd left Luca Romano, Gianni's father, because of her fear of the Wall of Death ride that he worked on at the family fairground. She didn't blame Sadie one little bit. It was bad enough thinking of Terry riding daily to Vauxhall and back on a flat road, without thinking about him doing it for a living. The walls of the wide barrel that Luca rode his bike around were steep, according to Sadie, several feet off the ground, and he climbed from the bottom, circling round and round until he arrived at the top, where the crowd cheered him on. Alice shuddered, thinking about it. If Luca fell from that height he could break his neck. It really didn't bear thinking about.

Brian clambered off and Terry climbed up onto the seat. He stood up on the pedals and waved at her. She felt an involuntary shiver run from head to toe. A little ghost running over her grave, as her ex-workmate Marlene would have said when anyone got the goosebumps.

Millie and Jimmy were joining them at five o'clock for a turkey sandwich and a glass of sherry. It would be lovely to see them.

Millie – who had left her job working with Alice at Rootes to sing with a band that went from base to base, entertaining the troops – had said over a recent cuppa that she was hoping to return to singing full time in dance halls up and down the country now that the war was well and truly over. She was a good hairdresser though, and in Alice's opinion, she'd be better off trying to get a job in a professional salon and training properly once she and Jimmy had decided where they were going to live when they were married. With Jimmy being a Blackpool boy they might even want to move away from Liverpool. How on earth the marriage would work if Millie *did* choose to sing professionally again, Alice didn't have a clue.

She finished the washing up, wiped the pots and hung the tea towel up to dry. She popped her head around the sitting room door. 'Shall I butter the bread ready for tonight's sandwiches?'

'Yes please, Alice.' Granny, whose head was swathed in bandages, looked up from the sofa, where she was lying down. 'That would be lovely. We're playing doctors and nurses. I'm the patient, as you can see. I do hope Cathy's bedside manner improves if she decides to take up nursing for real when she's older!' She stopped talking as Nurse Cathy rammed a toy thermometer into her mouth and said, 'Just be quiet, lady.'

Alice laughed and went back into the kitchen, leaving them to it.

*

'Canada? But what about your mam and dad, and your singing?' Alice stared open-mouthed at Millie and Jimmy, who were seated side by side on the sofa and had just calmly announced they planned to emigrate to Canada in a year or two.

'I'm sure she'll be able to sing over there, and her parents can visit us whenever they want to,' Jimmy said, taking hold of Millie's hand and lacing his fingers through hers.

'But why Canada?'

Jimmy shrugged. 'I met some real nice Canadian servicemen while I was in the army and they said their country is crying out for skilled tradesmen. I'm a bricklayer by trade, even though I worked in the family fishing business for a while before the war. I could get a really good job out there. Millie can work if she wants to, but probably won't need to. The houses look lovely on the pictures we've seen, and they're cheaper than here. I just think it will be a great start for us and a good place to raise any family we might have.'

Alice sat back and chewed her lip. She looked directly at Millie, who didn't quite meet her eye.

'But they need skilled bricklayers here with all the rebuilding that's going on.' She shrugged as Millie stayed quiet. 'Ah well, if it's what you *both* want, then I'm sure it will be a good move for you.'

Alice wasn't really convinced it was what her friend wanted. Millie was a real home-body and hadn't even got further than one station down the line from Aigburth in an abandoned attempt at joining the Land Army a few years ago. She'd travelled about with the band, but had always known she would be back in Liverpool every few weeks. There'd be none of that if she moved to Canada.

Jimmy nodded eagerly for them both. 'It is, and we've talked long and hard about it.'

Alice jumped to her feet and hurried into the kitchen before tears fell. Now that her friend was no longer on the road, she'd got used to Millie being at home; if she left Alice would miss her all over again, as would Cathy.

Millie appeared at the kitchen door. 'Why don't you and Terry think about emigrating? It would be amazing if we ended up in the same place.'

Alice shook her head. 'We can't do that. I don't want to uproot Brian right now. He's got important exams soon and we're hoping he'll go on to college and maybe university in a few years' time.

And Cathy starts school in two weeks. It's okay when you don't have responsibilities, like you and Jimmy.' She stopped as Millie frowned. 'Sorry if I sound all defensive, I don't mean to. But there's Terry's mother to think about too. He'd never leave her alone here. No, I'm afraid it's not for us, but I hope it works out for the pair of you. And I also hope it's what *you* really want, Millie, and you're not just going along with it for Jimmy's sake. You didn't seem too sure back there.'

'It is.' Millie nodded, her dark blonde hair bouncing on her shoulders. 'I got used to travelling around with the band. I feel a bit hemmed in when I have to stay in one place. It will do me good. Broaden my horizons.'

'Really?' Alice said. 'Two words: Land Army!'

Millie smiled. 'Ah well, that was different. The thought of cows and things, you know.' She changed the subject before Alice could say anything more. 'Here, let me help you take the sandwiches through and we'll celebrate what's left of Christmas.'

Alice shook her head after her as she waltzed out of the kitchen with two laden plates.

Chapter Four

January 1946

Alice looked at the little school uniform that lay over the back of the sofa and smiled proudly. Cathy would look a treat tomorrow, her first day at school. Alice had just finished stitching name tapes in everything. Two navy blue cardigans knitted by Granny Lomax, two navy gymslips that she'd bought a size bigger so that, with the hem taken up, they'd do at least a couple of terms, and two little white blouses. The navy blue coat with a hood she'd got from Paddy's Market; it was in good condition and spotlessly clean. That had been a stroke of luck as she was almost out of money, even after using her staff discount and a couple of clothing coupons for the rest. Christmas had taken a chunk out of what bit she'd put by. Terry had come home the other night with a tiny leather satchel that a workmate had passed on. It had a bit of ink-staining inside but he'd set to and given it a good clean. With a coat of wax polish, it was looking perfectly good enough for a little one just starting school.

'She'll look a picture tomorrow,' Terry said, looking up from his paper and flicking ash onto the hearth. 'I hope she settles okay.'

They were sitting in the front room with a roaring fire and the radio playing quietly in the background. It felt warm and cosy inside, but bitter cold outside with a fine dusting of snow. Alice hoped the snow stayed off for tomorrow at least. Cathy wanted to wear her new black shiny shoes and had put them by her bed ready. When Alice had told her she might have to wear her wellies there'd been tears before she'd fallen asleep.

'She will do,' Alice said. 'Keep your fingers crossed there's no more snow or I'll have a right time getting her ready.'

Footsteps sounded on the stairs and Brian popped his head around the door.

'Any chance of a mug of cocoa and some supper, our Alice?'

Alice smiled. 'I was just about to make some. Have you got your satchel packed ready and your uniform laid out?'

Brian nodded and came to sit beside her. 'All done. Can't wait to get back to it. I like the holidays, but it gets a bit boring after the first week, especially in the winter.'

Alice pushed his floppy fringe from his eyes and gave him a hug. He was a clever boy, her brother, and she was very proud of him, as she knew their late mother would have been too.

'Well, there's no more now until February half-term and that's only a short break. And we've got Millie's wedding to look forward to.'

*

'Can't believe she's starting school tomorrow,' Terry said as he and Alice lay snuggled together in bed later. 'I feel like I've missed out on so much with her. She's more comfortable with me now, but I wish I'd been there from the word go.'

Alice kissed him. 'It can't be helped, love. You're here now and that's all that matters. And when we decide to try for another, maybe later this year when we've got a bit more money behind us, you'll be with us all the way. And believe me, when the baby starts screaming with teething and colic, you just might regret what you wished for! You'll be desperate to get out of the house and go to work.'

He laughed. 'Never, surely? Although I've got to say, I *do* love my job. It was the right decision to accept it. They're a grand bunch of workers at Tate and Lyle's. All I need now is the bike on the road to save some time in getting back and to. I know it's only a few miles, but the bloody tram is stop–start all the way and I could get there and back in a quarter of that time.'

*

Dressed in her new uniform, and looking as smart as Alice had hoped she would, Cathy stood with her arms folded across her chest, a mutinous expression on her face. Alice had just told her to put her wellies on and the new shoes could be taken in a bag so she could get changed when they got to school. There'd been another snowfall overnight and although it was thawing a bit now, the pavements were slushy and slippery. Brian had already left for his tram to the grammar school, calling over his shoulder as Alice waved him off that it was a bit dangerous underfoot and to be careful. Cathy plonked herself down on the bottom stair and refused to budge.

'Right, well I'm just going to go without you then,' Alice threatened. 'I'll miss my tram to work and I don't want to be late. You'll just have to stay here on your own.' She put her coat and a warm scarf on and picked up her handbag. Calling Cathy's bluff might just do the trick. They had plenty of time, as Alice was going in a bit later today with it being Cathy's first day at school. But her daughter didn't know that. She went to the front door and opened it as Cathy let out a loud wail.

'I'm sorry, Mammy, I'm coming with my wellies on.' She ran down the hall, her plaits bouncing on her shoulders, dark eyes filled with worry at the thought of being left alone.

Alice lifted Cathy's coat down from the hall stand and Cathy slipped her arms into it. She pulled on her wellington boots while Alice put the shoes in a bag.

'Right, pick your satchel up and we'll slip the bag with the shoes inside it.' The satchel only just fastened with the shoes in it, but at least there was less chance of them getting left behind at the end of the school day. 'Come on then, let's go.'

They walked slowly up the street and out onto Lark Lane. The pavement was a bit clearer here and they picked up speed, crossing busy Aigburth Road and onto St Michael's Road and Neilson Street, where St Michael's Primary School was situated. The pavement was busy with mothers hurrying older children along, some pushing prams and dragging reluctant toddlers by the hand. Alice thanked God that, at the moment, she'd only got one to get ready in the morning; Brian was capable of seeing to himself. That would all change though when they decided to have another. But Cathy would be a bit older by then and more able to see to herself.

A tall woman with auburn hair was standing by the gate holding onto the hand of a little girl with the same colour hair. The little girl was crying and the woman also looked close to tears.

'Come on, Deborah,' the woman coaxed. 'See, here's a nice little girl who looks new too.' She smiled at Alice, who smiled back. Deborah peeped out from behind the woman and stared at Cathy.

'First day?' Alice said. 'Same here.'

'It's so hard,' the woman said. 'I've been dreading this day. I'm sure she'll be okay, but, well, you know. She's my only one.'

'I do. Cathy's an only one too. Cathy, say hello to…?'

'Deborah, or Debbie, as we call her,' the woman replied. 'I'm Clara, Clara Jones.'

'Alice Lomax, and this is Cathy. Hello, Debbie. That's a very pretty name. And what beautiful hair you have.'

Debbie smiled and her face lit up. 'It's not ginger,' she said.

Her mother rolled her eyes. 'A boy on the playground called her "ginger nuts" last year and she's not got over it yet!'

Alice nodded. 'It's auburn, and that's a very special colour.'

Cathy stood silently, staring at Debbie, and then moved forward to take her hand. 'Will you be my best friend?' she whispered.

Debbie smiled again. 'Yes please.'

Alice and Clara looked at each other. Clara waved her crossed fingers in the air and the foursome made their way into school to meet the teacher.

Sadie was waiting for Alice as she came out of the school fifteen minutes later with Clara Jones.

'How did it go?' Gianni had already been at school two years and had just started in class three today.

'Better than I was expecting,' Alice admitted. 'This is Clara, Cathy's new best friend Debbie's mum. This is Sadie, my friend and workmate. Her little boy Gianni is a bit older than our two so she's an old hand at this. Debbie and Cathy have gone in hand in hand and have been given desks next to each other. I think they'll be just fine.'

Clara nodded in agreement. 'Nice to meet you, Sadie. I feel a bit better than I did earlier. Thank goodness you came along when you did, Alice. I might just have turned tail and fled, the way I was feeling.'

Alice laughed. 'Be nice to hear their tales when they come home. I won't be here to meet Cathy as I don't get back from work until later. My mother-in-law picks her up, and Sadie's mam gets Gianni, but we'll see you again in the morning.'

'Well, it's been lovely to meet you both. I'll see you tomorrow.'

*

Alice looked at her watch halfway through her shift and sighed. They'd been busier than she thought they'd be, mothers enjoying a break from the kids, no doubt, and with coming in later and missing the morning break, it was almost dinnertime. She was just about to say something to Sadie when Millie and her mother appeared by her side.

'Thought we'd surprise you,' Millie announced. 'We've been shopping for my wedding outfit.'

'Oh, fabulous,' Alice exclaimed. 'What have you chosen?'

'Just a simple dress and jacket in cream,' Millie replied. 'We want to get married on Valentine's Day and churches don't do weekday weddings so it's at the same place you and Terry got married on Mount Pleasant. No point in having a long white dress for a civil ceremony. Besides which, I can always wear it again for special occasions.'

'Sounds just the job,' Alice said.

'How did you go on this morning with Cathy?'

'Oh, just fine, once we got there.' Alice told Millie about Debbie, the new best friend, and how Cathy had taken control of things and taken Debbie under her wing.

Millie laughed. 'That's my girl. Not much fazes our Cathy.'

*

Millie and Jimmy were married late afternoon on Valentine's Day. They celebrated afterwards with a small buffet at Millie's parents' house. Because it was a Thursday, and most of their friends were working and couldn't get the time off, the couple threw a party at the Legion the following Saturday night. Millie's band friends came up to Liverpool from their London base and brought their instruments, and although nothing had been planned, an impromptu session was played with Millie singing and providing the entertainment at her own wedding party.

Jimmy had only seen Millie singing with Alice and a piano accompaniment, and as she saw how impressed he looked by his new wife's amazing talent Alice went over to him and whispered, 'Don't let her lose this, Jimmy. Don't let it go to waste if you *do* go to Canada. Make sure she sings wherever she can.' She patted his shoulder and carried some empties to the bar, where Jack Dawson was working. He winked at her and she smiled.

'You okay, gel? I could say get behind here and give me a hand, but your hubby might not like it. We're short-staffed tonight with you partying instead of working.'

Alice laughed at his cheek. 'I can't be working at my best friend's wedding,' she said. 'Anyway, bartender, get me a large sherry, a small gin and orange and a pint of your best mild ale, please.'

Jack laughed. 'You've been seeing too many American films at the flicks, lady. Bartender, indeed.' He pulled Terry's pint and then poured Alice's sherry into a schooner. 'Do you want a small shandy for your Brian? He looks bored to death sitting with your ma-in-law. I'll stick a bit of extra gin in her glass; might put a smile on her face. Bit too uptight, that one. Always gives me a dirty look when she sees me. Think she has a notion that me and you might have got up to something naughty when I was walking you home in the blackout.'

'Jack,' Alice said, suppressing a giggle. 'Behave yourself, and be careful in whose earshot you say things like that. You know how quickly rumours start around here.'

Jack grinned and poured a small shandy for Brian. 'Put hairs on his chest, this will. He'll no doubt be doing a bit of courting soon. How old is he now?'

'Fifteen this year. And don't you be encouraging him. I want him to do well at school and not get involved with girls just yet.'

Jack raised an amused eyebrow. 'Boys will be boys. You can't stop nature taking its course, gel.' He put the filled glasses on a tray and carried them over to Alice's family table.

'Thanks, mate,' Terry said, handing his mother her gin and orange. 'Who's that small one for?'

'Brian,' Jack replied.

Brian's face lit up and he took the glass Jack handed him.

'I hope that's not got alcohol in it,' Granny Lomax said. 'He's far too young.'

'Alcohol? Nah, not that you'd notice, Gran,' Jack said, winking at Brian. 'It's mainly lemonade.'

Jack went back to the bar as Granny Lomax stared after him, her lips pursed. 'That young man is far too cocky and forward for his own good,' she grumbled. 'Oh, I know he's a good friend of the pair of you.' She looked at Alice and Terry. 'But it gives me a bad feeling in here each time I see him.' She patted her chest and picked up her drink.

Terry shook his head. 'Leave it alone, Mother. And you'd better get used to seeing Jack around because he's coming over next week to help me get the bike on the road again.'

*

Alice had to prise Cathy from her bed on Monday morning. Her daughter wasn't the best at getting up and on cold days she was worse than ever. But since starting school in January it had been a work of art trying to get her ready.

'Come on, Cathy,' Alice coaxed. 'Debbie will be waiting for you by the gates. We can't be late. Your chucky egg and toast is on the table with a nice cup of cocoa. And Granny said she's baking a cake today, a chocolate one. When she picks you up from school I bet she'll give you a piece with your glass of milk.'

The mention of cake did the trick and Cathy shot out of bed and allowed Alice to dress her in her uniform.

'Put your warm cardi on as well, it's cold today,' Alice said. 'And it's very icy outside again.'

Downstairs in the warm back sitting room Cathy tucked into her breakfast while Alice did her makeup and hair, ready for going on to work after she'd dropped Cathy off. Both she and Sadie started at ten and finished at four. Lewis's were very good at accommodating their working mothers with shifts that suited them best. Both children were picked up at three thirty by their respective grandmothers. By the time Alice had dashed over to Linnet Lane to get Cathy, she was always home when Brian got in from school. It was non-stop, but their hard work was paying off. She and Terry had replaced a lot of Mam's old furniture and carpets in the last few months. They'd even bought a gramophone and some records. When the kids were out of the way, Cathy in bed and Brian studying, they often rolled back the hearth rug and had a dance. The house was Alice's pride and joy and she loved cooking, cleaning and making everywhere look nice for her little family.

Cathy dragged her feet on the short walk to school but as soon as she spotted Debbie, standing at the gates with her mother, she picked up speed and the two little girls ran off together happily. Clara shook her head.

'Thank God for that. She was awful to get up this morning.'

'So was Cathy,' Alice said with a grin. 'It's Monday morning-itis, I think.'

Sadie was saying goodbye to Gianni, who always ignored the little girls when he was with his pals. She joined Alice ready to run and catch the tram into the city.

'Ready, gel?'

'As I'll ever be,' Alice said, linking her arm through Sadie's.

'Hope it's not too busy today,' Sadie said. 'I've got a banging headache.'

'Have you? Why is that?'

Sadie sighed. 'Well, apart from my monthly, which always gives me a bad head, I heard yesterday that someone who knows my mam has seen a poster near Sefton Park, advertising that Romanos' fair is coming to the area for Easter. I haven't slept with worrying about it. My mam says I should take Gianni out of the city for a few days while it's here. I've got an aunty in Chester who'll let us stay with her. Mam's writing to her today. I can't let Luca see Gianni. He might try and take him away. I couldn't bear it. And I really can't face seeing *him* either. I still love him, but I can't do that lifestyle and watch him taking his life into his own hands every day. It's not fair and it's not right. So I need to be gone for a while.'

'Oh, poor you,' Alice said with a frown. 'I understand though. You're probably better out of the way.'

Sadie nodded. 'If I let Gianni see Luca again, he might not want to come home. The fairground will seem so exciting to him. It's for the best.'

'I agree,' Alice said. 'I'm dreading my Terry getting his bike up and running again. But I need to get used to it because he's starting work on it soon with Jack. He's got all the new parts he needs now,' she finished as the tram trundled into view and the conductor shouted, 'Ranelagh Street.'

*

Alice wound the three yards of narrow pink and white lace trimming she'd just cut for her customer around her fingers and popped it into a small paper bag.

'And did you say a bobbin of white thread?' she asked the tall woman, bending to take a box of assorted bobbins from under the counter.

'Yes please, chuck,' the woman replied. 'I've just made a little underskirt and matching knickers from a length of parachute silk for my granddaughter's birthday, but they look a bit too plain so a nice bit of lace will pretty them up.'

'They'll look lovely,' Alice said, handing over the bag and giving the woman her change.

'Doesn't go far, does it?' the woman said, pocketing what was left of her half crown. 'Still, the silk was free so I mustn't grumble. Thank you, gel. I'll get on me way.'

Alice smiled and said goodbye. She turned to Sadie, who was sorting out hanks of wool to go on the shelves.

'That's a nice shade of lemon.' She picked up a hank. 'Might get some of that and ask Terry's mam to make a new cardi for Cathy.'

'Well, there's not a lot of that one, so don't wait too long. I'll put it at the back of a shelf just in case. Nearly break time. I could murder some toast and a gallon of coffee.'

'Me too. How's your headache?'

'It's going a bit now my mind's occupied,' Sadie replied. 'I can't help worrying though.'

'I know.' Alice rubbed her arm. 'But try not to. I'm sure things will be fine. Take a couple of Aspros with your brew.'

Sadie smiled. 'I'll give it a try, Nurse Lomax.'

'Oh, if only.' Alice sighed. 'But one day that might be my Cathy's title. Wouldn't it be wonderful?'

Sadie laughed. 'Well, let's just hope there are no more wars, and she doesn't get involved with a lad before she gets the chance, eh?' She looked at her watch. 'Here's our relief,' she said as a blonde-haired, gangly girl made her way to the counter. 'Let's get that coffee, gel.'

*

Alice stifled a grin as she heard her mother-in-law shouting at Terry, Jack and Brian as they washed their hands at the kitchen sink in an effort to remove the thick oil and grease. It was Saturday afternoon and they'd all had their dinner here at Granny's before the boys got to work on the motorbike. She looked up from her copy of *Woman's Weekly* as Granny Lomax flounced into the sitting room and patted the sofa for Cathy to come and sit beside her.

'I'll read Cathy her story if you'll make that dirty trio a cup of tea, Alice. And don't give them my decent mugs. There are some older ones in the cupboard. There's a piece of exhaust pipe on the draining board and an oily chain in the sink. Lord knows what will come inside next. I dread to think.' She shuddered.

Alice chuckled to herself as she walked into the kitchen. She gasped as she saw what had once been a spotless pink towel on the table, covered in oil.

'Oh no! You lot are for it now. She'll have your guts for garters. Get outside with your mucky boots and overalls and I'll make you all a hot drink.'

She shook her head as they trailed out of the kitchen, muttering something about women always being unreasonable for no good reason. Alice watched as they sat down on the garden bench and Jack offered his cigarettes round.

She was about to bang on the window to tell him not to give one to Brian when she saw her brother accept and light up in a way that told her it wasn't his first time. The look of bliss on his face as he closed his eyes and took a long drag made her smile. He was growing up and experimenting. But hopefully it didn't mean he'd go off the rails. When he went to college next year he'd be mixing with all sorts who probably got up to all sorts, as well. Maybe it was time for Terry to have a man-to-man talk with him about being sensible with girls.

When the tea was ready, she headed outside. Brian quickly hid his ciggie behind his back as Jack took a mug of tea from her and pulled a face. 'This mug has got a chip on the rim,' he said.

Alice tutted. 'Since when have *you* been so fussy, Jack Dawson? You three are not allowed the posh cups while you've still got oil on your hands. I've been told to hand out the old ones. Take it or leave it.'

'Well I guess that puts us in our place, lads,' Jack said with a grin. 'Tradesmen's entrance, chipped mugs! Don't think your ma likes me very much, Terry.'

'Nah, she loves you, mate,' Terry said. 'Just has a funny way of showing it.'

'Right, well I'll leave you comedians to it,' Alice said. 'And, Brian, you might want to rescue that ciggie from behind your back before you set fire to yourself! I'm taking Cathy back home now and getting her ready for bed. I'll see you two later, and I'll see you at the weekend, Jack.'

*

At the beginning of March the weather was still cold and warnings of fog and black ice on the roads made Alice feel glad that Terry's bike was still not quite ready for regular riding.

But as Alice was getting ready to take Cathy shopping on the Saturday morning, Terry announced that it was finished at last.

'Jack's doing the final brakes check this morning and then I'm taking it for a long spin,' he said. 'So don't worry if I'm not back by the time you have to go to work. I know you've got a big wedding on tonight at the Legion, Jack told me. Leave Cathy with Brian if you need to get going. I'll not be that much longer. Right, I'm off to my mother's now to give the bike a once-over and a good polish. I'll get a bite to eat there before I go for the test ride.'

Alice sighed as he kissed her goodbye. 'Please be careful, Terry. Watch out for any icy patches.'

'I'll be fine, stop worrying. Love you, see you later,' he said as he went to let himself out, calling goodbye up the stairs to Brian and Cathy first.

'Love you too,' Alice said as she waved him off. She went back into the sitting room and finished doing her hair in front of the mirror over the mantelpiece and then called for Cathy to come and put her coat on.

Down at the Lark Lane shops they bumped into Sadie and Gianni and had a cuppa in the small café at the side of the bakery.

'You look mithered to death,' Sadie said as she poured tea into two china cups from a little white tea pot while Alice buttered a toasted tea cake each. 'What's up?'

Alice cut a jam tart in two and gave a piece each to Cathy and Gianni. She licked her sticky fingers and sighed. 'Oh, nothing really. Just that Terry's messing about with his bike again today and I hate it. But I'm trying not to think about it. I'm taking Cathy to get some sturdy new shoes. Her feet have grown, even since January, and she's always complaining she's freezing. Her little patent ankle straps look lovely with nice white socks, but they're not really practical for this time of year. Don't want her getting chilblains at this age.'

'Oh no, you don't want that. Chilblains can be so itchy and painful. We'll come with you if you're going into the city. I fancy a rummage around Paddy's Market. I haven't been for a while. The aunty I told you I'm going to stay with at Easter is a great seamstress, so if I find anything I like she can make it fit me as though it were tailor-made. Do you fancy that, Gianni? Going shopping with Cathy and her mammy when we've finished here?'

'Can I have a toy then?' Gianni bargained, grinning at Cathy, who grinned back.

'We'll see. If you're a good boy.'

'An aeroplane?' He stuck his arms out either side and made dive-bombing actions, complete with sound, rocking in his chair and making Cathy laugh even more.

'I said we'll see. Now finish your tart and milk and then I can wipe your mucky face before we go.'

*

After saying goodbye to Sadie and Gianni and carrying her bags of bargains and Cathy's new shoes from the tram stop, Alice hurried back to Lucerne Street. It was late afternoon, starting to get dark and bitterly cold. Brian had banked up the fire in the back sitting room and announced he'd done all his homework as she came inside.

She smiled and dropped her parcels on the sofa. 'Good lad. Terry not back yet?'

Brian shook his head, cleared his books off the table and carried them upstairs to his room.

Alice heated the scouse she'd made last night and called Cathy and Brian to the table. She handed them laden plates and sliced some bread to mop up the gravy. She left the pair tucking into their meal while she went upstairs to get a quick wash and put her Legion uniform on. Downstairs, she brushed her hair in front of the mirror over the mantelpiece and glanced at the clock. It was almost half past five and Terry still wasn't back. He knew she started work at six so could have made a bit of an effort to be back before she left, even though he'd told her not to worry if he wasn't.

'I'm leaving to go to work now,' she told Brian. 'Make sure Cathy brushes her teeth when she gets ready for bed. Terry shouldn't be too long now. There's a low light under what's left of the scouse for his tea, Brian. But if he's not back in another fifteen minutes, turn it off or it'll catch the bottom of the pan. I'll see you two in the morning. Be a good girl for Brian, Cathy. Now give Mammy a big kiss.'

Alice closed the door behind her and hurried along the deserted street and out onto Lark Lane. It wasn't far to the Legion from here, but a fair bit further than when she lived at Granny Lomax's bungalow. Still, the exercise was good for her and now the blackout was over, it was good to see street lamps lit again. It was still freezing cold, and the bitter wind blowing up from the Mersey didn't help. She hoped Terry hadn't gone too far and got lost on his way back.

The Legion was heaving as she walked into the reception area. There were lots of people dressed up in wedding finery. Two Bootle brothers had married twin sisters from Aigburth this afternoon at nearby St Michael's church, so it was a big wedding to cater for. The steward, Arnold, and Jack looked rushed off their feet. Arnold's wife, Winnie, was red-faced in the kitchen, hurriedly filling plates for the buffet.

'Ah, Alice, thank God,' she said. 'Here, chuck, take some of these out there and put them on the table.'

Alice picked up two laden plates and carried them through to the room. The buffet tables were already dressed with white cloths and decorated with flowered garlands. Two white-iced wedding cakes stood in pride of place in the centre. Alice put down the plates and tweaked a garland into place. She hurried back to the kitchen and brought out more food. Another table that held the glasses for the toast also held small plates, napkins and neatly arranged cutlery. Winnie *had* been busy and Alice wished she could have come in a bit earlier to help her.

As the evening got underway, the room soon filled to capacity and the regulars were invited to join in the celebrations. The bar was busier than Alice had ever seen it. Tips were coming in thick and fast and her little pot was soon filled with sixpenny pieces and shillings. The money would go into their holiday fund. She and Terry were planning to take Brian and Cathy on a family holiday this year to Blackpool, so every spare penny was being saved towards it. She couldn't wait; even though summer was months off yet.

When a lull finally came she managed to ask Jack how Terry's trial run had gone.

'It was great,' Jack enthused. 'He seemed really pleased with the bike's performance. Haven't you seen him since he got home?'

Alice shook her head. 'He wasn't back when I left to come here.'

Jack frowned. 'He told me he was just popping to see a fella he works at Tate's with down near the Dock Road when he left me, and then going straight home. He should have been back well before you left. He must have got held up somewhere. He'll be back by now, I expect.'

'Well I hope so, because I left the kids alone and I haven't asked anyone to look in on them.' She looked at the clock above the bar and chewed her lip. It was now almost ten. None of their neighbours were on the phone so she was unable to check if Terry was home yet. He'd said only the other day that they should think about getting a phone put in. She'd remind him tomorrow to make enquiries.

Just before eleven o'clock, Alice was collecting glasses and putting them behind the bar to wash when the doors flew open and two serious-faced police officers hurried in accompanied by her mother-in-law. One look at Granny Lomax's pale and tear-stained face and Alice knew instantly that something had happened to Terry. Her hand flew to her mouth as the room spun out of focus and Jack caught her as she dropped to the floor. He carried her into the kitchen, beckoning the officers and Terry's mother to follow him. Arnold rushed in from the busy bar and asked what was wrong.

'We don't know yet,' Jack whispered. 'You go back out and see to the customers, or you'll have a riot on your hands. I'll stay here with Alice.'

Granny Lomax took hold of Alice's cold hand. 'You have to be very brave, Alice my love,' she began, her lips trembling. 'The officers came to tell me that Terry has had a bad accident on his way home from the Dock Road. He skidded on ice and the bike hit a lamp post. His injuries are serious and he's been rushed to the Royal Liverpool. He had no ID on him and it's taken them a while to find out who he belonged to. His bike is still registered to my address so they came to me and thankfully not to yours and the children. We're going to be taken to the hospital now.' She stopped and took a deep shuddering breath.

Jack gasped as Alice remained silent, just sitting there shaking her head in disbelief.

'Jesus. I'm so sorry to hear that,' Jack said, his colour draining. 'Is there anything I can do? Do you want me to come with you?'

Granny Lomax rounded on him. 'I think you've done quite enough, young man. If you hadn't encouraged Terry to get that damn bike back on the road this wouldn't have happened. You told him it was safe enough to take out today after you did the brakes.'

'And it was,' Jack said. 'He came back while I was still at your house and all was well. You saw that, before he went off again to see his mate, and I left to come here to work.'

'Madam, this isn't the time to lay blame,' one of the officers said. 'The roads are extremely bad tonight. I think we need to get this young lady to her husband's bedside. Would you like the young man to accompany us, Mrs Lomax?' He addressed Alice, who nodded.

'I'll just get my coat and let the boss know what's going on,' Jack said, glaring at Granny Lomax as he left the kitchen.

Alice looked at Granny Lomax, who was protesting loudly that she didn't think Jack should come with them.

'I want him there,' Alice said. 'He stood by me when my mam died and all the other times he's supported me. He's our friend and I need him there. Terry would want that too, I know he would.'

'Very well. I'm not arguing with you, Alice. I just think it's very inappropriate, this friendship you have with him.'

'Now hang on a minute, Missus,' Jack said, coming back into the room with his coat on and catching the end of the conversation. 'There's nothing inappropriate about me and Alice. We're good pals and we look out for each other, that's all. If she wants me there, then I'll *be* there. I've spoken to Arnold and he will sort someone out to go and stay with the kiddies,' he directed at a white-faced Alice as he helped her to her feet and handed her coat over. 'Freddie and his missus and Marlene are out there. He'll have a word with them. Come on, chuck, let's get going.'

Chapter Five

Alice and Terry's mother were taken to a side room on a busy ward. Jack took a seat in the corridor outside, telling Alice he'd wait there and to let him know if she needed him. Alice took one look at her white-faced husband, his head swathed in bandages, and burst into tears. His face was bruised, his chin bore cuts and his nose looked broken. She sat beside the bed, his mother on the other side. Alice wished she'd go away and let her have time alone with Terry, but she couldn't bring herself to say anything, as that would seem mean. He was her only child after all. She stroked his hand and willed him to open his eyes. There were things she wanted to say to him, to tell him how much she loved and needed him, but she wanted to say them privately.

Granny Lomax cleared her throat and dabbed at her eyes with an embroidered handkerchief. 'Alice, I'm just going to see if I can find the ladies'. I won't be long. Will you be okay for a few minutes?'

Alice nodded. 'Of course. I'll be fine.' She waited until Granny left the room and closed the door; then leant her head on the bed as close to Terry as she could. 'Oh, Terry, don't leave me. I couldn't bear it. I love you so much and I've only just got you back. Don't leave me, please.' She sobbed and clutched his hand but there was no response from him. 'We've got so many plans, Terry. The holiday with Cathy and Brian in the summer, and the new baby you want us to have. You need to get well and strong for us all.

We need you. I so wish you'd not gone on that bike. I just knew, a feeling deep down that something would happen.'

She stopped as the door opened and his mother slipped back into the room and resumed her place at the opposite side of the bed and took hold of his hand.

*

Terry passed away at six the following morning without ever regaining consciousness. The doctor explained to Alice and his mother that his head injuries were so severe that, even if he'd come round, there would have been every possibility he would have been in a complete vegetative state and unable to do anything for himself. The thought of her lovely, energetic and lively husband being incapable of even feeding himself was enough for Alice to know that Terry's death was merciful, if nothing else.

A white-faced Jack was called into the room after spending all night sitting on the chair in the corridor. He said his goodbyes to Terry's lifeless form and helped Alice and Granny Lomax to the family room, where a nurse brought cups of tea and plates of toast.

'Just take your time,' she said and closed the door quietly as she left.

'Sugar, Mrs Lomax?' Jack held the teaspoon aloft as she nodded her head, her face ashen.

'Put an extra one in,' Alice whispered. 'She's in shock.'

'And so are you, gel,' Jack said. 'Don't try and be brave, Alice. Is there anyone I can contact for you?'

Alice took a deep shuddering breath. 'There are only the children, and I'm hoping Arnold *did* get Freddie and his wife to call in and look after them after we left the club last night.'

Jack nodded. 'He will have done. Don't worry about the kids right now. They'll be fine.'

Alice sighed as fat tears ran down her cheeks. She felt totally empty and heartbroken. She and Terry'd had so little time together after all those years apart. It just felt so unfair to lose him now when they were on the verge of doing all they'd planned to do, before they were married and he'd had to go away. Brian and Cathy were going to be heartbroken too.

'I hope so,' she said. 'I expect Marlene will have gone with them too, so between her and Freddie, they'll have managed.'

*

After a lovely church service at St Michael's, attended by all their Lark Lane neighbours and friends, including some of Terry's ex-regiment and Alice's Rootes ex-co-workers, he was laid to rest alongside his late father in the graveyard. Alice had asked Arnold and his wife to put on a wake for Terry at the Legion and everyone was invited back.

'To think that my boy survived six years of being shot at by enemies abroad and then came home, only to be killed in his own city, beggars belief,' Granny Lomax said to Arnold as he poured her a third gin and orange. 'To say I feel heartbroken is an understatement. But life has to go on and Alice and the children need all the support they can get right now.'

'Aye, you're right, Missus,' Arnold said. 'And they'll get it. Me and the missus will always be there for her, and Jack's planning a fund-raiser to help her and the kiddies out.'

'Huh, Jack!' she grunted. 'Trying to salve his conscience, no doubt. If he hadn't sent my boy out on a bike with faulty brakes, Terry would still be here.'

'Well we don't know for certain that it *did* have faulty brakes, so it's not right to blame Jack,' Arnold said. 'He feels badly enough about things as it is. Maybe it's best to keep comments like that to yourself for now until we get a full report back from the police.'

Granny Lomax banged her glass down and shook her head. 'I don't need any police reports to tell me what I know is the truth.'

Jack, who was standing behind Arnold, shook his head. 'That's the drink talking. Don't let her have any more, Arnold. She's not used to knocking them back this early in the day.'

He signalled to Alice, who was sitting with Millie and Sadie, all nursing glasses of sherry, eyes red-rimmed from the tears they'd shed in church. She hurried over to the bar, wiping her nose on a soggy hanky.

'What's up, Jack?'

Jack pointed at Granny Lomax's back as she made her way to a table where her next-door neighbour was seated with his wife and Granny's farmer friend.

'Your ma-in-law is going on about faulty brakes again,' he whispered. 'People will start talking if they hear her. Try and persuade her to eat something. The gin's gone right to her head and loosened her tongue.'

Alice sighed. She filled a small plate at the buffet table, took it across to Granny and sat down beside her.

'I think you should try and eat something,' she said gently. 'It doesn't do to drink on an empty stomach. We don't want you being ill in front of Brian and Cathy. It might upset them and they've had enough of that this last couple of weeks.' She looked over at her brother and little daughter, who were at the next table, eating sandwiches. She smiled reassuringly at Cathy, whose lips trembled as she did her best to smile back. It was an effort to be brave for them and was going to be a long haul, but the three of them would pull together and cope. They were a team, and they'd manage, they'd have to.

Granny's neighbour patted Alice's arm. 'Don't you worry,' he said. 'We'll get her to have a bite to eat and then take her home with us. She needs a bit of time to herself.'

'Thank you,' Alice said. 'That's a weight off my shoulders. I'll go and see to my little girl now. She doesn't really understand what's happened and I have to put her first and look after her and my young brother too.'

She went to Brian and Cathy and took them to sit with Sadie and Millie. Millie lifted Cathy onto her knee and cuddled her. Jimmy came over from talking to Freddie and Marlene and asked if anyone would like another drink. They all nodded and he came back from the bar a few minutes later with a laden tray.

'Thanks, Jimmy.' Alice raised her glass, tears streaming down her cheeks. 'To Terry, the love of my life. May you rest in peace, my darling.'

*

The day after the funeral Millie and Jimmy came to the house. Millie carried a cake that her mam had sent round.

'I'll put the kettle on,' Alice said, leading the way into the back room. 'Have a seat.'

As they all sat around the table drinking tea, Jimmy cleared his throat. 'Er, we've something to tell you,' he began. 'We're moving over to Blackpool to my parents' place while we save up to apply to move to Canada. We can get there quite cheaply under the government immigration scheme, but we need savings for when we arrive.'

'Sorry we're dropping it on your toes now, Alice,' Millie apologised. 'It's not the right time, I know, but Jimmy has got a job lined up to start next week and he can do extra work at the weekends with his dad and the fishing business. So we have to go tomorrow to get settled in.'

Alice nodded, but felt too numb to properly take in what they were telling her. Life had to go on. Everything wasn't going to come to a stop because she'd been widowed. Millie and Jimmy had been there for her this last couple of weeks and she couldn't expect them to put their lives on hold indefinitely.

'You can always get the train over to see us when the weather gets a bit better. Maybe at Easter in the school holidays,' Millie suggested.

'Yes, we might do that,' Alice said. 'Write to me, won't you? Don't lose touch.'

'Of course I will,' Millie said. 'And we'll be coming over to see Mam and Dad so we'll always call in when we do that. And my mam said if there's anything they can do for you, you've only got to ask.' She put her arms around Alice and gave her a big hug as Alice fought back the tears that seemed never-ending at times.

*

Alice did her best to pick up the pieces of her life in the months following Terry's death. She struggled with her emotions and couldn't sleep at night. She tossed and turned and cried quietly into her pillow so the children wouldn't hear her. The awful feeling of knowing Terry was never coming home again washed over her each morning to the point that she didn't even want to get out of bed, but she forced herself to carry on for the sake of Brian and Cathy. She didn't want to end up like her mam after Alice's dad had died, staying in bed all day and getting more and more depressed as time passed.

Going back to work at Lewis's with Sadie had been a big help. And Marlene had offered her baby-sitting services on Saturday nights so that Alice could still work her shifts at the Legion. Everyone told her that keeping busy was the best thing for her and she had to agree that they were right. Having spent so much time alone while Terry was away, she knew she was quite capable of coping again, even though it was the last thing she felt like doing.

She threw herself into everything she could, so that not a moment of time was wasted on sad thoughts and what ifs. She had her memories to look back on when she was alone at night and she sobbed herself to sleep for her Terry, whose arms would never again wrap around her, whose lips would never demand hers again. But there were also times when she felt so angry with him for messing about with the damn bike, even though he'd known it worried her to death. If only she'd kicked up more of a fuss and demanded he got rid of it. But that would have made her a nagging wife, and he wouldn't have listened anyway, only laughed away her fears.

Cathy had taken to sharing her bed in the early hours, crying for her daddy. Granny Lomax said Alice was making a rod for her own back but Alice ignored her warnings; if it comforted both her and Cathy to cuddle up together then it was no one else's business but theirs.

*

Alice bent to pull a tray of buns out of the oven and popped them down on the worktop to cool. She'd ice them later. Sadie was coming over with Gianni for the afternoon and then, after tea, she and Alice were going to the Mayfair to see a late matinee while Brian looked after the little ones. Sadie had insisted it would do her good to come out for a while and she'd even offered to pay as a treat. They were going to see a George Formby film, *George in Civvy Street*. The girls at work had told them it was funny and Alice felt she could do with cheering up a bit.

Cathy came running in out of the garden, where she'd been playing ball with Brian. 'Need a wee-wee,' she said, jiggling from foot to foot.

'Well off you go then,' Alice said. 'And don't forget to wash your hands. You can help me ice the buns when you've finished. Shall we have pink or white icing?'

'Both,' Cathy said. 'And cherries on top.'

'We haven't got any cherries. Pink and white will have to do.'

Brian popped his head around the door. 'Want me to run round to Granny Lomax's and see if she's got any cherries?'

Alice shook her head. 'We'll manage, Brian. We can't keep running round there every time we run out of something and you've still got a bit of homework to finish before they arrive. Go and do it now, then you'll be finished in time for tea.' She'd made a pink blancmange, and with sandwiches and the iced buns, they'd have plenty.

Sadie and Gianni arrived at three and a giddy Cathy pulled Gianni into the front room to play tiddlywinks while their mothers set the table.

Alice had relied heavily on Sadie's support over the last few months, both in and out of work, and was always glad of her company. She poured two mugs of tea and they sat down at the table and waited until the heated game of tiddlywinks was finished.

'Is Brian doing his homework?' Sadie asked.

'Yes. He'll be nearly finished now.'

Sadie nodded. 'There was a letter waiting for me when I got home from work yesterday. I didn't get the library job I had the recent interview for, so you're stuck with me at Lewis's for a bit longer, I'm afraid.'

'Oh, I'm sorry you didn't get it. But I'm not sorry you'll be staying on at Lewis's, for now, anyway.'

'Well, there were ten applicants for the job. They're as rare as hen's teeth, so I won't be holding my breath. I'll probably still be with you for years.'

Alice was secretly glad to hear that. She'd feel lonely without Sadie when she moved on. Hopefully it wouldn't be for ages yet, especially now that Millie and Jimmy had settled in Blackpool. Millie's latest letter said that they were going to apply for their emigration later this year. Time was moving on for everybody apart from Alice, and some days were better than others. She kept busy by continuing to focus on making sure that Cathy and Brian had everything they needed, as best she could. Jack was being as supportive as ever, but after the accusations from Granny Lomax he seemed a bit withdrawn and not as relaxed with Alice as he had been before Terry's accident.

'Anybody would think I'd done something to the bike on purpose,' he'd said to her when he brought round an envelope of money that had been collected by the fund-raising event he'd organised. 'Your mother-in-law won't even look at me now. Not that she ever liked me anyway, but it's like I'm shit on her shoe these days.'

'I'm sure she doesn't really think badly of you, Jack,' Alice said, handing him a cup of tea. 'She didn't want Terry to do the bike up and because you were as enthusiastic as he was, and he isn't here any more, and you are, she needs someone to blame.'

'The police did a proper check and they said there was nothing wrong with the brakes,' Jack said. 'The bike was pretty mangled up when they recovered it, but from what they could tell it had been roadworthy prior to the crash. It was the wrong time, wrong place, just simple bad luck. A patch of ice and that was it.'

Alice nodded her agreement. 'Sadly, yes. That was all it took.' Just one patch of ice and Terry was taken from her forever.

Chapter Six

September 1946

Alice hurried an excited Cathy and Brian along to the corner of Aigburth Road. They were meeting Sadie and Gianni there to walk to Dingle station to catch the Dockers Umbrella, the overhead train, which would take them to the Pier Head. From there they would take a ferry across to New Brighton for the day. The long summer holidays were coming to an end and school was due to restart next week. Alice would have loved to take the kids on a short trip to Blackpool, like she and Terry had planned to do, but she didn't have the spare money now there was only one wage coming in. Granny Lomax had given her a few shillings towards their day out, and a three-bob rebate from the gas man when he'd come to empty her meter last week had been a nice bonus. Even though she knew she should have put it away for the winter months, when the meter gobbled up more than its fair share of her hard-earned money, it had gone into the pot to help towards the ferry fares. She'd worry about winter when it arrived.

She'd packed a flask of tea, a bottle of orange juice she'd ordered from the milkman, some beef paste sarnies, slices of sponge cake that Granny had dropped off and some apples Brian had picked from the tree in the garden. They wouldn't starve, and all being well she'd have enough left over after paying their fares for an ice-cream treat later. She smiled proudly at Cathy, who looked fresh and pretty in the blue and white gingham sundress and matching hat that Granny had made her. Brian had on shorts cut down from a pair of beige trousers he'd outgrown and a red and white striped T-shirt she'd bought him in the July sales. Alice's one and only pink cotton sundress was faded slightly now, but she'd whitened her peep-toe sandals, so at least they looked half decent. They all looked nice and summery, she thought, and the day was already bright and warm. Hopefully it would stay fine and they could all get a bit of colour in their cheeks. It had been a few months of ups and downs as they'd adjusted to life without Terry again. Making ends meet was a struggle that seemed never-ending. It was all work and no play at the moment, so this day off and going out on the trip was much needed.

Cathy squealed and let go of Brian's hand as she spotted Gianni standing by his mother. She hurtled towards him and flung her arms around him, nearly knocking him flying. She planted a sloppy kiss on his cheek and he grimaced and wiped his hand over his face.

Sadie and Alice laughed at his horrified expression.

'Gianni didn't like my kiss,' Cathy said, pouting.

Brian shook his head. 'Little boys don't like being kissed in the street, Cathy. A hug would have done.' He grabbed her hand and pulled her close. 'Come on, don't start bawling. Let's have a nice day with no falling out between the two of you.'

Gianni proudly stuck out his chest and pointed to a badge pinned on the brown sleeveless sweater he wore over his white cotton shirt.

'Oh, Gianni,' Alice said. 'Your badge came then? Your mammy told me you'd joined the Ovaltineys and were waiting for it to arrive.'

Gianni nodded, his brown eyes sparkling. 'I got a book too,' he said. 'I'll show you when we get on the train.'

'We'll have to join you up, Cathy,' Brian said, taking both children by the hand and leading them down the road.

Alice breathed a sigh of relief and linked her arm through Sadie's as they followed the trio.

'Thank God for Brian and his diplomacy,' Sadie said, laughing. 'Pity he's not older. He could have taken over from Mr Churchill.'

Alice smiled. 'He'll make a good politician, in time. It's something he's interested in as well, more so since Attlee got in. To be honest I don't take much notice, but Brian says he's rebuilding the country slowly but surely and promising all sorts of social reforms. Whatever that means. He talks about it with Granny Lomax, but she's a staunch Conservative. Brian says we have to give Mr Attlee a chance to prove himself. Since the Beveridge Report things have got better and there's that new national health service he's supposed to be sorting out where we can all get free care at the doctor's surgery and hospital. It won't be for a while but it sounds like a good idea to me and it'll save having to pay that few bob each month into the Lloyd George insurance scheme.'

'My dad was talking about it the other night,' Sadie said. 'He said nothing comes free and they'll find a way of making us pay for it somehow, through extra taxes or what-have-you. There was something on the news and he was shouting at the wireless. Mam told him to shut up because the newsman couldn't hear him.'

Alice laughed. 'My dad used to do that. Mam always rolled her eyes and ignored him. She said if it made him feel better about things then let him be. Right, here we are,' she said as they approached Dingle station on Park Road. 'Come and stand over here with Brian while we queue for the tickets, kids.' The station was busy with dock workers going on shift and families taking final summer days out.

Cathy's eyes grew round as the train rumbled into the dark underground station, creating a draught around their legs.

'Do we go in a tunnel all the way, Mammy?' she asked, shrinking back against Alice's legs.

'No, just for a short distance and then we're outside again.'

They found seats in a carriage near the middle of the train and sank down as it let out a belch of steam and chugged away from the platform. Gianni pulled out his Ovaltineys book and he and Cathy, heads bent low, studied the pages, laughing at things Gianni pointed out.

'Peace,' Brian muttered, relaxing back in his seat next to them and stretching out his long legs as the train emerged into bright sunshine and ran along the overhead railway track on its short journey to the bustling docks.

Alice stared out of the window at ships in the distance either approaching or leaving the dockside. She watched the *Queen Mary*, with its three red funnels belching steam up to the cloudless blue sky, making its slow passage down the Mersey towards the Irish Sea, from where it would head for America. She wondered what ship Millie and Jimmy would take when they eventually left England for Canadian shores, and blinked rapidly at the thought of her lovely friend moving so far away for good.

*

As they settled on the top-deck wooden seats of the *Royal Daffodil* ferry, Sadie pointed out to Alice the destruction of their once bustling city, stretching as far as the eye could see. Bombed and blackened buildings and flat areas where crowded tenements had once stood, the land now cleared for new housing stock. But the one thing they both remarked on was the amazing fact that, amongst some of the waterfront buildings that were intact, the Liver Building, with its mythical Liver Birds standing atop the clock towers, was undamaged and still stood as proud as it had ever done. A symbol of the freedom of Liverpool and treasured by all.

'Glad the Germans missed it,' Brian said, pointing to the building. 'All three of the Graces in fact. Imagine sailing into Liverpool and not seeing them any more. That would have finished us off for sure. See those big birds up there,' he said to Cathy as she squinted skywards at the Liver Birds. 'The day they fly away, Liverpool will be no more because the Mersey will burst its banks and flood the city and we'll all be drowned.'

'Oh, Brian,' Alice said as Cathy's lip quivered. 'Don't tell her things like that. She'll have nightmares. Rodney used to say it to me and it worried me to death for years. They can't fly anywhere, love,' she said to Cathy. 'They're only pretend birds.' She raised an eyebrow at Sadie, who was struggling to suppress a giggle.

At the pier docking point the ferry pulled in and Gianni and Brian helped Cathy down the steps. They ran along the length of the pier, Cathy in between them, racing to keep up, followed by Alice and Sadie.

'I'm surprised how busy it is,' Alice said as they made their way onto the already crowded sands. Couples were hurrying past, pushing trolleys piled up with babies and baggage, and dragging toddlers by the hand.

'Probably all like us. This is the nearest they'll get to a holiday, money being as tight as it is. And it's the last week before they all go back to school.' The unspoken 'thank God' hung in the air as Alice and Sadie laughed. 'I'm going to ask for more hours when we go in tomorrow,' Sadie said. 'I'm sure they'll give them to me as we'll be getting busy for Christmas and, with not getting the library job the other week, I could do with earning a bit more. I wonder where they'll put the grotto this year, if we even have one.'

'I might ask for a few extra hours as well,' Alice said. 'I need the money badly. I miss my Terry's wages, but not half as much as I miss him. Christmas will be so hard this year, remembering the last one, the only one we ever had. It's so unfair. But, come on,' she blinked away a tear. 'I'm not going to get all maudlin. I do enough of that when I'm sitting on my own at night. Let's enjoy our day.' She looked up as Cathy and Gianni came running back, panting and pointing to something going on down on the promenade to the left of the pier.

'It's Punch and Judy,' Gianni said excitedly. 'Can we watch it please?'

'Yes, of course you can,' said Sadie. 'Let's go and get some deckchairs for me and Alice and we'll have our dinner first and then you can watch this afternoon's show. If I remember rightly it starts again at two o'clock, so you can be first in the queue while we have a little sunbathe.'

Deckchairs in position facing the sea, Alice and Sadie set out the picnic on a cloth Sadie produced from her bag.

After every last crumb had been eaten, Alice tided away the cloth and empty flask and bottles and packed them away. Brian took the little ones up onto the prom to watch Punch and Judy and Alice and Sadie lifted their sundress skirts up slightly and stretched out their legs, loving the feel of the sun baking into their flesh.

'Get a bit of colour now and I won't need to wear stockings at work,' Alice said. 'I can save them for Saturday night at the Legion.'

'Are you going to keep both jobs on while you can?' Sadie asked. 'It's not just about the money; it's a bit of social life for you as well.'

Alice nodded. 'I will while I can. Brian's old enough to look after Cathy now and when he wants to start going out on a Saturday night with his mates, I'll have to think again. She can go to Granny's any time so I'm not looking to give it up just yet. I like the company and I like working with Jack. He makes me laugh.'

'I like Jack,' Sadie said. 'Not sure I'd trust him as anything other than a friend though. He's got too much of a roving eye.'

Alice grinned. 'He has. But he's a single man, so why not.'

*

Alice saw Brian out, all smart in his almost-new grammar school uniform. She felt proud as she watched him hitch his new satchel onto his back, a gift from Granny Lomax, and stroll confidently down Lucerne Street. This was an important year for him; the year he would take his School Certificate exams, which would ensure his future in further education. She closed the front door and went back into the kitchen to see to Cathy's breakfast.

Her daughter came trundling down the stairs, partially dressed and carrying the rest of her clothes with her.

'I can't do up my buttons,' she wailed. 'They keep going in the wrong holes.'

Alice smiled and fastened the shirt and then slipped a gymslip over Cathy's head.

'Go and sit down and I'll bring your breakfast through. No chucky eggs this morning until I do my shopping. Toast and jam will have to do.'

Cathy dragged her feet on the walk to St Michael's, but as soon as she spotted Debbie waiting for her by the gate, she perked up and ran to meet her best friend.

Clara Jones, Debbie's mum, smiled as Alice came to stand by her side. 'Thank the lord for that. I'm ready for a bit of peace – until the next holidays, that is,' she said. 'Here's your friend Sadie. No doubt you two are off to work? I sometimes wish I had a job, something for myself, but Arthur doesn't want me to work. He likes me to stay at home.'

Alice sighed. 'We have no choice in the matter. You enjoy it while you can, Clara. That's what I say.'

'But you two always seem to have much more fun. Ah well, I'd better get back to my chores. See you tomorrow.'

Alice raised an eyebrow after Clara's departing back. 'Much more fun? Who is she kidding? I wish I had her comfortable life.'

'Not sure about that,' Sadie said as they hurried towards the tram stop. 'Her hubby sounds a bit old-fashioned. He sounds like the sort who wants his tea on the table as soon as he comes in from work. Expects everything to be shipshape and Bristol fashion and his shirts ironed a certain way. We women have learned to be independent with the war years. We shouldn't have to go back to that old way of life just because men expect it. It's time we took a stand.'

Alice laughed. Sadie's face was alight and her expression one of determination. 'Maybe you should join the politics brigade as well. Fight to make life easier for women. Get it sorted for us all. A modern-day Emmeline Pankhurst.'

Sadie smiled as they jumped on board the tram. 'Well, let's see if I can persuade Lewis's to give me some extra hours first. I'll assert myself in store.'

Chapter Seven

Alice was crouched on the floor behind the counter, trying to entice a large spider away from making a web near the knitting needles. She wasn't a lover of the eight-legged creatures but didn't want to kill it. Wafting it with a sheet of paper wasn't making much difference as it was running up and down, weaving a new home to its heart's content. Sadie was terrified of spiders and wouldn't come back behind the counter until it was gone. The customer Sadie was serving from afar wanted size eight knitting needles and they were shelved right below the delicate web, which meant either destroying it and maybe having the spider leap at her in anger, or… well there wasn't an or. Alice tried to catch Sadie's eye to signal that she couldn't get to a size eight needle, but Sadie was looking in the opposite direction as she talked to her customer. Alice got to her feet and sidled past the web to the far end of the counter.

'I'm really sorry,' she began, 'but we appear to be out of size eights. We have an order due later today. Would you like to reserve a pair?'

The stout woman tutted and shook her head. 'I'll just take the wool then, chuck,' she said to Sadie. 'I'll borrow needles from Mavis, my next-door neighbour.'

Sadie handed the hanks of fawn double knitting wool to Alice, who bagged them up and took the woman's money. She reached for change from the till and handed it over.

The woman left with a smile and a nod.

'Is it still there?' Sadie hissed from the other side of the counter.

'Yes, and it's working hard.' Alice grimaced, looking down at the eight busy legs spinning the immaculate web.

'I don't care how bloody hard it's working,' Sadie muttered. 'I'm not coming back behind there until you get rid of it. It's already lost us a sale. Chuck me a duster and I'll polish the glass out front.'

Alice grinned and threw a cloth in her direction. 'Shall I ask someone to move it?'

Sadie looked around. 'I doubt any of the women will. We need a man and there's not much choice.' She bent to rub at some smudges on the glass-fronted cabinets while Alice kept a wary eye on the spider. By the time Sadie had finished the full length of the counter fronts it was almost break time and the girl who was taking over for fifteen minutes sauntered across.

'What's up with youse two?' Sally Ball asked, flicking her black curly hair over her shoulders. 'Youse both look dead shifty.'

Alice pointed to the spider and the girl jumped back and screamed. 'Oh bloody 'ell. It's as big as the one me dad just got rid of in our carsey back 'ome. I ain't going behind there until some bugger shifts it.'

Alice felt beads of sweat break on her forehead as Miss White, the floor supervisor, hurried over to the counter, her face pinched in a familiar lemon-sucking expression. Now they were for it.

'What on earth is going on?' Miss White demanded. 'Why did Miss Ball scream?'

'There's a spider, Miss White, and I'm terrified of 'em,' Sally replied.

'Oh, for goodness sake, girl,' Miss White muttered. She peered around the counter, keeping a dignified distance, gasped and signalled to a young man who was busy unpacking boxes on a counter across the other side of the floor. 'Malcolm,' she said as he hurried over. 'Get rid of that spider.'

Malcolm looked to where she was pointing and shuddered. His cheeks flushed as red as his hair and he took a deep breath. 'I, er, I can't, Miss,' he stuttered. 'I don't like 'em either.'

Alice was chewing her lip, trying not to snigger at his terrified expression, when a soft voice whispered in her ear, 'Perhaps I can help.'

She spun round to see Jack Dawson standing behind her, an amused expression on his face. 'Oh, Jack, you knight in shining armour,' she said. 'Thank you so much.'

Jack smiled. 'Can someone get me a glass or a cup and a postcard then?'

Malcolm went off to fulfil Jack's request and the spider was captured and dropped from a nearby open window. Jack wiped the cobweb away with his hanky and smiled. 'There you go, ladies. All in a day's work.'

'Thank you, young man,' Miss White said, her sharp features softening as she gave a rare smile.

'Thanks, Jack,' Alice and Sadie chorused.

Sally batted her eyelashes at him and he smiled.

'Any time, ladies. I was just looking at ties over the other side and saw something was going on, and then spotted you looking worried, Alice, so thought I'd come over and investigate.'

'Thank goodness you did. We'd better go for our break,' Sadie said. 'We're late as it is. Come and join us for a cuppa, Jack. You deserve one after your heroic act.'

'Don't mind if I do,' Jack said. 'Sticky buns are on me. Lead the way.'

*

Alice found a table while Sadie and Jack queued at the counter. She watched the pair in animated conversation and wondered what they were talking about. Jack swung around as though conscious of her eyes burning into his back. He winked and then turned his attention back to Sadie. Alice was surprised to feel a little flutter of jealousy wash over her as Sadie giggled at something Jack was saying. The pair made their way over to the table, Jack carrying the tray. Sadie slid into the seat nearest the window and Jack sat down next to her.

'Jack was just telling me that *The Big Sleep* is on at the Mayfair this week,' Sadie began. 'That new Humphrey Bogart and Lauren Bacall film.'

'Really? Oh, I'd love to see that. Haven't been to the pictures since we saw George Formby,' Alice said.

'Well now's your chance, because Jack just asked me if I thought you'd like to go with him. I told him you'd probably say no but that I would give you a gentle push, because I know how much you like Humphrey Bogart.'

Alice spluttered on the mouthful of tea she'd just taken. 'I can't. What about the kids?'

'Ah, well that's sorted because once I've got Gianni to bed my mam will keep an ear out for him and I'll pop around to yours to make sure Brian and Cathy are okay. It will do you good to get out, Alice.'

Alice looked at Jack, who sat there smiling as though he knew what the outcome would be. 'Did you set this up?' she asked. 'Plant the spider and then pretend to be buying a tie?'

Jack laughed. 'Don't be so daft. I was getting a new black tie for Arnold because he's going to a funeral this afternoon. And how would I know you two are scared of spiders anyway? It's not a subject we've ever brought up. No, I just told Sadie I felt a bit shy about asking you to come with me, that's all, and she said leave it to her.'

Alice smiled. 'Now there's a first. You, shy, I mean. But yes, actually, I would love to go and see the film with you.'

What harm could it do? It was only the pictures. Jack had always been there for her in the past few years and looked out for her, so it would be a nice change, a couple of old pals going to see a film.

Jack grinned. 'That's grand,' he said. 'So what about Wednesday, then? I've got the night off. I can pick you up at seven.'

Alice nodded. 'Wednesday is fine.'

*

'What can I wear?' Alice asked as she and Sadie took their places back behind the now spider-free haberdashery counter. 'I've hardly got anything that doesn't have darns in it and isn't faded. I've got a black skirt that's half decent, but nothing to go with it.'

'I can lend you a nice pink and white striped blouse,' Sadie offered. 'We're the same size, so it should fit you nicely. I'll bring it round later, after we've had our tea.'

'Oh, thank you. That's really kind of you. Oh, God, I feel all nervous now. I shouldn't have said I'll go.' Alice twisted her hands anxiously together.

'Alice, you'll be fine. Jack's a good friend and you've known him for years now. He'll be lovely company for you.'

'Terry's mother will go mad. She'll read all sorts into it.' Alice chewed her lip.

'It's got nothing to do with her. You're entitled to a life, for goodness sake.'

Alice drew a deep breath. 'I am, aren't I? But I know she still blames Jack for Terry's death. Don't say anything in front of the kids tonight. I'll tell them on Wednesday just before Jack comes to the house for me. Granny may pop in tonight or tomorrow to see how they got on at school and I don't want them saying anything to her.'

'My lips are sealed,' Sadie said with a grin and turned her attention to a customer who was looking at the knitting patterns spread out in a fan-shape on the counter.

Alice spotted Miss White making her way over to their counter and put up a hand to gain her attention.

'Yes, Mrs Lomax?' Miss White glanced at the clipboard she was carrying. 'Make it quick as I have to attend a meeting in another department in a few minutes. I just wanted to make sure you were both okay after this morning's, er, unfortunate incident. Although I have to say,' she lowered her voice, 'with the amount of building work going on around us, I would imagine all sorts of insects and creatures are looking for new homes. Just keep a close eye on things.'

'We will,' Alice said as Sadie's customer went on her way. 'Sadie and I were wondering about the possibilities of us both having a few extra hours' work each week.'

Miss White's face brightened. 'I'm sure there is some. Would that be here on haberdashery?'

'Are there any vacancies in cosmetics?' Sadie asked, crossing her fingers behind her back.

'Not at the moment, but I will certainly bear you both in mind when there are. I can currently offer another two hours a day on here.'

Alice and Sadie smiled and nodded.

'I'll have a letter sent out to you detailing your new hours to start next Monday then. Now I must dash.'

'Well, that's better than nothing,' Alice said as Miss White hurried away.

'I'll say. An extra few bob will come in handy. Cosmetics don't know what they're missing, mind. Hopefully we'll get something in there soon.'

*

Sadie's pink and white striped blouse with a neat white Peter-Pan collar fitted her perfectly and looked lovely with the straight black skirt with kick-pleated hem, Alice thought, as she twisted this way and that in front of the full-length mirror in her bedroom. In spite of her earlier apprehension, she was looking forward to going out with Jack tonight. Cathy was tucked up in bed already – she'd almost fallen asleep with her head in her bowl of soup. Brian was in his room doing homework and would listen out for Sadie knocking. He'd told her to go and enjoy herself when Alice had informed him that Jack was coming later to take her to the pictures. Cathy hadn't been told as she was too tired to take anything in, which suited Alice, as the less she knew the better. She picked up her jacket and handbag from the bed and knocked gently on Brian's door.

'I'm going downstairs now to wait for Jack,' she whispered. 'You'll need to lock the door behind me and don't forget to listen out for Sadie in a bit.'

'Okay, our Alice. Have a good time.' Brian gave her a hug.

Alice smiled. 'I'll try.' As she walked downstairs a gentle tap sounded on the front door. Jack was standing on the step, a broad smile on his face.

'You look nice, gel,' he said.

'Thank you, and so do you.' He was wearing a navy suit and white shirt and his black boots were highly polished, his dark brown hair neatly brushed and his blue eyes twinkling.

She closed the door behind her and they walked down Lucerne Street together. Alice felt a bit self-conscious, but no one was out on the street to see them. On Lark Lane Jack offered his arm and she slipped hers through his at the same time as the newsagent's wife came outside to take in the A-board with its advertisements for newspapers. Her eyebrows practically vanished up her forehead as she observed them walking along. Alice avoided eye contact with the woman. By tomorrow morning her mother-in-law and half the neighbours in the vicinity would be talking about her. Ah well, she'd just have to ignore them. All they were doing was going to see a film. It was no one's business but theirs.

'Mate of your ma-in-law's?' Jack said with a grin.

'Yes.' Alice sighed. 'And the biggest gossip for miles.'

'Ah well, don't let her spoil our night. It's bugger all to do with the neighbours. And we're doing nowt wrong.'

The queue outside the Mayfair stretched down the street. Half of Aigburth appeared to be there. The film was proving to be popular up and down the country and Humphrey Bogart and Lauren Bacall were big stars. Inside, they followed the usherette, who led them to their seats halfway down the stalls. They sat down and Jack handed over the bag of Chocolate Limes he'd managed to get. Sweets were still on ration so they were a real treat. Alice handed one to Jack. She popped one into her mouth, savouring the sharp lime flavour with the milky chocolate. They settled back to watch the Pathé news, which was mainly about politics, ongoing plans for the proposed new health scheme and the countrywide rebuilding of thousands of new houses and flats to replace all that had been lost during the war.

'Do you want an ice-cream now or in the interval?' Jack asked as two usherettes made their way to the front with laden trays.

'Let's wait for the interval. Tell me what the film is about. I've heard it's good, but to be honest I've no idea what the story involves.'

Jack nodded. 'I read the book a while ago and really enjoyed it. The story is written by Raymond Chandler and it's about a private detective called Philip Marlowe. But I won't tell you the plot, because it will spoil it for you.'

Alice smiled. As the lights went down she turned to look at Jack, whose animated face was fixed on the screen. His right cheek with the scar he'd received in a fight during his youth was in her vision and she felt the urge to gently stroke it, but forced herself instead to concentrate on the film. At the interval they had a tub of vanilla ice-cream each and as the lights went down for the second half, she felt her tummy fluttering at Jack's close proximity, and then immediately felt a pang of guilt as the thought of Terry crossed her mind.

*

Alice gritted her teeth as she knocked on the door of Granny Lomax's bungalow the following day. The door was flung open and she was invited in, but the look on Granny's face made her heart sink.

'Tea, Alice?' Granny led the way into the lounge, where Cathy was sitting on the sofa with a book.

'Er, no thank you. I need to get home. I've a lot to do. Cathy, come on, let's get your coat on.'

Cathy ran towards her and gave her a hug. Alice popped Cathy's coat on and bent down to fasten the buttons. 'Pick your school bag up and then we can get off.'

Granny was standing in the doorway with her arms folded. 'Did you enjoy the film last night?'

'Yes thank you. It was very good,' Alice said, hoping her cheeks weren't as red as they felt. She'd been ready for the question so had mentally prepared herself on the tram journey home.

'Well, I hope it's not going to be a regular occurrence, you going out with Jack Dawson, I mean.'

Alice felt a rush of anger. The blooming gossips had no doubt had a field day. Why shouldn't she go out with Jack again? Not that he'd asked her yet, but it was no one's business other than theirs. And if he did ask her out again she would definitely be accepting. She'd enjoyed his company, he'd made her laugh, and lord knows she needed to. There had been nothing inappropriate in his behaviour.

She grabbed hold of Cathy's hand and pulled her down the hall towards the front door.

'It might be,' she said. 'A regular occurrence, I mean. We enjoy each other's company. But I have no immediate plans at the moment. We're both very busy people with work commitments and I also have the children to look after. From next Monday I've got a couple of extra hours a day at Lewis's. I don't want to put you out, so I'll ask Brian to collect Cathy on his way home from school.'

Granny snorted as she opened the front door. 'Cathy could still stay with me while you do extra hours. But with regards to the other matter, I thought you had more sense than that, Alice. After what that man has done to this family as well.'

Alice gritted her teeth. Terry's mother would never let that one go, in spite of being told time and again that she was wrong to blame Jack for the accident.

'Not in front of Cathy, please. And as I said, Brian will collect her and then I can just go straight home after work. We'll see you tomorrow.'

Chapter Eight

December 1946

Alice sat down on the front sitting room rug, in front of the dying embers of the coal fire, finishing wrapping the few presents she'd managed to buy for Cathy and Brian. It was a far cry from last Christmas, when Terry had been here and they'd managed to treat everyone to something decent. This year's gifts were more necessities than luxuries. The small tree in the corner was a second-hand artificial one from Paddy's Market and two of the lower branches looked as though a dog had chewed them, but she'd positioned it so that they were at the back and draped them with tinsel to cover the bald bits. It was okay, but nowhere near as grand as last year's tall pine-scented tree. Her heart wasn't really in the festive season but she would do her best for the kids.

They were having dinner and tea at Granny Lomax's on the day, which would save Alice some money at least. Cathy was as excited as any other five-year-old and Alice tried hard to match her enthusiasm, but it wasn't easy. She got up and made herself a cuppa and brought it back into the front room. As she sat watching the last glow in the coals disappear, tears ran down her cheeks. It was always going to be hard, but this first Christmas without Terry would be the worst of all. Last year she'd thought they'd have many more to look forward to, with an expanding family to enjoy it with. Even when he was away there was always the dream to hold onto; always the thought that when he came home they would do this and that, making plans for the future. Now there was nothing. No hopes and dreams, just emptiness stretching ahead for years to come.

*

Christmas dinner at Granny's was a sombre affair in spite of Granny's generous portions and her insistence that they all have seconds, which only Brian took advantage of. Alice felt tired. It had been a very late finish at the Legion as Arnold had insisted that she and Jack join him and Winnie for a sherry and a mince pie, once the customers had gone home and he'd locked up. Winnie had given her a bag containing three gaily wrapped parcels for under the tree, and then Jack had walked her home and given her a small parcel that he'd pulled from his pocket.

'It's not much, Alice. But I know it's one you like to wear,' he'd said as they stood on the front doorstep.

'Thanks, Jack. That's very kind of you. Look, I know you're having dinner with Arnold and Winnie tomorrow, but why don't you come here for tea on Boxing Day? Sadie and Gianni are coming too.'

'I will. Thanks, gel.' He'd given her a peck on the cheek and a hug and hurried on his way.

*

Alice felt her head had hardly touched the pillow before Cathy was clambering on her bed the next morning, excitement in her big brown eyes.

'Come on, Mammy. Let's see if he's been.'

Alice had groaned. All she wanted to do was curl into a ball and cry. It hardly felt like five minutes since last Christmas morning, when Terry was here and they'd opened their gifts in front of a roaring fire. But she had crawled out of bed and discovered that Brian had already crept downstairs and had the fire going and a pot of tea brewed. He was doing his best to be the man of the house and she plastered on a brave smile for him and sat down on the sofa to watch Cathy tearing the wrapping paper from her gifts. Alice opened hers and, amongst them, was delighted to find a little blue bottle of Soir de Paris in Jack's parcel, and a beautiful red and cream silk headscarf from Arnold and Winnie.

*

'Are you okay, Alice?' Her mother-in-law's voice broke her thoughts.

Alice nodded. 'Just feel a little out of sorts. My head's not really in the place it should be.'

'That's understandable, love. I feel the same. Brian, when you've finished eating, help me clear the table and then you and Cathy can open that compendium of games I gave you.'

'I'll only play with her if she doesn't cheat,' Brian teased, pulling on his little niece's pigtails.

Cathy stuck out her bottom lip. 'That's mean. I don't cheat.'

Brian laughed. 'Yeah, you do.'

Alice got to her feet before they started arguing. 'Behave, you two. Do you mind if I go and sit in the lounge?'

'Not at all. Off you go and I'll bring you a nice cuppa through when I've finished washing up,' Granny replied.

Alice sat down on the sofa in the festively decorated room and let her head fall back against a cushion. The scent of the pine tree in the bay window made tears tumble down her cheeks. Every anniversary, birthday or Christmas Day would be difficult to get through. She'd been doing so well up to today. People had told her it would get easier given time, but how? So many women had been widowed by the war and they just had to get on with it. At least she'd had her Terry back for nine months, a privilege denied to many others. She'd always treasure her memories of those few precious months.

Granny Lomax came into the room with a tray of tea and mince pies. She put the tray down on the coffee table, fished an envelope from her skirt pocket and handed it to Alice.

'It's what's left of the policies I cashed in after Terry's death,' she explained. 'I settled up the funeral bills, and thought the rest would help you out over the next few months. I've been meaning to give it to you for a while, but there never seemed to be the right time. It's not a lot, but it might come in useful.'

Alice stared at the envelope and then at Granny Lomax. She peered inside and took a deep breath. There were six five-pound notes folded together. Thirty pounds. A small fortune that would see her through the winter months for extra coal and making sure the kids were warmly dressed. It would be a huge help.

'Thank you so much. But are you sure?'

Granny nodded. 'Your need is greater than mine, Alice.'

'I don't know what to say. It's a lovely surprise and it will certainly help us through the next few months. Thank you.' Alice felt overwhelmed. Granny had spent a lot of money on presents for the kids and had given Alice a new pink sweater and some silk stockings. She'd been more than generous. All Alice had been able to afford for a gift was a box of ladies' embroidered hankies, but they'd been received with good grace and enthusiasm and Alice knew they'd be used. Granny always liked a fresh hanky in her handbag each day.

'Why don't the three of you come for tea tomorrow? We can have the left-over turkey and I'll make a trifle.'

Alice chewed her lip. 'Er, why don't you come to us? We've got Sadie and Gianni coming for tea, and, erm, Jack is popping in too.' No point in not telling her because he would be there, Alice was certain.

Granny pursed her lips. 'I'll leave it, thank you. I can't sit in the same room as that man, especially not this year, and at Christmas too. I'm surprised at you, Alice.' She got to her feet and walked out of the lounge, leaving Alice's thoughts in turmoil.

She couldn't do right for doing wrong. But Jack would be all alone if she hadn't invited him. And he was her friend, after all. He'd looked after her and it was the least she could do.

*

Alice, Jack and Sadie sat around the dining table, drinking sherry and chatting comfortably, while the children played games in the front room with Brian. Before Jack had arrived, Alice had told Sadie about her little windfall and how Granny Lomax had refused to come for tea because Jack was invited.

'I felt really bad,' Alice said. 'Especially as she'd just given me the envelope of money.'

Sadie sighed. 'It can't be helped. One day she'll realise that Jack wasn't to blame for Terry's death. But for now she needs to put the blame on someone. Don't worry, Alice. She'll get her head around it eventually.'

Alice nodded and threw some coal on the fire. 'Maybe.'

Jack had arrived just after five o'clock with three small Rowntrees selection boxes for the children, who'd whooped with delight as he'd produced them from behind his back.

'Thank God for my mate who works down at the docks,' he'd whispered to Alice as she let him in. 'Couldn't come empty-handed and, with no shops open, I had a dilemma.'

Alice laughed as he dropped a kiss on her cheek. 'They'll be thrilled to bits. I've never seen so much chocolate in one place since before rationing started. Thank you so much, Jack. It's very thoughtful of you to go dashing around to find something for them.'

'My pleasure, gel,' he'd said, reaching into an inside jacket pocket and producing a bottle of sherry. 'For the ladies.'

'So, what plans do you gels have for the next year?' Jack asked now, raising a toast to the three of them.

Sadie shrugged. 'Keep applying for library jobs and saving a bit each week to get me and Gianni a little place of our own.'

Alice shook her head. 'I'm too scared to make plans. After the last year I've had, just to get through each week will be enough. As long as I can keep the roof over our heads and food in the kids' bellies, that will be enough for me. Brian's got a busy few months coming up with all his studying for his mid-year exams. And then if he passes, I'll worry about that when the time comes. It'll just be work, work, work for me, I'm afraid.'

'Well, me and Sadie will always be there for you, gel, you know that,' Jack said, patting Alice's hand. 'As will all your friends. You only have to ask if you need anything.'

Alice smiled and raised her glass. 'To good friends who've never let me down. Thanks for always being there for me.'

Chapter Nine

July 1947

One Saturday morning, halfway through July, Alice picked up an official-looking envelope from the mat behind the door and felt a little thrill go through her, mixed with apprehension at what it might contain.

'Brian,' she called up the stairs. 'I think it's here.'

The sound of a door being flung open and footsteps thundering on the stairs broke the silence and Brian hurtled into the back sitting room, his brown hair standing on end and sleep in his blue eyes. Alice had placed the envelope on the table. She pointed to it and his eyes opened wide.

'Go on,' she urged. 'Don't keep us in suspense any longer. I can't bear it.'

Brian chewed his lip and tore at the envelope with shaking hands. He removed a sheet of paper and stared at it, his anxious face relaxing into a wide smile.

'Oh my God! I've done it, our Alice. I've passed the School Certificate. I've got credits in all five of my subjects.'

Alice's eyes filled and she pulled him into her arms. 'Oh, well done, Brian. I am so proud of you. I know Mam, Dad and Rodney would be too if they were here.'

'And Terry,' he said, his voice husky.

'Well that goes without saying, my love.'

'Granny Lomax will be chuffed to bits as well,' he said as a sleepy Cathy shuffled down the stairs on her bottom and slunk into the room. 'I've passed my exams, Cathy,' he said, scooping her up and waltzing her around the room.

She stared at him as he put her down. 'Is that good? Do we get a present for it? Can I have my chucky egg now, Mammy?'

Alice rolled her eyes and laughed. 'I suppose so. And it's Brian who should get a present, not you, Madam.'

After breakfast, once Brian and Cathy had left to go and tell Granny Lomax the good news, Alice took a pad and pen from the kitchen drawer and started to jot down figures. Brian's passing his exams was great news, but meant an extra financial headache in that he would now stay on at school for a two further years to take his Higher School Certificate, which could potentially lead to him gaining a university place in two years' time. It was what she wanted for him more than anything, and she knew it was what he wanted too. But financing it was the problem. Even with her extra hours at work, they were more than on the breadline.

The thirty pounds she'd received from Granny Lomax last Christmas had been very useful in helping to pay the bills for the last few months, but now it was almost gone and she was struggling more than ever to make ends meet. Brian would need books and all sorts and the cost was out of her reach. Granny Lomax would no doubt offer to help a little, but although Alice had tried to remain friendly with her since the first time she went out with Jack, the close bond she and her ex-mother-in-law had shared in the past was no longer as strong as it used to be. Brian wasn't a blood relative of Granny's and she was under no obligation to help.

Alice chewed the end of her pen as the figures she'd written down swam before her eyes. They simply wouldn't balance. But by hook or by crook her brother was going to stay on at grammar school and eventually become a teacher or a professor or whatever. She would never let him throw his future away, no matter how hard she had to work. There must be a way, but God only knew what and how. She would talk to Jack tomorrow when they went out for the day, see what he thought. Cathy was spending Sunday with Granny, as had become the usual pattern lately, and Brian was going out with his pals to the boating lake at Sefton Park. Jack was borrowing Arnold's car for the day and he'd asked Alice if she fancied a trip to Blackpool with him. She'd agreed. She'd not had a proper break since taking the kids to New Brighton last year, so a nice day out was something to really look forward to. They'd rung Jimmy's parents' house from the Legion's phone and he and Millie were going to meet up with them. Alice was looking forward to catching up with her friend again.

*

'I'm not sure how I'm going to manage,' Alice told Jack as they sat side by side on two deckchairs on the crowded sands in Blackpool. The day was hot and she slathered her arms and neck in Nivea cream and made Jack put some on his face to protect the area of scarring on his right cheek. A tram tooted loudly, passing behind them on the promenade on its way to the south pier. Millie and Jimmy were due to join them in half an hour and the foursome planned to have fish and chips in a little café on the prom.

'But I've got to do it somehow,' Alice continued, pulling the straps of her blue and white floral sundress back up onto her shoulders. 'Brian has worked so hard for this. I can't fail him now.'

Jack nodded. 'I agree. He's a good kid and he deserves to do well, but you can only do for him what you can afford to do, chuck. He's a very lucky lad to have a big sister like you looking after him. Without you he'd no doubt have been shoved in an orphanage long ago.'

'I know, and I've done my best. But the cost of the bills keeps going up and up and food is getting more expensive. They both eat like horses. School uniforms cost a packet. I've got to admit it; I'm really struggling at the moment, Jack.' Her voice wavered and she sniffed back a tear.

Jack stared at a seagull swooping and calling above their heads, before diving into the sea for food. He lit a cigarette and blew a cloud of smoke in the air.

'You know what I think you should do?'

'No, what?'

'Have a serious think about getting married again. It would make your life a whole lot easier.'

Alice stared at him as though he'd gone mad. 'Married again? Don't be so blooming daft, Jack. Terry's only been gone sixteen months. And anyway, married to who? Who'd be mad enough to want to take on two kids and me?'

Jack looked at her and frowned. 'Do you really need to ask that, Alice? We've been getting closer over the last few months and I love being with you. After all this time, you must know how I feel about you, surely? And you also know that Terry wouldn't have wanted you to struggle on your own forever.'

Alice's jaw dropped and she stared at him. 'Jack Dawson, are you pulling my leg here, or are you actually trying to propose to me?'

'I guess I must be, gel, proposing, that is.' He dropped onto the sand and tried to balance on one knee, but his lame foot wouldn't hold him up and he grabbed her arm to save himself from falling over, but ended up by pulling her down with him, laughing helplessly as her face broke into a wide grin. 'Well, that's made a bugger of that!' he said.

Alice giggled until her sides ached. Her arms were covered in sand that had stuck to the cream she'd put on.

'Oh, Jack, what are you like? I don't know what to say.'

'You could try saying yes,' he teased.

'Well, yes. I would love to marry you. But we've only been casually seeing each other, I didn't realise you had proper feelings for me. We've only had the odd few kisses. I mean, I know we've been best friends for ages, and you're always there for me, but you might not like me that much if we were to get married.'

'Alice, shut up wittering, woman, and give us a proper kiss right now.'

Alice melted into his arms and Jack held her tight as they shared a passionate kiss that went on for ages. She came up for air and looked into his eyes, shocked by the intensity of the feelings she had just experienced.

'Do you still want to marry me?' she whispered. 'I mean, do you love me?'

Jack smiled and kissed her again. 'What do *you* think? And what about you, do you have feelings for me?'

'Well, you've taken me by surprise... but yes, of course I have feelings for you, Jack. I can't imagine a life without you in it now.' Alice wasn't sure if her feelings amounted to love just yet, but she really couldn't imagine not having Jack in her life. Maybe love would grow as time went on.

'There you go then. I know I'm not the most romantic bloke in the world, but we might as well be together as apart.' He looked up as someone called their names, and waved at Millie and Jimmy, who were making their way across the sands to join them. 'We can have a chippy tea celebration with this pair.'

'We got an earlier tram,' Millie said. 'Why are you two on the floor?' She eyed them curiously as she and Jimmy drew level. 'You've got sand all over your arms, Alice. And were you just kissing one another?'

'Aye,' Jack said, taking a towel from the carrier bag between the deckchairs and handing it to Alice. 'We were. Shall I tell them, or will you?' he directed at Alice.

She smiled and rubbed at her arms. Millie knew she'd had the odd night out with Jack, but Alice had always kept things close to her chest because she didn't think Jack was serious.

'You can tell them,' she said.

'Alice has just agreed to marry me,' Jack said, grinning from ear to ear.

'What?' Millie squealed and dropped to her knees. 'Oh my God.' She gave Alice a big hug and Jack a kiss on the cheek. Jimmy shook his hand and gave Alice a kiss.

'Congratulations, both of you,' Millie said, beaming. 'I can't believe it. Now that means we have *two* things to celebrate.'

'Two things?' Alice frowned, shaking sand off the towel and then rubbing at her arms again. 'God, this is worse than being sandpapered.'

Millie nodded while Jimmy smiled. 'I'm pregnant,' she said, grinning. 'Two months. And because of that we've decided we're not going to Canada after all.'

Alice flung her arms around her friend and burst into tears. 'Oh, I'm so happy for you, and also I'm *really* glad that you're not going to Canada.'

'So are my mam and dad,' Millie said. 'As soon as I found out a baby was on the way I realised I couldn't do it to them. They've only got me, and this will be their first grandchild. It would be cruel to deprive them of seeing it growing up and it would be such a long way for them to travel at their ages too.'

Jimmy nodded his agreement. 'We're going to move back to Liverpool, so Millie can be near her parents. There's a lot of rebuilding going on in the city. I'm sure I'll get fixed up with a bricklayer's job easily enough. We're moving in with Millie's mam and dad next week but one for now, but if you hear of any little houses going for sale or to rent in or around the Lark Lane area, will you let us know?'

'There's nothing at the moment, but I'll keep my eyes open,' Alice said, thrilled with the events of the day, and how everything was looking so rosy for them all.

'There are a lot of new estates being built by the corporation, Jimmy,' Jack said. 'They're crying out for skilled brickies. You'll get fixed up right away.' He got to his feet and brushed sand from his smart flannel trousers. 'I think we've had enough of the beach today. Let's go and celebrate all our good news with a nice fish and chip tea.'

*

When Alice and Jack took Arnold's car back to the Legion they told him and Winnie their good news. Alice felt her cheeks heating and her stomach flipping as Jack held her hand and sat close beside her on the sofa. It had all felt wonderful, sharing their news with Millie and Jimmy and making plans on the drive home. But now the reality was hitting her and she was worried about what everyone would say. Terry was never coming home, but even so, she hadn't been widowed very long. His mother would go mad of course; she didn't like Jack as it was. Alice took a deep breath as he squeezed her hand reassuringly. This was their lives and she had to do what was best for her, Jack and the children. And having extra money coming in from Jack's wages would help her to carry on doing the best she could.

'Well I'll be,' Arnold declared. 'But I didn't think it'd be too long before you two got together. Summat's been brewing for years.'

'Oh congratulations, luvvies,' Winnie said, getting to her feet and giving Alice a hug and Jack a peck on the cheek.

Alice felt her cheeks getting hotter still at Arnold's comment. She wondered how many other people had the same thoughts.

'Get the sherry out, Arnold,' Winnie ordered. 'We need to raise a glass to toast the pair of them.'

After the toast, Alice told them about Brian's achievements and how Jack's proposal had come about.

Arnold nodded and scratched his chin thoughtfully. 'The house you live in on Lucerne Street, Alice, do you own it outright?'

She nodded. 'Yes, I do, well, along with my brother, that is.'

'Have you ever thought about selling it and going into business?'

'No, never.' Alice shook her head. 'Why, what sort of business do you have in mind?'

'Well, me and her ladyship,' he began, nodding at Winnie, 'we've been thinking about retiring very soon, as you know, and we'd love it if Jack could take over from us. But he needs a bond for the brewery that owns the business. Now, you can see how big this flat is up here, plenty of room for a family, and there are three big bedrooms too. It's all rent- and rates-free. If you sold the house, you could put money aside for your brother's education from his share, pay the bond and all move in here. Jack could run the place, you could work when you wanted to, like my Winnie does, or you could get a woman in to help with the cleaning and catering side. You could still do a bit at Lewis's then, because I know you enjoy your job there. It'll be up to you, chuck, of course, but you'll be quids in and have a nice big home as well. What do you think?'

'It's a lot to take in.' Alice looked at Jack, whose face had lit up at Arnold's suggestion. 'Jack, what do you think?'

'It's up to you, love. It's yours and Brian's house and he'll need to be in agreement. But it's a great suggestion. Our own business, a lovely big flat, freedom from bills we'd maybe struggle a bit to pay. Brian can stay on at school. It's a good start for me and you and a solid future for us all.'

Alice chewed her lip. Jack was right, but a couple of things bothered her and maybe she shouldn't have accepted his marriage proposal without thinking long and hard about it first.

'You don't really like kids, and Cathy will be living with us,' she said. The fleeting memory of Terry saying Jack would drink a business dry crossed her mind, but she dismissed it as quickly as it had come. He'd change if they were married, she was sure. He only drank because he was lonely.

Jack laughed. 'I can get used to anything, given time. And Brian and Cathy will be at school most of the day. We'll not be having any babbies of our own, though. We'll be far too busy building a future.'

Alice nodded. She wasn't that bothered about having any more children. She'd rather be working and taking care of Cathy and Brian and now she could look after Jack properly too and make a nice home for them all.

'All we've got to do now is tell your ma-in-law and the kids and we're sorted. We can book a date for the wedding and start making plans.'

Alice grimaced at the mention of telling her mother-in-law. She was absolutely dreading it. Granny would go mad. She might never speak to Alice again. But at the end of the day, if she could give the kids all they needed, and Brian his all-important education, then she had to put them first. She was sure she would be very happy with Jack. That passionate kiss on the beach and the promise behind it, the long friendship they shared, his supporting her through the aftermath of losing Terry – surely it was meant to be. And she smiled as the memory of Millie and Jimmy wanting to rent or buy a house in Aigburth popped into her mind. With a bit of luck, things could fall into place perfectly for them all. She'd talk to Jack about that when he walked her home.

'If Brian agrees to me selling the house, then we'll do it,' she said. 'And to be honest, I really can't see him objecting if it means he can eventually go to university. Refill those glasses, Jack, and we'll toast Arnold and Winnie's retirement and our own happy future.'

Chapter Ten

'Do you want me to stay while you talk to the kids?' Jack asked as Alice relaxed in his arms on the sofa in the small front room. 'I'll need to get back to the Legion for work at seven though.'

She shook her head and looked at the clock on the fireplace. It was just gone half past six. She couldn't believe how much her life and future had changed in the few short hours since they'd left the house for Blackpool that morning.

'They'll be home any minute. Brian was going to pick Cathy up from Granny's and no doubt she'll have saved him something to eat. I'll get Cathy ready for bed and out of the way while I talk to him. Telling her we're getting married can wait until after school tomorrow. If Brian says yes about the house, I'll write to Millie and Jimmy later and let them know we'll be selling it. I'll post the letter tomorrow rather than phone them from a phone box with Cathy's little ears wagging beside me. They'll get the letter on Tuesday, Wednesday at the latest, and meantime I can get someone in to tell me how much the house is worth.'

Jack nodded. He pulled her close and kissed her passionately, his hands running thought her hair and over her body.

'You have no idea how many times I've wanted to do this,' he whispered. 'Just to hold you really close and kiss you properly. I've always held back because I didn't want to overstep the mark and frighten you away. As soon as you've told people, we'll book our wedding. I've no one to tell, so it's just your side. We can live here until everything's sorted. I don't want to wait too long, Alice, because I need you, gel, and the sooner the better.'

Alice caught her breath as she looked into his hungry blue eyes. He was studying her intently and her stomach flipped. It was a feeling she hadn't experienced for a while. She needed him too. As he'd just said, the sooner they were married the better. She jumped as the front door was flung back so hard it bounced against the hall wall.

'Mammy,' Cathy called out, running into the room. She stopped dead and scowled as she saw Jack sitting close to her mother. Brian popped his head around the door and greeted Jack in a friendly manner.

'Hiya, kids,' Jack said. 'Nice to see you both, but I'm afraid I'm just off back to work. Me and your mam have had a lovely day in Blackpool. Next time we'll take the pair of you with us. Bet you'd like that, eh, Cathy? Playing on the sands with your bucket and spade and having donkey rides.' He got to his feet and Alice jumped up with him, smoothing the skirt of her dress straight. She saw him to the door and he gave her a quick kiss, whispered, 'Good luck, gel,' and closed the gate behind him. He turned to wave and she called quietly to him, 'Jack, pop in on your way home.'

'Are you sure?'

She nodded. 'Yes, and then I can tell you what Brian said.'

'Okay. See you later then.'

*

Alice rubbed Cathy's freshly washed hair with a towel and ran the brush through it. Her daughter squealed when the brush hit a tangle.

'Sorry, sweetheart,' Alice apologised and dropped a comforting kiss on Cathy's cheek. She pulled a clean pink nightie over her daughter's head and sent her downstairs to sit with Brian while she tidied the bathroom. She folded the damp towels and picked up Cathy's dirty clothes from the floor, her thoughts tumbling over and over in her mind. Was she doing the right thing? This house was the only security her family had. It wasn't worth a fortune, but it was their home. Then she thought about how she would never move on unless she was prepared to take a chance and make some changes. And also she didn't want to remain a lonely widow forever; she was too young to give up on that side of life. The nice big flat, her own business – well, her and Jack's – meant a more stable and secure environment and future for the kids, and a new life was just what they all needed. It would be good for Jack as well to belong to a family and have someone take care of him.

She didn't have quite the same strength of feeling for him that she'd had for Terry, but she hoped that would grow given time. It was all new and not every relationship would be the same, all hearts and flowers. But Jack had excited her when he'd kissed and caressed her and she wanted more. Millie had thought herself in love with Alan, until he dropped her for a nurse he'd met in France, but it hadn't stopped her marrying Jimmy as soon as the war ended and they were happy together. Millie never mentioned Alan now. Alice knew she'd never forget Terry – how could she when she had his mirror image in Cathy? – but she could put her pain to one side and make a real effort with Jack.

'Mammy, are you making my cocoa now?' Cathy's piping voice called up the stairs, breaking her thoughts.

'Yes, I'm coming, love.' She hurried down the stairs and into the kitchen to put the milk on the stove to heat. 'Brian,' she called out, 'would you like some cocoa as well?'

'Please,' Brian called back from the front room, where he was listening to the wireless. 'Have we got any biscuits, Alice?' he said, coming into the kitchen behind her. 'I'm proper starving.'

Alice nodded. 'You always are. We have some ginger nuts in the tin. But didn't Granny feed you? She usually does on a Sunday.'

Brian grinned and Alice thought how handsome her younger brother was these days. He was getting to look so much like their late brother Rodney. His eyes the same shade of blue and his hair thick and dark. Her heart skipped a beat as she thought of Rodney and how much she missed her big brother.

'She gave me a roast dinner that she'd kept warm in the oven. It was lovely, but I'm peckish again now.'

Alice laughed. 'Help yourself to biscuits then.' He'd always had a good appetite. Hollow legs, as their mam used to say.

She made the cocoa and they took their mugs into the front room, where Cathy was curled up on the sofa with a picture book, struggling to keep her eyes open. Good. She could go up to bed as soon as she'd finished her drink while the subject of the house was broached with Brian.

*

Alice chewed her lip as Brian sat quietly beside her on the sofa while he mulled over what he'd just been told.

'I'll leave you to have a think for a while and go and wash these,' she said. She picked up the empty cocoa mugs and took them into the kitchen. While she was filling the sink Brian came to stand in the doorway.

'Not much to think about really, is there?' he began. 'Let's do it. Sell up and move, I mean.'

'Do you really mean it?' Alice smiled and gave him a hug. 'And me marrying Jack, how do you feel about that?'

Brian shrugged. 'It's fine by me if it's what you want, our Alice. He seems a nice enough chap. I've always got on really well with him. Granny will go mad though, you do know that, don't you? She can't stand him because of what she thinks he did to Terry's bike.'

Alice sighed. 'Oh, I do know, love, and I dread telling her. But this is our life and I have to do what's best for us three as a family, not her. She's had her life and done what she considers best for her since being widowed. Now it's my turn for me to do what's best for us. With your half of the house money put away in a separate account for your future, you can do what you like then. Make no mistake, Brian, there's no way we could afford to put you through university if we don't sell this place. And it's what I want for you more than anything; you know that, don't you? I think Jack and I will be very happy together and I'm sure Cathy will take to him once she gets to know him better. She's a bit shy around him at the moment, like she was with Terry at first, but time will sort that out.'

'She'll be fine,' Brian said. 'Jack might give me a job collecting and washing glasses at weekends. I can earn a bit of pocket money then. No, you go ahead, Alice. Don't let Granny or anyone else stand in your way. And if Millie and Jimmy buy the house, then we're all sorted. It can all be done dead quickly.'

Alice blew out her cheeks. 'I'll tell Granny tomorrow when I pick up Cathy after work. I was waiting to hear your thoughts first.'

Brian gave her a hug. 'Right, I'm going up to my room to do a bit of studying. Greek mythology! Oh, the joys.' He rolled his eyes. 'See you in the morning.'

'You will. Goodnight, Brian, don't stay up too late. I'm going to iron yours and Madam's uniforms for school tomorrow and get a quick bath. Jack's popping in on his way home to see what your thoughts are on our plans.'

*

Alice yawned and stretched her arms above her head. The wireless was playing softly in the background and her *Woman's Weekly* magazine was on the floor by her feet. She must have dozed off for a while. Jack would be here soon. Her heart did a little skip and her tummy fluttered at the thought of seeing him again. It was a nice feeling. She'd had a bath and written the letter to Millie. It was on the mantelpiece ready to post in the morning. A slight tap on the window made her jump and she edged the curtain back to see Jack's smiling face. She hurried down the hall to let him in, conscious of the fact she was wearing her blue silky nightgown that matched her eyes.

'Thought it best to tap quietly on the window rather than wake up the kids by banging on the door,' Jack said as she let him in and led him into the front room. 'Any joy with Brian, then?'

She nodded, smiling, conscious of his eyes on her. She could smell whisky on him, but it wasn't as strong as on previous nights, the scent of Old Spice shaving soap stronger.

'Yes, Brian is fine with the idea, more than fine, in fact. He's dead keen. I've written to Millie and I'll call into Shaw's tomorrow before I go to work, and ask them to give me an idea as to what sort of price I should ask for the house in case she and Jimmy want to buy it.'

Jack swept her into his arms, his smile lighting up his face. 'That's marvellous, Alice, bloody marvellous. I can't believe it. Me and you getting wed, gel, and business partners as well as partners for life.'

Alice nodded, unable to speak and conscious of Jack's hands running up and down her body through the thin fabric of her nightdress. He dropped his lips to hers and kissed her passionately. She could feel his arousal as he pressed himself ever closer, clutching her buttocks.

As they came up for air Jack said, 'Tell your ma-in-law tomorrow, please. I need you, gel, and I can't be held responsible for my actions when you come to the door dressed in something as skimpy as this nightie.'

Alice grinned shyly. 'Behave yourself.'

'I don't want to,' he teased. 'But seriously, will you tell her?'

'Yes, I intend to. And then we can go and see the registrar and book the wedding.'

'And I'll tell Arnold and Winnie we'll have the club. They can arrange to have the paperwork drawn up and start looking for a new place. Winnie said she saw some newly built bungalows for older people, near Hoylake, in tonight's *Echo*. She fancies one. Arnold just rolled his eyes and nodded.' Jack laughed. 'He's right under the thumb, that one. I'd better go. I can't hold you much longer like this and be expected to control myself! Can't wait to marry you and make you mine.'

'Me too,' she said and stood up on tiptoe to kiss him again.

'Wish I didn't have to go,' he whispered, squeezing her backside again. 'But let's try to keep it all above board and decent until we're legal. I don't want any of the bloody neighbours gossiping about you for having me stay over before we're wed. Walls have ears round here, as we know.'

She nodded. 'It won't be for long. Take care on your walk home. Call in tomorrow before you go to work at seven if you can. I'll be able to tell you how it went with Granny then. Wish me loads of luck. I'll need it. Goodnight, Jack.'

'Goodnight, gel, and good luck by the bucketful.'

*

Jack lit a cigarette as he limped away down Lucerne Street and out onto Lark Lane. He felt really pleased with himself. He and Alice would rub along just fine, he was sure. They'd been friends for ages now and that would stand them in good stead. He'd been desperate to get his hands on the Legion, and by a strange quirk of fate, with her having financial problems brought on by having a clever brother, he was almost there. He was confident he could make an even bigger success of the place than Arnold and Winnie had. He had big plans in his head. He'd book good turns for every Saturday night like other social clubs did. There were some smashing artistes around now the war was over and they were all looking for a venue to sing in. And hopefully Millie would become one of his regular acts when she was back in Liverpool. He'd run weekly bingo and whist nights; get the bowling green overhauled and back to grass. During the war it had been given over to the WI for growing vegetables and since then Arnold hadn't bothered with it, but bowling teams would flock to a decent green and they could serve tea and sandwiches. Maybe even do regular dinnertime bites to eat as well. Nothing like a nice pie and chips with a decent midday pint. With plenty of booze on tap for himself, the world was his oyster. He'd just need a couple of good barmaids and a regular cleaner. He was sure Alice would want to stay on at Lewis's, but that wasn't a problem to him. She'd be with him at night to enjoy and then he could more or less do as he pleased during the day.

Jack wasn't the type of man that liked being bossed around by women. Alice would soon know her place. He cared for her, of course he did, and loved her in his own way, and he'd look after her the best he could. He was grateful that she wanted to be with him and was willing to give her share of the house towards making his dreams come true. But he hoped she wouldn't expect too much in the mushy words and flowers department. It wasn't his thing. As far as *he* was concerned, you showed a woman love with actions, not words. And if it was anything to do with him she'd not be going short of the former. He'd waited a long time for Alice, and he couldn't wait to make her his and to show her what she'd been missing.

Chapter Eleven

Alice caught up with Sadie at the tram stop the following morning. She'd just popped into Shaw's and Mr Shaw had arranged to come over to the house tomorrow afternoon. Hopefully she could get off work a bit earlier. She'd met Sadie outside school, but told her she'd got an errand to run and would see her at the stop. She posted Millie's letter after queuing for a stamp, avoiding eyes that tried to make contact, and then puffed up to the stop in time for the tram that got them to Lewis's just before ten o' clock.

'Sorry about that,' Alice said. 'I'll explain when we're sitting down and I get my breath back.'

'Sounds mysterious,' Sadie said, raising an eyebrow as the tram squealed to a stop. They jumped on board, found seats upstairs and sat down. 'Right, come on. What have you been up to?'

Sadie's jaw dropped as Alice told her some of the weekend's events. 'Bloody hell. I knew he fancied you, he told me. But a few dates with him and you're getting married?'

Alice shrugged. 'We've had a few nice times, yes, and we've been really good pals for years. He stood by me all through the war, and as you know he was there for me when Mam and Terry died. It just feels the right thing to do. There's no point in us waiting ages.'

'But selling your house and living at the Legion, isn't that rather drastic?'

Alice finished her tale of how the decision had been made and why. 'So you see, it's the best thing all round. Brian gets his education;

we get a lovely big flat to live in and also a decent business to run. Well, Jack will do most of that because I love working at Lewis's and I might as well keep it on for the bit of extra money. I'll help Jack out at the weekend. He'll get barmaids in during the week. We'll manage just fine and I'll be better off than I've been for a long, long time.'

Sadie nodded. 'Sounds like you've got it all worked out. Wish I was in a position to buy your house for me and Gianni.'

'Ah, well, that's the next bit of news I was going to tell you. Hopefully, Millie and Jimmy will buy it, and very soon at that.' She told Sadie what was happening with the pair and their plans to come back to Liverpool.

'Flipping heck! You lot are full of surprises. Well, let's hope it all falls into place. Fancy Millie being pregnant. That's lovely. Bet she's thrilled to bits.'

'She is. I am, too, and I'm so glad she's coming home.'

'So when are you and Jack setting the date?' Sadie asked as the conductor came upstairs and shouted for any more fares. 'Two to Ranelagh Street, please.'

Alice took the tickets from him and handed over her fare with Sadie's. 'As soon as we can. I'm telling Terry's mam tonight when I go to pick Cathy up. I'm not looking forward to it, but it has to be done, and then that's it, there's nothing to stop us. I think the banns have to be up for twenty-eight days and then we can get married as soon as the time's up and the registrar can fit us in. Hopefully we'll be married by the end of August and move into the Legion very soon after. I know it'll be a mad rush and people will be raising eyebrows, but Jack and I haven't done anything yet and we won't until after the wedding. He said he doesn't want people talking and he also made it quite clear that he doesn't want us to have any kids.'

'And how do you feel about that?'

Alice shrugged. 'Fine. I think. I always wanted more kids with Terry, but Jack and I will have enough on our plates with Brian, Cathy and the business.'

'I'm inclined to agree with you,' Sadie said. 'But in that case don't leave it all up to Jack to be careful, because you know what men are like. Look how easy you and me copped for Gianni and Cathy.'

Alice nodded. 'I'll have to read up and see what I can do as an extra precaution. I don't want anything happening to spoil things before we start.'

'Very wise,' Sadie said as the conductor called, 'Anyone for Ranelagh Street?'

'Here we are. Let's get to it, gel.'

*

Lewis's haberdashery department, close to the top of the stairs, was buzzing with mid-morning shoppers as Alice and Sadie took their places behind the counter. A short queue had formed and a tall skinny woman with a red jacket and matching headscarf caught Alice's eye.

'Can I help you, Madam?'

'You can, chuck. I'd like a pattern for a matinee jacket and bootees for a new baby please,' the woman replied.

'Certainly.' Alice reached under the counter and lifted out a box of baby knitting patterns. She leafed through several and selected a handful, laying them out on the glass counter top. 'These are all from birth to six months,' she explained.

'I don't want owt too complicated,' the woman said, sifting through the patterns. 'Me daughter's in the family way, so it's me first grandchild and I've never really knitted before, just socks for the soldiers and them was never quite right, looked more like mittens than socks, the WI woman in charge told me. But the other grandma is knitting like it's going out of fashion and I don't want 'er showing me up, like.'

Alice nodded, trying to suppress a grin, remembering how Terry's mum and her own mother had gone into competition overdrive to knit when Cathy was on the way.

'I'm sure you'll do her proud. All new mums are very grateful for everything you grandmas do for us.'

The woman smiled. She chose a pattern and handed it to Alice. 'Do you think I'll manage this one, queen?'

Alice chewed her lip, trying to think of a tactful answer other than no. 'Erm, you might find it a bit too complicated with that lacy yoke. What about this?' She handed a simple stocking-stitch jacket pattern to the woman.

'It's too plain.' The woman pursed her lips.

'But if you choose your wool in a nice pastel shade, pretty buttons and white ribbon to trim it with, I think you'll be on to a winner. And your daughter will be thrilled to bits that you've made an effort. She does know you're not an experienced knitter, doesn't she?'

'Aye,' the woman said. 'She told me to buy something ready-made, but I'm determined that 'is mother's not going to push my nose out. Now what colour wool do you think it would look nice in?'

'I always think lemon is a safe bet until a baby is born,' Alice said. 'With white ribbon threaded through the neck and cuffs, it will look lovely.'

'Righto then, gel. I'll take your advice and can you sort me out the right size of knitting needles as well?'

Alice parcelled up the woman's purchases and handed over her change. 'Good luck to you, and congratulations in advance.'

'Thanks, chuck.'

Sadie nodded after the woman. 'I know her. I'm sure her daughter was in our class at school. Marilyn something or other. You know, always had her hair in plaits, sort of pale gingery colour, and she had loads of freckles.'

'Marilyn Dawes?'

'That's her. Wonder who she's married to?'

Alice shook her head. 'No idea, but if Mrs Dawes comes back for more wool we can ask; although I wouldn't hold your breath on that score. Her grandchild will be starting school by the time she's finished knitting that jacket.'

'I have to say you were very diplomatic there, Alice. I'd have sent her up to babywear for a ready-made one.'

'Mrs Lomax, Mrs Romano, I need a word with you please.' Miss White, the supervisor, came over to them, brandishing a clipboard and pen. She pushed her glasses up her nose and gave her usual half-smile that didn't quite reach her steely grey eyes. 'We're moving your counter across to the back of the floor by the lift for the time being. We need to make a bit more room for school uniforms. It's coming up to that busy time of year, as you know, and we're really struggling for space. We've a new contract for more grammar schools and I've a fresh batch of blazers coming in. They need to be placed centrally where they can be seen. Management have decided this is the ideal spot because it's close to the stairs. I'll have some boxes sent over in a short while and you can begin to pack your stock. Make sure you label each box so that you can locate things easily enough. Give me a shout when you're all packed and ready and I'll get a couple of men to carry the boxes across the floor. There's a counter and some shelving back there with more storage space than you have here. Everything will need a good clean because of all the dust that's in the air. We all have to do the best we can for now.' She sighed. 'Sadly it's looking like it's going to take a few more years before the store is anywhere near back to normal again, much longer than we first thought.'

Alice nodded. This was the second time they'd had to move their counter since she'd been working here, but with two-thirds of the store being rebuilt there wasn't a lot of choice. No doubt they'd still be over by the back wall once the Christmas stock started to arrive in the autumn and Miss White would want the prime spot again for that. God only knew where the grotto would be located this year, or if there was even going to be one. Nothing had been said.

'I know it's a bit early, but go and have your break,' Miss White said. 'I'll hold the fort and the packing boxes will be here for you to make a start when you get back.'

'Before we go, can I please ask a favour?' Alice said. 'I need to finish a bit earlier tomorrow if possible. Will that be okay?'

Miss White raised an inquisitive eyebrow. 'It's a bit short notice, Mrs Lomax?'

Alice nodded. 'I know, but I wouldn't ask if it wasn't important. I have an appointment, you see.'

'An appointment?' She looked Alice up and down. 'Mrs Lomax, you shouldn't really make appointments during your working hours. I presume that as you have done, it must be something important. I do hope it's nothing serious health-wise.'

Alice knew she wouldn't get away without telling the supervisor what sort of an appointment she had made.

'No, nothing serious and it's not a doctor's appointment either. I'm hoping to sell my house. I have a man coming to discuss it with me tomorrow afternoon. It's the only time he can fit me in this week.'

That wasn't strictly true, it could have been any afternoon – tomorrow was just the soonest he could do and she was keen to get the information she needed as soon as possible.

'Oh, I see. You're moving then?'

'Eventually,' Alice replied. 'But not from the Aigburth area.' That was it. She was saying no more, otherwise it would be all over Lewis's by dinnertime and before she had a chance to talk to Granny Lomax. People would insist on giving her advice and telling her she was being impulsive to think about marrying Jack with no lengthy courtship behind them, and not to give up her only bit of security for anyone. Maybe she *was* mad for going ahead with the idea, but she was still going to do it anyway.

'Very well, Mrs Lomax. Maybe you can make up the time another day rather than lose your pay.'

'Yes, thank you. I'll arrange to do that.'

Sadie linked Alice's arm as they made their way to the cafeteria. 'Did you cop her raised eyebrows? Bet she thought you were in the family way and you with no man in tow. Well, not one that anybody knows about yet, anyway. Sticky bun with your brew?'

Alice laughed. Sadie's observations were probably right. 'Oh yes please. I'll find us a place to sit.'

She grabbed a table by the window that four girls were just vacating and sat down, looking out at the street below where some workmen were carrying hods of bricks and others, standing on scaffolding, were throwing chunks of damaged masonry down to the area of pavement that was fenced off from public use. It was such a shame. The damage to the store was so extensive, it might have been easier to demolish the lot and rebuild from scratch. But at least they had jobs and that was something to be thankful for. Many women who had held things together while the men were away fighting had since found themselves out of work, losing the jobs they'd loved to the returning male workforce.

'No sticky buns so I got a couple of scones,' Sadie said as she came to the table with a tray. 'Hope that's okay?'

'Fine by me,' Alice said. 'I'm starving.' She yawned. 'Oh, do excuse me. I'm feeling really tired. I didn't sleep too well last night. My mind was going over and over everything.'

'I'm not surprised,' Sadie said. 'You're about to take a bloody big step into the unknown. Marrying a man you've not really spent a lot of time with and taking on a business as well. Oh, I know he cares about you, but I'd still be having massive panic attacks if it was me.'

Alice shrugged. 'If you think about it, I've actually spent more time with Jack than I ever did with Terry. I know him really well. We get on just fine. Okay, I know he likes a drink or two, but I'm sure that's only because he's lonely when he's at home on his own. Maybe it helps him to cope. I bet he'll cut right down once we're married.'

Sadie raised an eyebrow. 'Maybe he will. But he is a bit of a ladies' man, don't forget. He's got a right roving eye. I hope that stops too when you're married.'

'Oh, I'm sure it will. He was single up until yesterday and men have all got roving eyes when they're not with someone special.'

'And are you?'

'Am I what?' Alice sipped her tea and stared over the top of her cup.

'Are you Jack's someone special?'

Alice lowered her eyes and split her scone in two. 'He hasn't told me that he loves me if that's what you mean, well not in so many words, but he's sort of implied it and his actions make me think he does.'

'And have you told him you love him?'

Alice shook her head. 'Not yet. It's not like it was with Terry. That was proper love, you know. This is – well – I suppose this is convenience for us all. It's something I just have to do. Love will grow in time.'

Sadie shook her head as Alice looked away. 'I hope you're right, Alice. I really do.'

*

Granny Lomax stared in horror at Alice. The cup she'd been drinking tea from lay on the hearth rug in a puddle, along with the saucer and a shortbread finger that had been balanced on one side. Alice leapt to her feet and ran into the kitchen for a cloth to clean up the spillage before it left a stain on the light-coloured rug. Cathy was in the back garden with her little friend Debbie, who had come to play after school. The pair were sitting on the lawn with a collection of Cathy's dollies and toy pram and cot. Alice took a deep breath and walked back into the lounge. She knelt down in front of her silent mother-in-law and proceeded to mop up the spilt tea.

'I don't know what to say,' Granny Lomax eventually spluttered, her face as white as the hanky she was using to mop at the tea splashes on her beige pleated skirt.

'I'm sorry my news has given you such a shock,' Alice said, trying to stay calm and in control of the situation. 'I know it won't be easy for you to accept, but it's what Jack and I both want.'

Granny shook her head. 'Well, for what it's worth, I think you're making a dreadful mistake. There's something about that man I just don't trust. And to think he'll be moving into the house my Terry was so happy in. How could you even think of letting a relationship develop beyond friendship, never mind agreeing to marry him, Alice?'

Alice drew a deep breath. She really didn't want to fall out completely with Granny, but she was determined not to let her spoil the plans she'd made for the future.

'He won't be living with me in the house for long, none of us will. I'm selling it, hopefully to Millie and Jimmy.'

Granny looked puzzled. 'I thought they were moving abroad?'

'They changed their minds. They're staying in England now and moving back to Liverpool. Millie is expecting a baby and wants to live a bit closer to her mam and dad.'

'I see. So where will you go if you sell your house to Millie? And what about the children? What do they think?'

'The children will be with me and Jack, of course. Brian is fine about it all and we'll tell Cathy tonight. We're taking over at the Legion and will be living in the accommodation above the club. It's a huge flat and will give us so much more space than we have at the house. My share of the sale will pay the bond we need to get into the business. I'll help Jack run the club when I can, but I'm going to stay on at Lewis's for now as I love my job. Another thing we need to plan for is Brian's education. I can't afford for him to go to college and university if I don't sell the house. His share will be put to one side to help with the cost of it all. I swore I'd do my best for him when Mam died, and that's what I'm going to do. Jack will back me all the way with that. He and Brian get on and always have done. Jack's as keen as me that my brother finishes his education and gets a good job in time.' Alice took a deep breath to stop herself waffling on, and looked at her mother-in-law.

Granny Lomax pursed her lips and nodded slowly, a smug look on her face. 'Ah, I see it all clearly now. Jack wants your money so he can take over the running of the club. I always knew he had his eyes on you, Alice. I think he deliberately got rid of my Terry so he could also get his hands on you. The thought of my little granddaughter living under the same roof as the man who was responsible for the death of her father makes me feel sick to my stomach. I wouldn't trust him as far as I could throw him. I've heard bad things about him. I've kept my mouth shut as I try hard not to fall out with you. You always seem to think the sun shines out of his backside. But I know better. I've heard that he mistreats women when he's had a few too many. Well, he'd better not lay a finger on my Cathy or he'll have me to answer to. I think you're being very foolish, and if it's money for Brian's education you want then I could help a bit with that and you could work full time at Lewis's to earn more. I can look after Cathy for longer than I do. We'd manage between us. You don't need to sell your house or marry the man who killed my son.'

'No, you're right, I don't,' Alice protested. 'But I want to marry him, and I will do. I'm not falling out with you over this. It's my life, mine and the kids', and I'll do the best I can for them both. And how dare you imply that Jack got rid of Terry deliberately? That's slander, and you've no right to say anything like that. If Jack heard you he wouldn't be very happy. The police proved the bike was roadworthy, you know they did. And Jack doesn't mistreat women either. There were rumours years ago but they were always unfounded. Jack has never given me any reason not to trust him. I'm going now because nothing I say will be right. I'm making sacrifices for the children. I loved Terry but he's not coming back and I can't afford to keep both kids for the next umpteen years on fresh air, no matter how many hours I work. We'll have a bigger home, a business and enough money for a much better way of life. Why would you want me to deny them all of that? You either accept that Jack is in our lives to stay or you don't. It's up to you.'

Alice left the room to call Cathy and Debbie inside. She went back into the lounge, where Granny was still sitting tight-lipped and white-faced.

'I'll see you tomorrow,' Alice said as the little girls came running indoors. 'Say goodbye to Granny, Cathy. We need to take Debbie home now.'

Granny gave Cathy a kiss and a hug. 'I'll still help you with Cathy,' she directed at Alice, 'but I want nothing to do with that man whatsoever. He's not, and never will be, welcome in my home.'

'Fair enough, it's your choice,' Alice said over her shoulder as she followed the girls down the hall. She knew for a fact that Jack wouldn't care less about that. 'I'll see you tomorrow,' she repeated. 'Oh hang on, no I won't. I'll pick Cathy up myself as I'm finishing early. I've got the estate agent coming at two. We'll see you on Wednesday.' And with that, she left the house, the girls happily chattering away to each other.

Chapter Twelve

On Tuesday afternoon Alice dashed home from work and tidied up the bedrooms the best she could. They really were struggling for space, with Cathy's toys piled on the end of her bed and in every corner of her tiny room, and Brian's books all over his bedroom floor. He could do with a desk for his studies and a small bookcase. She'd be able to buy him both of those things when they moved. She couldn't wait to make the flat above the Legion into a lovely, comfortable home for them all. A little thrill of happiness ran through her as she thought about the future.

Downstairs she plumped up the red cushions on the front room sofa and chairs and straightened the half-moon hearth rug. If Millie didn't want the house she'd have to ask the agent to sell it for her, so the nicer it looked today the better. When Jack had called round last night she'd told him about the argument with Granny Lomax and he'd told her he'd fully expected her to kick off, and not to worry. She'd either come around to the idea or she wouldn't. But he said he wasn't going to kowtow to the woman. She could like it or lump it as far as he was concerned.

He was calling in again later on his way to his evening shift at the Legion so Alice could let him know how she'd gone on with the agent. He'd told her not to let on to Mr Shaw that she might be selling it privately, in case he refused to tell her what it was worth as he wouldn't be getting any money out of it. She took a final look around the two downstairs rooms and dashed into the kitchen to put away the breakfast pots that were stacked on the draining board. She opened the back door to let some air in and, satisfied that everywhere looked the best it could, she went to stand by the front room window to keep an eye out for Mr Shaw's arrival. On the dot of two o'clock the doorknocker sounded and she rushed to answer it.

'Please come in.' Alice ushered the portly little man into the front room.

He removed his trilby hat and smiled. 'Good afternoon, Mrs Lomax. May I?' He indicated the coffee table to put his briefcase on and Alice nodded. He removed a notebook, pen and metal tape measure and asked her to show him around.

He followed Alice, nodding, measuring and taking notes. Upstairs he smiled and indicated the two windows in the large front bedroom.

'These properties are ideal for partitioning off into two smaller rooms at the front,' he said, making a note in his book. 'Very popular with larger families. The parents can then take the middle room.'

'Oh, we never thought of that,' Alice said. 'I lost my husband last year and we were always saying we need another room as my daughter's room at the back is quite tiny. But that's an idea that never crossed our minds.'

She finished showing him around and then took him outside into the small back garden that Brian looked after. Thankfully it was tidy and her dad's old bench still sat near the wall, with a small apple tree overhanging it.

'A nice shady place to sit with a cuppa when it's sunny,' she said, pointing. 'My dad made that bench out of bits of old wood many years ago. I'll be taking it with me though. It's special.'

'Where are you moving to?' Mr Shaw asked, as he scribbled into his notebook.

'I'm getting remarried,' she replied. 'My new husband and I are taking on the Legion club and we will live in the flat above it.'

'Very nice.' He nodded and followed her back inside. 'Well, it's all in very good shape, clean and freshly decorated in the main. A good-sized family home. I would say it would fetch in the region of eight hundred and fifty pounds.'

Alice nodded. That amount of money would do them very nicely. There would be something left over after paying the brewery the cost of the bond, enough to buy a bit of furniture at least, and do a few jobs around the Legion that Jack wanted to do. Brian's share would cover the next few years until he was able to start work in his chosen career.

'Lark Lane is a good area and anything in the streets just off it always sells well,' Mr Shaw continued. 'We didn't get too much war damage in these parts, apart from the Princess laundry of course, and we're close to Sefton Park and nice schools. All important factors to consider when thinking of buying a house. I'll draft up a letter and get my secretary to type it and pop it through your letterbox tomorrow. Let me know as soon as possible if you decide to go ahead. I have landlords on my books that are always looking out for houses in this area so I'm sure we can find you a buyer very quickly. I'll leave you in peace to think about it and discuss it with your future husband.'

'Thank you, Mr Shaw,' Alice said, showing him to the door. 'I'll be in touch.'

As she was waving him off Millie's mam came hurrying towards her, red-faced and out of breath as she reached Alice's door.

'Come in, Mrs Markham,' she invited and showed Millie's mam into the front room. 'Would you like a cuppa? I was just thinking of making one before I leave to pick Cathy up at half three. We've plenty of time.'

'I'd love one, chuck. Oh, Alice, I'm that excited,' she said, following Alice through to the kitchen.

Alice laughed and filled the kettle. 'I bet you are. Congratulations on your expected grandchild.'

'Thank you. Well,' Mrs Markham took a deep breath. 'I've just had our Millie on the phone and she's all of a dither. She got your letter this morning and her and Jimmy are over the moon and want your house. They're driving over tomorrow and will pop in after tea when you're home from work to talk about it with you. She told me to come round right away and tell you in case that estate agent bloke persuades you to let him sell it for you.'

Alice flung her arms around Millie's mam. 'Oh, I am so happy. Everything is just falling into place for us all.'

'It is. And our Millie said that when she's had the baby she'll go back to work and leave it with me. I can't wait to look after it. She also said she'd like to work at Lewis's with you and Sadie. Now wouldn't that be lovely? All three of you, working as shop girls together.'

'Oh, it would. It'll be just like old times. And hopefully we can get into the cosmetics department, Millie always wanted a job in there, she'd love it and so would I.'

Alice brewed a pot of tea and carried two mugs through to the front room. 'Have a seat and get your breath back. All this excitement is making us giddy.' She couldn't wait to tell Jack later. He'd be over the moon.

'And what about you, chuck?' Mrs Markham said. 'Getting remarried, eh? How do you feel about that?'

'Happy,' Alice replied. 'Quite excited. Can't believe it's happening. I'm a bit nervous of course, it's a big step to take, but I'm sure it will all be fine. And we've the Legion to run between us so we'll be really busy. And I like that thought.'

She wanted and needed to keep busy, because it stopped her dwelling on how things might have worked out with Terry. She would always love him, but she had to do what she could, for her own happiness and that of her family.

'Our Millie is really thrilled for you about it all. She said she'd like to sing there again if Jack ever wants her to.'

'Oh, he definitely will. Jack thinks the world of Millie and her wonderful voice.'

'Well, I'm very happy for all of you. Here's to a rosy future. Cheers, my love.' Millie's mam raised her mug to Alice's and smiled.

*

Alice met Cathy from school and then hurried her home before she could kick up a fuss at not being allowed to go to Debbie's to play. Alice had warned Debbie's mother that she had to take Cathy straight home after school as she needed to talk to her privately. She'd popped into the bakery on the way to school and bought a small sponge cake. Back at home, she ordered Cathy to get changed out of her school clothes and made herself a brew. She poured a glass of milk for Cathy and sliced the cake, then sat at the table and waited for her daughter to join her.

Cathy bounced downstairs and smiled at the sight of the cake. She sat down opposite Alice and took a swig of milk, a white moustache forming on her top lip.

Alice took a deep breath and began. 'We are going to move out of this house soon and go to live somewhere much bigger.'

Cathy's eyes grew round. 'To a palace, like the King?'

Alice tried not to smile. 'No, love, not a palace. But you'll have a much bigger bedroom and there might even be space in it for a dolly's house. Remember how you said you'd like one, but we have no room for it here?'

Cathy nodded, her mouth full of cake.

'And something else nice is going to happen too. Mammy is going to get married again, to my friend Jack. Maybe you could be a bridesmaid. Would you like that?'

Cathy shook her head and her lower lip trembled. 'Jack's a bad man.'

Alice's jaw dropped. 'Jack's not a bad man. He's a very good man. Who told you he's a bad man?'

'Granny doesn't like Jack. She said he hurt my daddy.' Fat tears rolled down Cathy's cheeks as Alice stared at her.

'When did Granny say that to you?'

'She didn't,' Cathy sobbed. 'She said it to you ages ago.'

'Oh, sweetheart, Granny didn't mean it. She was upset about Daddy and I'm sorry, I didn't know you'd heard her saying that. You should have told me.'

Cathy shook her head. 'I don't like him.'

Alice sighed inwardly. 'Cathy, listen to me. Jack did not hurt Daddy. Daddy hurt himself by going off on that silly motorbike. Jack is a good man and he will look after us all. We'll have a nice home and there's a big garden to play in too. We'll all be very happy together. Brian is happy for us and he wants to move so he can stay on at school. It's very important that we all do this, okay?'

Cathy nodded, looking uncertain, but Alice breathed a sigh of relief and hoped that would be the end of the matter. She cut another slice of cake and gave it to Cathy.

*

Late Wednesday afternoon Jack knocked on the door and waited for someone to answer it. He didn't like to walk straight in, on the off-chance Terry's ma was lurking. Although from what Alice had told him yesterday, it was unlikely, but even so. Alice needed the old bag's help with Cathy while she worked, so he didn't want to upset the apple cart by offending her with his thoughts if she had a go at him, as he was certain she would do, given half a chance. That could wait. He'd bide his time.

'Come in, Jack, it's not locked,' Alice called from somewhere at the back of the house.

He walked in and she hurried to meet him. 'Sorry, I was just bringing the washing in off the line.' She reached up to kiss him and he grabbed hold of her and pulled her close. His lips came down on hers, hard and demanding, and she melted into him.

He held her tight. 'I can't wait to be married to you, gel,' he whispered into her hair.

'Nor I,' she whispered back. She chewed her lip and looked down.

'What's up?' He lifted her chin with a fingertip, hoping she wasn't having second thoughts about selling the house.

She took a deep breath. 'Brian's just told me he's going away at the weekend with his mate and his mate's parents on a camping trip. I'm going to ask Granny if Cathy can stay over while I work and then I'll pick her up on Sunday morning.'

He raised an eyebrow. 'I know what you're gonna suggest, gel. But are you sure?'

Alice nodded. 'You'll be walking me home anyway, so you might as well stay with me. No one needs to know.'

'Then I will. And I'll sneak out before the street wakes up. Keep your reputation intact.' He kissed her again and gently slapped her backside. 'Now go and put that kettle on. A man could die of thirst waiting for you to brew up.'

She laughed and led him into the back room. 'Sit down while I do it then. I've made lamb scouse for tea. I know you like it.'

He nodded. 'I do, and it smells really good.' Alice had invited him for tea tonight, and after she'd put Cathy to bed, Millie and Jimmy were coming over and they were all going to talk business. Jack had managed to get the night off, explaining to Arnold why. His boss had been happy enough to oblige. Jack had assured him that things were moving forward and that Alice hopefully now had a buyer for her house.

All was well with the world at the moment and life was about to get a whole lot better. Jack was feeling quite contented with his lot and now that Alice had asked him to spend Saturday night with her he could make her his at last. A regular woman in his bed was something he hadn't had for a long time and he couldn't wait. He was sick of one-night stands and fickle women who always wanted more than he could give them and had nothing to give him back in return, except mither. It was time to put some roots down.

*

Alice dished up the meal and sat down at the table. 'Get stuck in. Oh, Brian, bring the bread through, love, I've forgotten it. Cathy, stop fidgeting and sit still.'

She'd seen Jack staring at her daughter, who was glaring at him and now complaining that she didn't like scouse and wanted a chucky egg. He didn't look too happy.

'You *do* like scouse, so get it eaten or you can go to bed without,' Alice warned.

Cathy glared at her mother and kicked the table leg. 'I don't like it. And I don't like *him!*' She pointed at Jack, who looked at Alice and raised his eyebrows.

'Right.' Alice dragged her daughter from the chair, slapped her legs and marched her into the front room. She sat her on the chair under the window, where Cathy stared sullenly, her arms folded. 'Now stay there, until you are prepared to say you're sorry to Jack. That was very naughty of you and I won't have it.' She slammed the door closed and went into the back room. 'I'm so sorry, Jack. I don't know what's got into her. It was very rude of her to speak to you like that. Little madam.'

Brian looked up from his already empty plate. 'Can I have hers if she doesn't want it? Shame to let it go to waste.'

Alice sighed and sat down next to Jack. 'You might as well, Brian. I'll make her an egg later.'

'My ma would have made me go to bed with nothing if I'd behaved in that way and my dad would have taken his belt to me,' Jack said, wiping around his plate with a chunk of crusty bread. 'That was delicious, Alice. Thank you.'

Alice half-smiled. Maybe she *had* spoiled Cathy, overcompensating for Terry not being around. And Granny had always given in to her every whim. But being rude to a guest was unacceptable. Jack wasn't that keen on kids to start with. She didn't want to put him off and have him changing his mind at this stage; Cathy would just need to learn to do as she was told.

'Would you like seconds? There's a bit left in the pan.'

'I would, gel. But I'll get it; you stay there and eat yours before it goes cold.'

'Just put a light under it for a few minutes,' Alice instructed as Jack left the table. She didn't feel like eating now. The mood of the evening had been spoiled. Brian was eyeing up the remains of her meal and she pushed her plate towards him. 'I can't believe she did that.'

'I can,' Brian said. 'After you spoke to her yesterday about you and Jack getting married she told me she wants to go and live at Granny's house and not in the new flat with us. She said Granny doesn't like Jack so *she* doesn't have to like him either. You can bet your life she's said something to Granny today after school.'

Alice frowned. 'Well, Granny didn't say anything to me when I went to pick Cathy up after work. But she was a bit funny with me, although I put that down to the conversation I had with her on Monday. I hope she's not been poisoning Cathy's mind with lies. I'm going to have to have a word with her.'

Jack came back into the room carrying his plate of seconds. 'I'd leave it, Alice. I overheard what you both just said. Cathy will come round to the idea soon enough. We'll have to put our foot down. We can't let a kiddie ruin our plans. We've got Brian to think about as well. It's not fair that he should miss out just because Cathy wants her own way. If you drag Terry's mam into it even more, you don't know what she might say to upset things further. Let's just keep things close to our chest for now.'

Alice chewed her lip. She wasn't used to someone telling her how to deal with her own child, and she wasn't too sure how to react. But maybe Jack was right, and she didn't want to undermine him. He'd be having some say in how their household was run in the future, so best to start how they meant to go on.

'Okay.' She got up to clear the table. 'Shall I make her something to eat then, or what?'

'Just make her some toast and then get her to bed,' he said. 'She needs to learn that she can't have it all her own way, or we'll make a rod for our backs before we even start our new life.'

Brian got to his feet and helped Alice clear the plates away.

'Thanks, Brian. You get off upstairs and do your homework now. I'll see you later. Millie and Jimmy will be here soon.'

Jack finished his scouse and brought the plate into the kitchen. He dropped it into the sink of soapy water.

'I'll make Cathy's toast,' he said. 'Where's the bread?'

Alice nodded towards the breadbin. 'She likes a mug of cocoa before bed too. She might as well have it to fill her up a bit and then I can get her settled before Jimmy and Millie arrive.'

'I'll do it, gel,' Jack said. 'You finish off in here and then we're ready for our visitors. She might play you up if she sees you again.'

Alice wasn't sure that was a good idea but she kept her mouth shut and let Jack get on with it. After all, he'd be helping her with the kids once they moved so he might as well get used to it.

*

Jack carried the small mug of cocoa, a plate with one slice of buttered toast balanced on top, into the front room. Cathy looked up at him as he came inside and kicked the door closed again with his foot. Her eyes wide with fear, she shuffled back into her chair and whimpered, 'I want my mammy.'

'Mammy's busy,' he said. 'Now get this down you and then you are going up to bed.' He lowered his voice to a threatening whisper. 'And you listen to me, young lady, don't you ever go telling your granny anything you see or hear in this house or in our new flat. I don't like kids that tell tales. Do you hear me?'

Cathy nodded tearfully.

'Right,' he continued quietly. 'Any nonsense from you in the future and I will send you away to the naughty girls' home. Me and your mam are getting married, whether you like it or not, understand?' He pointed to her mouth. 'You keep that shut or I'll give you something to cry for. Now eat that toast, drink your cocoa and I'll be back in a few minutes to take you up to bed, and I might read you a story if you're good. We don't want to hear a peep out of you tonight, right?'

He left the room and went back into the kitchen, where Alice was wiping the pots.

'Is she all right?' she asked, a worried look on her face.

'Smashing, gel. She's eating her toast and I said I'd take her up to bed and read her a story before Millie and Jimmy arrive.' He slipped his arms around Alice's waist from behind and nuzzled her neck. 'Don't you worry, chuck. I think me and Cathy are going to get on just fine.'

Chapter Thirteen

Brian was in his bedroom studying and Cathy was tucked up in bed after Jack had read her *Goldilocks and the Three Bears*. In her own bedroom, Alice stood on tiptoe in front of the mirror that was a bit too high on the wall. Terry had hung it there to suit his height and not hers. She hadn't got around to moving it yet and she supposed there was no point now if they were off to pastures new very soon. She brushed her hair, touched up her lippy and then got changed into a full-skirted navy and white dress she kept for best and that Jack had told her he liked a while ago.

Cathy called out to her as she was going down the stairs. Jack had nipped out to the off-licence on Lark Lane for a bottle of sherry for Alice and Millie and some brown ale for him and Jimmy. Alice went into Cathy's room and saw that her daughter was sobbing into her pillow. She sat down on the bed and Cathy clung to her neck, tangling her hands into Alice's hair.

'What's wrong?' Alice said, trying to prise her hands loose.

'I want my daddy,' Cathy howled. 'Not Jack. He's nasty. I want my proper daddy.'

Alice choked back the lump in her throat. 'I'm sorry, Cathy, but you know Daddy isn't coming back. You have to be a brave girl. You've got Brian and me and Granny, and Jack, who will love you just as much as Daddy did.'

'I don't want Jack,' Cathy screamed so loud that Brian came hurrying out of his room, a worried look on his face.

'What's up with her?'

'She wants Terry,' Alice said, feeling helpless as a knock at the door sounded. 'Go down and let Millie and Jimmy in, Brian. Jack's gone out to the off-licence.'

Brian ran down the stairs and Alice heard him letting their visitors in, then Jack's voice greeting them too. He must have arrived back as Brian let them in.

'I need to go down now,' she said to Cathy. 'Would you like to go and sleep in Brian's room for a while?'

Cathy nodded and wiped her tears away on the corner of the sheet.

Brian came back upstairs as Alice settled Cathy on his bed with her teddy bear. 'I'll transfer her to her own bed later,' she whispered to Brian. 'I don't think it'll be too long before she falls asleep. Just keep an eye on her and let me know if she cries.'

Alice ran down the stairs and greeted her friends. Millie was flushed with excitement and Jimmy was smiling broadly. At least someone was happy, she thought as she told them to sit down while they sorted out drinks. She followed Jack into the back room, got the glasses out of the sideboard cupboard and put them on the table.

'What were you doing?' Jack asked as he poured a measure of sherry into two small glasses and filled two bigger ones with ale. 'Why did Brian let us all in?'

'I was settling Cathy down. She was crying for Terry. I've put her in Brian's room for now.' She left out the comments that Cathy had made about Jack being nasty. He'd read her a story while Alice was with them and Jack had been nothing but kind to her daughter. It would only cause trouble if she told him.

Jack nodded. 'You're too soft with her, Alice. She runs rings around you. You need to be a bit firmer.'

Alice took a deep breath. 'I'm trying. She's had a lot of changes to deal with. We need to be a bit more patient with her.'

Jack picked up the glasses of ale and indicated for her to carry the sherry. Alice sensed he was angry by the colour that flushed up his neck, and felt like piggy in the middle. She was sure that Cathy would be fine, eventually; it would take time for them all to adjust. Jack wasn't used to kids, but he'd learn to be patient, she hoped.

'How long do you think it will be before you can move into the Legion?' Jimmy asked after he and Millie had agreed that the price Mr Shaw had suggested was a good one for the house. His dad, who owned a couple of properties in Blackpool, had recently sold one of them and had offered the money to his son and Millie as an interest-free loan to buy Alice's house. 'We have the money waiting in the bank to buy this place. So we're ready to move as soon as you are.'

'You need to get a solicitor to sort out the legal side and transfer the deeds,' Jack said. 'And we'll need one as well to make sure our side goes through smoothly. Me and Alice will go to the registry office and put the banns in tomorrow for the wedding. It takes twenty-eight days and then we can get married as soon as they can fit us in. We'll book it tomorrow.'

Alice nodded. 'Yes, and then we can start planning. We'll see if Arnold can suggest a good solicitor, Jack. And then he and Winnie can get the transfer sorted out for us to take over the Legion.'

Jack nodded. 'I reckon by early September it'll all be done and dusted.'

'We'll raise our glasses to that then,' Jimmy said as they all lifted their drinks in a toast. 'Millie here can't wait to be back near her mam and dad. Is there room for a shed out in the back garden, Jack? I've got quite a lot of tools to bring with me.'

'There is. Come on, I'll show you and we'll have a fag out there while these two catch up on the gossip,' Jack said.

As the pair went outside Millie turned to Alice, her eyes shining. 'I'm so excited, I can't wait.' She stopped and looked at Alice. 'You okay? You're a bit quiet tonight.'

Alice nodded. 'I'm fine. Just a lot on my mind and there's so much to do.'

'I'll bet. The wedding to plan, the move to sort out and then getting to grips with the business and your lovely new flat. Are Brian and Cathy excited?'

Alice chewed her lip. 'Brian is. Cathy, well, I'm not too sure.' She looked over her shoulder to make sure Jack was still outside and told Millie about Cathy's outbursts. 'Don't say anything to him. I can't work out if he's upset about it or just really annoyed. Terry's mother is fuming about the whole affair. She's pretty much washed her hands of me, but said she'll still help me with Cathy.' Alice told Millie what else Granny had said on Monday.

Millie puffed out her cheeks. 'She obviously sees Jack as replacing Terry in your lives and it must hurt. But it's unfair to hold grudges and blame Jack for something that wasn't his fault. He'll be feeling really bad deep down and he doesn't need her to keep bringing the bike accident up and neither do you. No wonder Cathy is acting up. Maybe Granny is saying things out of order to her when you're not there. Making out that Jack's the bad man in all this.'

Alice shrugged. 'Maybe she is, but how would I know? I'm not there when she has Cathy all to herself.'

'Can't you get someone else to pick Cathy up from school and look after her for a few hours and then just let her visit Granny once a week with you in tow? That way you can keep an eye on things. Keep an ear open for anything said that you feel is out of order and nip it in the bud right away.'

'That's a good idea, Millie. Maybe Debbie's mother would do it for me and Marlene might do the odd time too. She's at a loose end now she's not working at Rootes. Once we're in the flat they could always drop her off with Jack. Debbie's house is just around the corner from the Legion. Cathy can play out in the garden then or sit at one of the tables and draw. There will be people around who could keep an eye on her until I got home. I'll see what Jack says later after you and Jimmy have gone.'

Millie raised an eyebrow. 'Is Jack living here with you now then?'

Alice blushed and looked at the ceiling. 'No, he's not. We haven't even spent any time alone yet because of the kids. It's all been such a rush since he proposed. But I've asked him to stay over on Saturday. There'll be no kids around, thankfully.'

Millie smiled. 'And will it be your first time with him?'

Alice nodded. 'It will, and I feel very nervous about it. I've only ever been with Terry and we were still learning to please each other. I feel so naïve. What if Jack doesn't like my body? He might compare me to other women he's been with and then decide he doesn't fancy me after all, and this will all be for nothing.'

'Oh, Alice. Don't be silly. He'll love you to bits. Talk to him about things. Spend a bit of time here on the sofa getting to know each other. Take your lead from Jack. He's the one with the experience, if what we've heard about his ways with women is to be believed.'

Alice took a deep breath and nodded. 'I will. He calls in each night after his shift, so we've a few more nights before Saturday. The kids are always in bed; he could stay a bit longer.' She jumped as Jack called out from the back room.

'Do you girls want a refill? Bring your glasses through if you do.'

Alice smiled and picked up the empty sherry glasses. 'Refill, Millie?'

Millie shook her head and rummaged in her handbag, producing a packet of Rennie's. 'I've got a bit of heartburn, but I'd love a cuppa if there's one going.'

Alice rolled her eyes. 'Oh God. I remember it well! And it gets worse. I don't envy you. I'll join you in a brew though. Back in a minute.'

*

'Right, what's on your mind, gel?' Jack asked as he closed the door after seeing Millie and Jimmy out. 'You've looked mithered to death most of the night.'

Alice chewed her lip and sat down on the sofa. She patted the seat next to her. 'Can we talk for a bit?'

'Course we can.' He sat down beside her and took her hand. 'Come on, out with it.'

Her voice faltering, Alice told him how she was worried about letting him down. 'I'm just bothered that once you see me properly, you won't fancy me. I've got a few stretch marks from having Cathy and my tummy isn't as flat as it used to be. You're used to having single women who still have perfect figures.'

Jack shook his head. 'Not all of 'em, chuck. And there's nowt wrong with your figure at all. You go in and out in all the right places and you'll do for me. That first day I met you at the Legion a few years back I thought then what a nice figure and legs you had and you still do. I fancy the arse off you, Alice, so give us a kiss and let me show you how much,' he said, looking deep into her eyes.

'What, here?'

He nodded. 'Kids are asleep, the curtains are shut, there's nobody around but us two.' He got up and pushed one of the armchairs behind the door. 'And they can't get in now even if they did wake up.' He sat back down beside her again and took her into his arms, pushing her back against the cushions and kissing her passionately.

'Don't you want to wait until we have the house to ourselves?' she whispered as Jack's hand slid up the skirt of her dress and caressed her thighs above the tops of her silky stockings.

'No, I want you now, gel.' He silenced her with more kisses and unbuttoned the front of her dress. There was no way he was waiting. He'd have her tonight and then she was his. Alice wasn't the sort to let a man down once he'd had his way and she was succumbing nicely to his charms, sighing and moaning at his touch like they all did when they were desperate, and Alice had gone without for a good while now. She certainly wasn't being shy with him either, reaching to unzip him without him having to hint at it. It was good to know he hadn't lost his touch, even though it had been a while since he'd last enticed a woman into his bed. Alice would do for him all right and the feelings he had for her were stronger than he'd ever had for anyone else.

Chapter Fourteen

Saturday night in the Legion was really busy and Alice didn't have a minute to herself until Jack told her to take a break. She'd spotted Freddie and his wife Rose, along with Marlene and her husband Stan, sitting near the windows overlooking what used to be the bowling green. She poured a small sherry and took it over to sit with them. They greeted her enthusiastically and Freddie pulled up a spare chair.

'How you doing, queen?' he asked, giving her a hug. 'Busy in here tonight.'

'It is,' Alice said. 'Millie and Jimmy are coming in soon as well. They were going to the Mayfair pictures and then coming in for the last hour. And I'm fine, by the way.'

'We know,' Marlene said, raising an amused eyebrow. 'A little bird has told us a few secrets.'

Alice glanced across the club to Jack, who grinned and winked at her. She felt her cheeks heating as they all looked at her, waiting for confirmation. 'He's told you, has he?'

'Depends what you mean by that,' Freddie teased. 'He told me the bowling green will be reinstated when he takes over the running of the club. Which is great news, because I've really missed my Saturday bowling matches.'

Alice nodded. 'And what other secrets has the little bird told you?'

'That he's getting married and he and his new wife and her little family are moving into the flat above here. Congratulations, chuck. We're all very pleased for you. Not surprised, mind. We always thought summat were on the cards with you two.'

Alice felt her cheeks getting hotter still. Had the spark between her and Jack been that obvious? Surely not when she'd been married to Terry? Although Arnold had made a similar observation when they'd told him and Winnie of their intentions. It was no wonder that Granny Lomax wasn't too happy with the situation, she must also be thinking along the same lines. Alice chewed her lip as Freddie raised his glass and they all said cheers. She didn't tell them Millie's news. Millie could do that for herself when she and Jimmy arrived. There had been no mention of Alice selling the house either. Maybe Jack had kept that to himself. She hoped so. She didn't want their financial situation bandied around Aigburth.

She turned to Marlene. 'I was hoping I'd see you tonight, Marlene. I'm wondering if you could do me a favour. I'm going to carry on with my job at Lewis's for a while when we move in here, and I'm afraid I've had a falling-out with Terry's mam over things. I could do with a bit of help in getting Cathy picked up from school and then bringing her back here until I get home.'

Marlene's face broke into a big smile. 'You've no worries on that score, queen. It'd be my pleasure. My lot are all at work now, me mam and dad are in an old people's 'ome and Stan 'ere is back working on the trams. It'll give me summat to look forward to each day. I'll take 'er back to mine and then we can spend some time reading and colouring and whatever else she likes to do. Then you can come and pick 'er up on your way 'ome. Saves Jack 'aving to be mithered with 'er 'ere when 'e's busy. 'Ow does that sound?'

Alice felt like crying with relief. Her old friend had never let her down. Marlene had even delivered Cathy in the air raid shelter at work when Alice had gone into labour in the middle of an air raid.

'Thank you so much. You have no idea what a weight that is off my mind.' She got to her feet and gave Marlene a hug.

'I can start on Monday if you want,' Marlene said. 'Might as well, then she gets used to being with me. School 'olidays start at the end of next week, so it'll give us a few days.'

'That's great. Thank you. Right, I'll go back behind the bar and catch up with you later.'

Jack greeted her with a light kiss on the lips as she joined him behind the bar. He squeezed her backside out of view of the customers.

'Jack, behave yourself,' she whispered, suppressing a grin.

He laughed. 'Well if a fella can't cop a feel of his future wife it's a poor show,' he said. 'And you have no idea how hard it is to keep my hands off you after the other night. I can't wait until we get back to yours. I think a repeat performance is in order.'

Alice rolled her eyes in amusement and turned to serve a large man who'd banged his empty pint pot down on the bar. 'A refill, Harry?'

'Aye, chuck, please.'

A new pianist was in tonight and he was busy tinkling the ivories in the background with no one paying that much attention to him. While she pulled Harry's pint of mild ale, Alice realised he was playing one of her current favourite songs and hummed along to 'I'll Hold You in My Heart (Till I Can Hold You in My Arms)'. She had treated herself to the gramophone record from Epstein's in town recently and thought the singer Eddy Arnold had a lovely voice. Perhaps Millie knew the song and would sing it for them when she came in. That would have the punters paying full attention and help the new player gain a bit of recognition. As if on cue the doors flew open and Millie and Jimmy walked in. They hurried over to the bar and Alice pointed to the pianist and asked Millie if she knew the song.

'Yes I do and I love it,' Millie said. 'Just let me have a quick drink and then we'll ask him to play it again and I'll accompany him.' She looked around the large concert room, which was buzzing with life, and smiled. 'This is what I've missed so much,' she said. 'And baby or no baby, I want to sing again at the weekends if Jack'll let me.'

Alice laughed. 'That's a definite. If Jimmy has no objections, that is.'

Jimmy shook his head. 'I doubt I'll get much of a say in things. I'll be the one left at home holding the baby.'

'Oh, Mam'll do that for you. You can come and watch your wife entertaining,' Millie teased. 'Then you can walk me home in the moonlight and I'll sing just for you.'

Alice smiled. It was lovely to see her best friend so happy. 'Freddie's waving at you.' She pointed to their ex-foreman. 'Go and tell him your good news and that you are moving back home and having my house. And then you can sing. By the way,' Alice lowered her voice. 'Marlene will take over with Cathy from Monday. Tomorrow I have to pluck up the courage to tell Terry's mother when I go to collect Cathy, because she's staying with her all night.'

'That's good. And, oh yes,' Millie said, grinning. 'You've got an empty house and company tonight, haven't you?'

'Shh,' Alice said, although there was no one in earshot and Arnold and Winnie had taken the night off to visit Winnie's sister, so there was only Jack and her behind the bar.

'Did you talk to him the other night like I suggested?' Millie asked.

Alice felt her cheeks heating and looked away. 'Er, yes, I did.'

'Oh my God!' Millie clapped a hand to her mouth. 'You did more than talk. I can tell by the blush creeping up your face. Was everything okay?'

'Very okay, thank you,' Alice whispered, her heart skipping a beat as she thought back to Wednesday night and how Jack had made her feel like she was the best lover in the world, restoring her confidence. 'I don't know why I was worrying.' She pulled Jimmy's pint and poured a small sherry for Millie and they took their drinks across to Freddie's table.

'Is she going to sing for us?' Jack asked, nodding his head towards Millie, who was being swept into an embrace by Freddie and then Marlene.

'She is, when she's finished her drink.' Alice washed the dirty glasses waiting on the bar. 'Why don't you take a bit of a break,' she suggested to Jack. 'Oh, and by the way. Marlene has agreed to help out with Cathy. Picking her up from school and keeping her until I finish work.'

Jack frowned. 'What about Ma Lomax? Won't she go nuts if she can't see the kid? She'll blame me for that as well.'

'She won't,' Alice replied. 'I just feel it's best if she has a bit less control over Cathy, and then she won't be as spoiled for us. I thought you'd think it was a good idea.'

'Okay. Whatever you think is best. We'll give it a try, see how it goes.'

Alice picked up a tea towel and started to dry the glasses. 'I'll tell Granny tomorrow when I go and pick Cathy up.'

'Righto, gel.' Jack poured himself a large whisky and carried his glass over to where Millie and Jimmy were sitting.

Alice saw him speaking to Millie, who nodded, and then he walked over to two women, whose faces lit up as he approached. One of them got up to give him a peck on the cheek and he sat down at the table with them, his back to the room. Alice wondered what the trio were talking about but couldn't hear anything above the babble of voices and the piano man. One of the women, a thin-faced girl with ginger hair piled up on top of her head with loose curly tendrils falling onto her cheeks, was talking animatedly and nodding at whatever Jack was saying. The other woman joined in and smiled at him as he got to his feet and came back to the bar.

'Just got us a barmaid and cleaner lined up for when we move in,' he announced and slipped his arm around Alice's waist. 'Sheila, the red-head, she's the new barmaid and Gloria, the chubby one, she's going to clean for us.'

Alice stared at him, her mouth open. 'Aren't you jumping the gun a bit? We haven't even signed up yet. And shouldn't we decide between us who we employ?'

She looked across and caught the red-head looking over. The woman looked quickly away, but not before Alice saw the jealous look on her face. She wondered if she was one of Jack's conquests and felt a bit uneasy. Was that the reason he wasn't bothered about Alice keeping her job on at Lewis's? So that he could have time alone with Sheila while Alice was at work. She mentally shook herself. What a stupid thing to think when she was about to marry the man.

Jack shrugged in reply, seemingly unbothered by her concern. 'They're good workers. Sheila knows the trade well. She lost her job when her place of work was bombed out, a pub down near the docks. And Gloria is in the same boat. We don't need to make decisions together. I'll be running this place and I'll choose who I'm going to work with. You'll only be down here on the odd night to help out.'

'I'll be here at the weekend,' Alice protested. 'I thought that was the plan.'

'But you might want to spend time with the kids. Or be too tired after working all week. I don't want you wearing yourself out. This way I know I've got reliable staff coming in if you're not feeling up to it. I want to make a success of this place, Alice. You need to back my decisions, gel.'

She nodded. 'And I will. Here's Millie. Go and sort out with the pianist what she's doing.'

'Just one more thing before I do,' he said, pulling her into the kitchen area. He took her into his arms and kissed her. 'Take your rings off,' he whispered. 'You're my woman now. I don't like you still wearing Terry's rings. It doesn't feel right.'

Alice chewed her lip. Her wedding and eternity rings had not been off her finger since Terry put them there. She hadn't had the heart to remove them since his death. But Jack was right, she supposed. She *was* his now after the other night, although he could have asked her away from work and given her time to consider it. She swallowed hard and did as he requested. She slipped the rings into the pocket of her coat, which was hanging from a hook on the back of the kitchen door.

Jack took her hand and smiled. 'Thank you. That makes me feel better. You'll soon be wearing mine. It won't be long now, gel. Right, I'll go and talk with Millie. See you in a bit.' He slapped her gently on the backside and walked away.

Alice blinked back threatening tears, took a deep breath and went out to the bar area.

*

Millie sang her heart out and the crowd whistled for more. She took a bow and blew kisses like a real star, then she beckoned Alice to join her and the pair sang one of their favourite Andrews Sisters songs, 'Don't Sit Under the Apple Tree'. Applause and loud wolf-whistles followed and the pair came off the stage, Millie to a proud and smiling Jimmy, who gave her a hug and covered her face with kisses, and Alice to a scowling Jack, who was looking threateningly at a young man propping up the bar and eyeing her up. Once again Jack pulled her into the kitchen.

'That's the last time you sing with Millie,' he said. 'I'm not having lads ogling my future wife. That lad at the bar's tongue was hanging out the whole time you were on the stage. You're mine now, Alice. Your flirting days are over.'

'But, Jack, I wasn't flirting,' Alice protested. 'I never do. I didn't know he was looking at me.'

Jack's answering smile didn't reach his eyes. 'You don't flirt? Alice, you've flirted with me since the first time I set eyes on you. Anyway, there'll be no more of it. You behave with dignity once we're running this place. Have you ever seen Winnie giving the glad eye to a fella?'

'Well, no,' Alice faltered. Winnie was at least twice her age anyway, but even so, Alice was unaware that she'd given *anyone* the glad eye, as Jack put it. She could hear someone shouting 'Bar' from the other side of the door.

'Right,' Jack said. 'Get out there and serve our customers and I'll go and collect the empties. Stay behind the bar now tonight, we've only half an hour left anyway.'

Alice felt embarrassed as she served the young man who'd whistled. He seemed harmless enough but she couldn't meet his eyes as she handed him his change, in case Jack was watching her. She wished she'd not asked him to stay over now. His behaviour tonight had felt a bit controlling and it bothered her. Terry had never been like that. But if she told Jack she'd changed her mind and didn't want him to stay, he wouldn't be happy and she couldn't run the risk of *him* changing *his* mind about wanting to marry her. So much depended on that happening now; Brian's future, for one, as well as her own happiness. This feeling was just a blip. They usually had lovely times together. Maybe he was feeling a bit insecure. That would go once they were married, she was sure.

Her mind was in a whirl as she totted up the cost of the drinks she'd just pulled for another customer and she hoped she'd added it up right. Jack came back with his hands full of glasses. People were starting to leave the club as Alice plunged her hands into soapy water, conscious of her missing rings, which nearly always worked their way up her finger as she washed up. Millie and Jimmy came over to say goodnight and she hurriedly grabbed a tea towel and dried her hands, hiding her naked ring finger under the towel. Millie would be sure to notice her lack of rings and say something; although she hadn't commented when they sang together, Alice assumed she had been too busy singing and hadn't noticed her ringless finger.

'I really enjoyed us singing together,' Millie enthused. 'It was just like old times. We must do it again. Good luck tomorrow with

Terry's mam. Let us know as soon as you can about the house and where things are up to. We go back up to Blackpool tomorrow to pack our stuff and then we'll move into Mam and Dad's. So we'll see you later next week most likely.' Millie gave Alice a hug and pecked Jack on the cheek. 'See you soon.'

Alice waved until her friends were out the door. A few stragglers left their empties on the bar and called goodnight. Jack locked the doors and checked all the ashtrays were empty. Alice finished the glasses and took a cloth to all the tables. She felt weary as she wiped up sticky messes and rinsed the cloth in the bowl of water she'd carried with her. As she bent to pick up the bowl Jack grabbed her from behind, making her jump. He laughed and spun her around to face him.

'I can't wait to get back to yours,' he whispered and kissed her. 'If I wasn't expecting Arnold and Winnie back any minute I'd take you right now, gel, I'm that desperate,' he said, pushing her back against a table and grinding his hips against hers. As if on cue, lights shone in through the windows as the boss's car pulled up outside. 'Right,' Jack said, releasing his firm hold on her, 'take the bowl back to the kitchen and let's get off.'

Chapter Fifteen

Alice sat with her back against the wooden headboard as she listened to Jack whistling while washing himself in the bathroom. It was only seven am, but as good as his word, he was leaving early before the neighbours roused, although no doubt the Sunday paper delivery boy would be out on his rounds. She was glad Jack was going now, as she needed to get her head in place to go and pick up Cathy from Granny Lomax's. She was dreading it, but it had to be done. She was Jack's future wife now and it was time to move on and take control.

She smiled as he strolled back into the bedroom and pulled on his discarded clothes. She watched as he sat on the side of the bed and carefully pulled a sock over what was left of his right foot. It wasn't a pretty sight and made her stomach roll; there were only two toes left intact, the big toe and the one next to it. All the outer foot and the rest of his toes were gone and the scarring was red and ugly. Last night had been the first time she'd seen it properly and she'd held her breath as he'd told her she might as well look and then she'd get used to it. When he'd made love to her the other night downstairs they'd both been still partially clothed and the foot hadn't been mentioned.

He'd told her last night that, although it wasn't painful most of the time, the nerve endings still tingled and at times it felt like his foot was on fire when he'd been working all day. She'd done her best to look as sympathetic as she could. Rumours were still bandied around occasionally that he'd shot himself to get out of being sent abroad with the army. But Jack had always denied the rumours and Alice didn't believe for a minute that anyone would be so stupid as to deliberately injure themselves in that way when there was a chance they'd arrive home safe and sound, like Terry and Jimmy had done.

Jack put on his boots and jacket and leant over to kiss her goodbye. He smelled of Dentifrice toothpaste and she wondered if he'd used her brush.

'Thanks for thinking, gel, and putting that blue toothbrush out for me to use,' he said, smiling. 'I forgot to bring me own. I'll get on me way now and I'll call in tonight on the way into work. See how you got on with your ma-in-law. Perhaps you can save me a bit of dinner. And thanks for a great night. I think me and you are well-suited, Alice. Stay in bed and I'll lock the door and put the key through the letterbox. It's really early so you might as well have another hour's kip.'

'Okay.' Alice nodded. 'I'll see you later. I'm really tired.'

He laughed, a wicked glint lighting up his blue eyes. 'That's because I kept you awake for most of the night. Better get used to it, gel. I'm a hot-blooded man.'

Alice smiled wearily and lay back on her pillows as he left the room. He wasn't wrong there. She felt exhausted. They'd made love for most of the night. He'd been as tender as the other night at first and then quite demanding the second time and then tender again earlier this morning. He still hadn't said he loved her though and she wondered why when his actions had been so passionate and loving. Terry had always said it when they'd made love. Her eyes filled as she thought of Terry and his gentle ways and she blinked to clear the tears. Jack excited her and she loved being in his arms, being at one with him. And, like he'd told her, she'd better get used to it. She was marrying him soon, no matter what anyone else thought. She wasn't going to lie in bed wallowing in thoughts of what used to be. She needed a bath. She felt sticky and Jack hadn't used any protection like he did the night before. She knew she should have said something, but she hadn't liked to bring up the subject in case his mood changed. He'd been a bit off-hand last night at the club, and then when he'd practically dragged her back here and up the stairs to bed, she'd just kept quiet. She wasn't frightened of him, but there was something about him, a controlling thing almost, that made her think he wouldn't take too kindly to being questioned too much about anything. He was different to Terry, but her feelings for him were strong enough to cope with that. From what she knew of his early life, he wasn't from a very close family; he might not have been shown much love as a child and so might be unsure how to express it. Hopefully he'd learn from her, given time. And they had plenty of that.

But he was the one who didn't want any kids, so she needed to sort out some form of birth control and pronto. If Jack wasn't going to take responsibility then she would have to do it herself, or they'd soon be knee-deep in babies. She'd speak with Sadie tomorrow, see what she could advise. She was more clued up than Alice on such matters. She just hoped to God that last night hadn't left her pregnant as she was worried that Jack would scarper if that was the case and she'd be left with no money, no future and no education for Brian, plus another mouth to feed. Then there was the shame she'd have to endure. It didn't bear thinking about. She dragged herself out of bed, feeling a bit weary, and hurried into the bathroom.

The blue toothbrush Jack had used was in the holder and Alice felt tears springing to her eyes again. It was Terry's brush, and she just hadn't had the heart to remove it. She couldn't believe that Jack had thought it was one she'd bought for him. She'd just assumed he'd bring his own and a change of clothes, but he'd come empty-handed. She felt suddenly overwhelmed, and sat down on the side of the bath and burst into tears.

'Terry, why did you leave me?' she wailed. 'Now I've got all these responsibilities to deal with and I have to marry Jack just to make ends meet. I hate that damn bloody bike for taking you away.'

She knew she was being melodramatic now and pulled herself together, beginning to fill the bath. She didn't *have* to marry Jack at all; she was doing it because she *wanted* to marry him.

She looked at her bare left hand with no wedding and eternity rings and blinked away more threatening tears. Her head was banging, she felt a bit sickly, and the last thing she wanted to do today was go and see Granny Lomax. But it had to be done. She turned the bath taps off and tipped some bubble bath into the water. A good soak, as hot as she could stand it, would help and by her reckoning it was a safe enough time in her monthly cycle. Hopefully she'd be fine, but it didn't stop her feeling worried.

*

Granny Lomax handed Alice a mug of tea and a small plate with a buttered scone. Cathy was outside playing in the garden. Alice put the plate down on the coffee table and tried to keep her left hand by her side. Damn, she'd intended to slip her rings back on when she came here, but her mind was all over the place and she'd forgotten. Her ringless finger hadn't gone unnoticed.

'Hmm,' Granny snorted. 'It didn't take *you* long to take my Terry's rings off, did it?' she said, a catch in her voice.

Alice chewed her lip and stared at the floor. 'It's not appropriate that I wear them now I'm marrying Jack,' she muttered. 'He, er, he didn't like it.'

'I bet he didn't.' Granny sipped her tea and stared at Alice over the top of her mug. 'But you're not married yet so it could have waited, surely. For Cathy's sake if nothing else. That poor little mite has been very unsettled this weekend, and,' she lowered her voice, although Cathy was nowhere in sight, 'she wet the bed last night. That's not like her. She's fretting and she's unhappy and she seemed scared to me when I mentioned Jack's name.'

Alice sighed. 'I'm sorry. Would you like me to take the bedding home and wash it?'

'It's already on the line, drying. I've tried to get her to talk, but she just clams up.'

'Talk about what?' Alice asked, stiffening. 'She's fine. Stop making out there's a problem. It'll take a while for her to get to know Jack, and he's not used to kiddies, but he's doing his best. Making her supper and reading her bedtime stories.'

Granny pursed her lips. 'I'm just telling you that I sense something is wrong. I don't want you to marry that man.'

Alice slammed down her empty mug. They'd be going around in circles forever at this rate. 'And I'm just telling you that if I don't sell my house and move in with Jack, Brian will have to leave school and get a job. I can't cope on my own any longer. It's not easy for any of us, but it is happening. I know you think you mean well, but I'll thank you to keep your nose out of my business. Tomorrow Jack and I will be putting in the banns for our marriage. By the end of August we will be man and wife and living at the club as soon as the house sale goes through. Millie and Jimmy will be living there.'

Alice took a deep breath. Might as well as get it over now that she was on her high horse. 'And from tomorrow, Marlene will be looking after Cathy. Now I'm doing all the extra hours at Lewis's I feel it's too much for you. Marlene's fitter and younger and hopefully I will soon be working full time if I can get it.'

This wasn't all strictly true, but she would ask for further hours if Jack was in agreement and didn't need her to work on the bar. The more money coming in the better, so they could all enjoy a nice comfortable lifestyle and never have to worry about money again.

A crimson flush appeared on Granny's cheeks and she jumped to her feet, her hands shaking.

'I knew this would happen now you've got involved with that man. Taking my only grandchild away from me. She's all I've got left of my Terry. After everything I've done for you and your family, this is how you repay me. I didn't think you had it in you to be so cruel, Alice.'

Alice chewed her lip. She hadn't meant it to come out the way she'd said it. Her words had sounded harsh, even to her own ears.

'I didn't mean you can't see Cathy at all. It's just that if I work full-time hours, Marlene can cover them with no problem. I can bring Cathy here every Sunday afternoon to see you. And you are always welcome to come and visit us at the Legion at any time.'

Granny shook her head. 'I will not be setting foot in any establishment run by Jack Dawson. I can assure you of that.'

Alice nodded. 'It's up to you, but it's Cathy's birthday at the end of August and we'll be having a little party for her. We'd like to see you there, at the house, that is. We won't be moving out until September at the earliest. I doubt Jack will be there as he'll be working, it being a weekend afternoon.'

Granny drew a deep breath. 'We?' she said. 'When you say *we* won't be moving does this mean that man is already living under your roof? Before you are legally married?'

Alice could feel her cheeks heating. 'No, of course he's not. By we, I mean Brian, me and Cathy. Jack visits us, but he's not living with us.'

'Hmm. Yet. I suppose it's only a matter of time.'

Alice got to her feet. 'I'd better go. Brian will be home soon. I've got things to do. Shall we see you next Sunday then?'

Granny nodded. Alice called for Cathy to come inside. Her daughter ran into the lounge, pigtails flying out behind her and smelling of fresh air and grass. 'Say goodbye to Granny. Give her a kiss.'

'Bye bye, Granny. See you tomorrow,' Cathy said, throwing herself at Granny's legs.

Granny's agonised sob was more than Alice could bear and she grabbed Cathy's hand and pulled her towards the door, mouthing over the top of her head, 'I'll tell her when I get her home.'

She marched swiftly towards Lark Lane, dragging a protesting Cathy by the hand.

'Why is Granny crying?' Cathy said. 'Let's go back and love her better.'

'We have to get home. I've got to cook a dinner and Brian will be back soon as well. And, er, Jack is coming on his way to work to have something to eat with us.'

Cathy stopped dead and stamped her feet. She snatched her hand from Alice's and folded her arms across her chest. 'I'm going back to Granny's. I don't want Jack to come round. He's a nasty man.'

'Cathy, now enough of that nonsense. Has Granny been saying something to you about Jack?'

Cathy clamped her lips together and glowered at her mother from beneath a thick fringe that needed a trim. 'I'm not telling you. It's a secret.'

Alice sighed wearily. 'Right, well I'm going. So you either come with me or you stay there.' She walked slowly away, knowing that eventually Cathy would follow her.

*

Cathy's lips trembled as she watched her mammy walking slowly down the road. She felt torn between wanting to go home with her and going back to see if her granny was okay. She wondered why Granny had cried. Something had made her sad. Maybe it was because Cathy had wet the bed last night and it had upset her. But she couldn't help it. She had dreamed a nasty dream where Jack Dawson was dragging her by the arm to the big house on the road near where he lived. He said she was a very bad girl and nobody wanted her so she was being taken to live at the naughty girls' home, just like he'd threatened the other day. He told her she could never come home again and he and her mammy would have lots more children to love instead of her. Cathy told him she needed the lavvy but he ignored her and she'd wet herself and then woken up screaming in bed at her granny's house and then Granny was there cuddling her and telling her not to worry. Granny had asked her if she was worried or frightened about something. But she'd said no. Because she knew that Jack would send her away if she told Granny anything about him and what he'd said to her, and then her dream would come true. She wiped her eyes on her cardigan sleeve and shouted, 'Mammy.'

Alice turned around and held out her arms. Cathy hurtled towards her and the pair walked home hand in hand.

*

There was no sign of Brian as Jack let himself in and hung his jacket on the hall stand. He popped his head around the front room door, where Cathy was playing hospitals with her dollies on the rug.

'Hiya, gel,' he said quietly and smiled with satisfaction as she looked terrified and shrank back against the chair. Good, he'd soon have the little madam under control. 'Where's your mammy?'

'In-in the kitchen,' Cathy stammered.

'Right, well you stay there then and don't you come out until she calls you.' Satisfied that she'd not move until told to, he closed the door and walked into the kitchen, where Alice was running water into the sink. Lids were clattering on top of the boiling pans on the stove so no wonder she hadn't heard him come in.

'Boo,' he said, coming up behind her and slipping his arms around her waist. 'How's my gorgeous gel, then?'

'Oh, Jack, I didn't know you were here,' she said, turning in his arms. He held her tight and kissed her. 'Careful, Cathy might see us.'

'She won't,' he whispered, nuzzling her neck. 'She's playing at nurses with her dolls in the front room. Proper engrossed in her game, she is. I just had a little chat with her and she's happy enough.'

'Oh, well Brian's due back at any minute. In fact, he's later than I was expecting him.'

He frowned and squeezed her tight. 'Playing hard to get, gel? Thought you'd be ready for a repeat performance by now. Sooner that ring's on your finger the better.'

'Er, no, I'm not playing hard to get, but I'm trying to cook a meal and, well…'

'I'm teasing,' Jack said, laughing. 'You'll get used to my sense of humour in time. Ah, there's the front door. That'll be Brian. I'll go and help him with his stuff while you carry on in here.' He released her from his grip and left the kitchen. 'How you doing, Brian?' he greeted the young lad, who beamed at him. 'Had a good time?'

'Very, thank you. I've fished and rowed a boat and we walked for miles. It was lovely. The Peak District, they call it. You should take our Alice there for an afternoon out one day.'

'Maybe I will,' Jack said. He liked the lad. Keep Brian sweet and on his side and he wouldn't go far wrong. 'I've been thinking, when we move into the Legion, and you've finished your homework for the night, you can do a bit of pot collecting to earn a few bob. How does that sound?'

'Smashing. I was hoping you might suggest that. I would have asked you anyway.'

'Good. Me and you are going to get on just great, lad.'

Chapter Sixteen

Jack met Alice from work on Monday afternoon. He greeted her with a kiss and she was glad to see that he'd made an effort and was clean and presentable with a shirt and tie on and no trace of alcohol on his breath. All she could smell was his lovely Old Spice shaving soap.

The pair made their way to Mount Pleasant registry office, where they spoke to a woman on reception. She filled in the forms with them and then told them the banns would be put up that day. She booked their wedding at a cost of seven and sixpence, for the licence. The date was set for Saturday August 30th at two o'clock. Alice felt uncomfortable that Jack had decided this was the best place for them. He wasn't religious so had told her he didn't want a church wedding, and she wasn't too sure that she would have even qualified for one either, with her having been married before. But, although Jack probably had no idea, as it had never been mentioned, Mount Pleasant was where she'd married Terry in 1940. The memories came flooding back as she stood waiting in the reception area with Jack. The air raid siren had sounded as soon as they were married and they'd spent the first two hours of their married life in the nearby shelter. All they'd had was the one precious night together and that had been it for over five years until Terry had come home. She mentally shook herself and tuned in to what Jack was saying as they left the building. It wouldn't do for him to know where her thoughts had been.

'Let's go and celebrate with a quick drink in the Phil,' he suggested, grabbing her hand and leading her in the direction of the Philharmonic pub on Hope Street. 'Also, we need to get you a wedding ring. I could do with a new suit too. Not had one for years and this one is too shabby for getting wed in. We'll make a list. I've a bit of money put by that I was saving for the bond, but I won't need that now you're paying it with the house sale money, so we can use my money for stuff for the wedding.'

'Well, if you don't mind,' Alice said. 'I don't have a spare penny until we get the house money. Shall we have this drink, then get the tram back to Aigburth and tell Arnold and Winnie we've booked a date? We also need to call in on the way back and see that solicitor on Lark Lane that Arnold recommended. I've got all the house deeds and papers in my handbag ready.'

'Sounds like a good plan, gel.'

*

Arnold and Winnie hugged the pair of them as Alice and Jack told them their latest news.

'We've set the ball in motion for the house sale as well,' Alice said, smiling.

'We went to see the solicitor on the way back here,' Jack told them. 'Because it's just the one house with no hold-ups it will go through very quickly. You can start packing now, Winnie.'

'And I will, my love,' Winnie said, beaming. 'Oh, I'm that happy for the pair of you. He's a good lad, you know, Alice. Just needs a bit of taming and looking after. I'm sure he'll look after you and you'll both be very happy.'

Alice grinned as Arnold handed her a glass of sherry and raised a toast. At this rate she'd be tiddly by the time Marlene brought Cathy home. Jack had insisted she have a large sherry in the Phil and this one was large too. Drinking in the afternoon was not something she was used to. *And* she had an empty stomach. But she felt quite mellow and relaxed and also happy. Jack had been in a really great mood all afternoon and she knew for certain that marrying him was the right thing to do. Not just because it would make life a whole lot easier financially, but because she loved him and wanted to spend the rest of her life with him.

'Now, me and Winnie will put on a buffet here for you as our wedding present,' Arnold said. 'We'll do the cake, the lot. We want you to have the best start possible and it will be our pleasure to do it. Jack's been like a son to us and it's only fitting that we should do for him what we would have done if we'd had a lad of our own.'

Winnie nodded her agreement. 'It'll be the finest wedding party this club's ever seen. All you two need to do is turn up, dressed for the part.'

Alice laughed. 'Oh, and we will. But you will come to the registry office first to see us taking our vows, won't you? We have no parents between us, so it would be lovely if you can be there.'

'Of course we'll be there,' Winnie said.

*

'What time is Marlene bringing Cathy back?' Jack asked as he and Alice walked home hand in hand up Lark Lane.

'She said she'd give her some tea when her lot gets in from work,' Alice replied. 'And then bring her back about half six-ish. I told her I wasn't too sure how long we'd be out for this afternoon.'

'And Brian? What time is he usually in?'

'He's having his tea at his pal's today and then they're going straight to the lads' club boxing session at the church hall. He'll be back about seven.'

Jack pulled her close and whispered, 'So I've got you all to myself for a good hour, gel. Good, cos I'm feeling hungry.'

Alice nodded. 'Shall I get something nice for our tea from the bakery? Perhaps a nice potato and meat pie?'

'Not that sort of hungry,' he said, grinning and pulling her along.

'Jack Dawson, you're insatiable.'

'It has been said before. But you're the only one for me now, Alice.'

As they laughed and held hands, turning the corner into Lucerne Street, they bumped right into Granny Lomax. She stopped dead in her tracks. Alice gasped and tried to free her hand from Jack's but he held on tight and stared at Granny.

'Alice,' Granny snapped. 'I wanted to talk to you. But I see you're busy.'

'Er, yes,' Alice mumbled, feeling her cheeks heating as Jack dug his fingernails into her palm. 'We, er, we have things to discuss.'

'And where is Cathy?'

'With Marlene. She'll be back later.'

'And Brian?'

'He's having tea at his friend's.'

'I see. Well, what I have to say won't take long. I was hoping to find you on your own. Could I perhaps come in for a minute if *he's* going?'

'Listen, Missus,' Jack butted in, annoyed that his bit of time alone with Alice was under threat. 'I'm going nowhere. Whatever you want will have to wait. I need to get back to work shortly and Alice and I have some private stuff to sort out first. Why don't you come back tomorrow when she's got more time? You can see the kiddies then as well.'

Alice nodded her agreement but Granny Lomax rounded on Jack, wagged a finger in his face and shouted, 'You stink of alcohol. How dare you interfere between me and my daughter-in-law? It's got nothing to do with you.'

'But she's not, is she,' Jack yelled back. 'Not any more. She's my wife-to-be. So whatever you have to say to her has everything to do with me from now on. She'll see you tomorrow, like I said. Oh, and I've had two drinks and so has she. Not that it's your business, but we've celebrated the fact that we've booked our wedding.' He dragged Alice away before anything else could be said, leaving Granny staring after them, shaking her head.

Alice silently chewed her lip as Jack unlocked the front door and then locked it again once they were inside.

'I'm not having that old bag interfering in our lives,' Jack said. 'We've had a nice afternoon and she comes along and bloody spoils it. Well, I'm not putting up with it.'

'Jack, calm down and come here.' Alice put her arms around him and he sighed into her hair. 'I'll speak to her tomorrow after work. I'm surprised she came round after yesterday. Maybe it's best that she stays away from the house for good now. You'll be here most of the time and we've got work to do: helping me to get ready for the move.'

'I know,' Jack whispered and kissed her. 'I'm sorry, gel. I'm calmer now. It just annoys me because I know she still blames me for Terry's death and it's not right. Make me feel better, Alice. Come and love me while we've got the time.' He took her hand and led her upstairs.

*

'So will you help me choose?' Alice asked Sadie as they travelled to work on the tram the following day. 'Jack's given me some money from his savings to buy the dress. I don't want anything expensive or too fancy, just something nice and summery that I can wear again.'

'Of course I will.' Sadie squeezed her arm. 'How exciting. I haven't been to a wedding for ages.'

'Will you stand for me?' Alice asked. 'You know, be my witness?'

'Me? But what about Millie? Won't she feel hurt if you don't ask her? And maybe Jimmy could be Jack's.'

Alice shook her head. 'Jack thinks we should ask someone new as Millie and Jimmy were witnesses at mine and Terry's wedding.

He doesn't think it's right to have the same people. He said it might bring bad luck.'

Sadie laughed. 'Well, flipping heck. I never had Jack Dawson down as being superstitious. But yes, count me in and thank you. Any excuse for a new dress, eh, gel? And who will stand for Jack?'

'He's asking Arnold.'

'Oh, that's nice. Arnold is lovely and he'll be thrilled to bits.'

Alice nodded. As the tram trundled on towards the city centre, her thoughts turned to yesterday afternoon and how loving, gentle and careful Jack had been in bed compared to the previous night when he'd taken too many chances. How, after making love to her, he'd tied wool around her finger to get the right size for her wedding ring. And how later, after work, he'd come back and handed over some money to buy a dress for the wedding. She wondered how he could be so loving one day and a bit off-hand and possessive on others, like after she'd sung with Millie. Terry had always been even-tempered, so it was difficult to understand, but maybe time would mellow Jack. He still hadn't told her that he loved her, but his actions spoke volumes so she could live in hope.

'Come on, dreamer.' Sadie nudged her elbow. 'You were miles away. Conductor has just shouted Ranelagh Street.'

They hurried off the tram and Alice linked her arm through Sadie's. 'When we get to break time I need to talk to you privately. I'd like some, er, advice.'

'From me?' Sadie raised an eyebrow. 'About what?'

'Birth control and what I can use,' Alice whispered as they entered the building.

'Ah, okay. Well, I'll do my best. You look a bit worried though. Hope it's not too late.'

Alice rolled her eyes. 'You and me both, Sadie.'

*

The haberdashery department shelving units had been moved across near the lift area and were now fixed firmly to the walls. Alice and Sadie began to unpack their stock and reposition it. They were able to make a display of knitting patterns on the wall and Sadie artfully wound a rainbow of woollen hanks around some hooks that were sticking out of an abandoned peg board.

'That looks really nice.' Alice nodded her approval. 'You can see what colours we're stocking much easier now and it brightens the bare wall up.'

Miss White strolled across the floor towards their display, nodded her head with approval and almost half-smiled. 'That looks very nice, ladies. Well done.'

'Thank you,' Sadie said and pulled a face behind the woman's back as she swanned away. 'Bloody sourpuss. No wonder she's still single.'

Alice grinned and turned to a stout woman who was eyeing up Sadie's wool display. 'That looks grand,' she began, 'but I want boring black for socks for my old fella. Have you got any, gels?'

'We have.' Alice reached on the shelves behind her. 'Two ounces?'

'Best give me four, chuck, then I've got spare for darning. His hobnail boots don't half wear his socks out quick. Mind you, his bony feet and long toenails don't help either. Funny how you never notice stuff like that in the first flush of love. Mind you, that were over thirty years ago. Good job my eyesight's not as good as it used to be. What I can't see I can't fret over. You young ones enjoy yourself while you can. Getting old's no fun.' She pocketed her change and picked up the bag of wool and waved goodbye.

'Well, she's a bundle of laughs,' Sadie said. 'Puts you right off, thinking of men getting old and their horrible feet, doesn't it? Don't honestly think I can be bothered again after Luca. He was the one, but it wasn't meant to be. Although part of me wishes I'd stayed around now and gone to see him when the fair was in town at

Easter. But still, what would have been the point? I couldn't have gone back to that lifestyle and he may be with another woman now for all I know. No, it's just me and Gianni from now on, and that's that.'

Alice nodded, thinking of poor Jack's lame foot, and how she'd have to avoid looking at it until she too couldn't see, but understanding just what Sadie was saying.

*

'So you think that would be the best method then?' Alice asked as she and Sadie sat by the window in the temporary canteen on their morning break, enjoying a toasted tea cake split between them. There was hardly a soul around so it was a good opportunity to talk about personal things.

Sadie shrugged. 'Well, I used one occasionally and I never got caught again after Gianni. Luca is Catholic and doesn't believe in contraception so it was down to me and I didn't tell him I was using it. Although how he couldn't tell I don't know. But he never said anything.'

'Hmm.' Alice took a sip of tea. Sadie had suggested she ask at the doctor's surgery for a diaphragm, which she said was like a rubber cap that stopped pregnancy. Alice didn't fancy the idea but didn't feel she had much choice in the matter. Jack's aversion to using a rubber on occasion was nothing to do with religion, just carelessness, but she couldn't take that chance again until they were at least married. It was him that didn't want kids, but she would feel more comfortable about discussing matters once they were wed. She'd have to do her best for now by making sure the kids were always around until after the wedding day. That wouldn't be too hard, with a bit of luck. But for now she'd see about this method Sadie had suggested on the off-chance he told her he was coming round on his way home from work at night when the kids were in bed. At least she could be prepared before he arrived.

On their dinner break, Alice and Sadie went upstairs to the ladies' clothing section. It was much smaller than it used to be, but there were still a few nice dresses left on the summer rails.

'I like this.' Sadie held up a pale blue dress with a sweetheart neckline and small white pearly buttons to the waist, the full skirt falling in soft folds to just on the knee. 'You could wear your white peep-toe sandals with it and I've got a white handbag you can borrow and a white silky jacket that would go lovely.'

Head on one side, Alice looked at the dress. It was perfect and the blue would accentuate her eyes. 'I'll try it on. Come with me.'

They hurried over to the fitting rooms and an assistant showed them to a curtained-off cubicle. 'Sorry it's a bit makeshift, ladies. But, well, you know.'

'We do,' Alice said. 'We're from haberdashery and keep getting moved from pillar to post. We've just unpacked again this morning. Right, I'll go and slip this on.'

Sadie waited outside, talking to the assistant while Alice got changed. As the curtain slid back she gasped. 'Alice, you look lovely. It's perfect.'

The assistant nodded. 'It looks very nice. Is it for a special occasion?'

'My wedding,' Alice said. 'It's my second time around, so it's a bit informal. I'm widowed, you see.'

'Sorry to hear that, love. Did you lose him abroad? I lost mine in Germany just before the war ended.'

Alice shook her head, feeling tears welling. So many women were in the same boat as she was.

'Sadly no. He came back safe and sound, and then got badly injured in an accident on the Dock Road. His motorbike skidded. He died not long after. I'm sorry you lost your husband out there. I lost my brother in Germany.'

'Well, at least you've got a second chance at happiness, love. You make the most of it. And if the dress is for a wedding, I've got just the thing over in lingerie to go with it.' Alice and Sadie followed her across the floor to a glass counter, where she rummaged underneath and pulled out a box. 'Here you are: a blue lacy garter, a bit of extra "something blue" for you.'

Sadie smiled as Alice blushed. 'That'll get Jack going,' she teased. 'Not that he needs it,' she added.

Alice rolled her eyes as the woman wrapped the dress and garter in tissue paper and placed them in a box, then slid the box into a large carrier bag. She totted up the total and knocked Alice's staff discount off. Alice pocketed the change from the five-pound note that Jack had given her. She could afford some new stockings now as well. She had some almost-new white lacy underwear that she'd hardly worn and it would look lovely under the dress, and if she borrowed Sadie's white jacket, there would be just enough money left over to get Cathy some new socks and hair ribbons, and Brian a nice tie to wear. Cathy had a pretty summer dress made by Granny that would do nicely and Brian had a decent white shirt and grey trousers. There was a grey tweed, double-breasted sports jacket of Rodney's still hanging in the wardrobe that was in almost-new condition and might fit Brian now. It would be better than him wearing his school blazer, the only jacket he possessed. At least then he'd look smart and presentable for the occasion.

Chapter Seventeen

Alice's late August wedding day dawned bright and sunny. Millie came round mid-morning to do her hair and paint her nails. As she left to go back to her mam's to get herself dressed for the occasion, promising to be back by one with Jimmy, her parents and the cars to transport them all, Sadie arrived, with a spick and span Gianni, to help Alice into her outfit. Earlier Cathy and Brian had been to the flower shop on Lark Lane to pick up the small posy of white roses fastened up with blue ribbon that Alice had ordered, along with pink and white carnation buttonholes for their guests. The box of flowers was waiting on the table in the back sitting room.

'You okay?' Sadie asked as Alice slipped her arms into the white silk jacket that Sadie had brought with her.

Alice nodded, turning this way and that to check herself in the long mirror on the wardrobe door.

'Just a bit nervous,' she admitted. 'But otherwise I'm fine.' She took a deep breath. 'How do I look?'

'Fabulous. Jack's a very lucky man.'

'Do you really think so?'

'Of course. He's getting a beautiful wife and a lovely little family, not to mention his dream coming true in stewardship of the Legion. I know he's wanted that for a long time. Without you it wouldn't be possible.'

Alice sighed. 'I know a lot of people think I'm mad. I see it when I go into the local shops and everyone stops talking as I walk in. I'm obviously the topic of conversation, even though no one actually says anything to me. Jack said to ignore them and that it's probably all down to Granny Lomax saying things out of turn. But I don't know that she'd do that.'

'Have you heard from her since the last time she tried to visit you?'

Alice shook her head. 'Last time I took Cathy round to the bungalow it was all locked up and her neighbour told me she'd gone away to visit friends for a week or two.'

Sadie smiled. 'She's too nosy to keep away for ever. She'll be round when she gets back, you'll see.'

'Maybe. She won't come if Jack's here and we'll be moving late next week. I can't see her coming over to the club either.'

'No, but she can phone you there at least. So, are you looking forward to your honeymoon?'

Alice nodded. 'Blackpool will be busy at this time of year, but I'm sure we'll enjoy ourselves. It's only two days anyway as we need to be back for the move.'

'And is Marlene definitely looking after the kids?'

'Yes. She's going to stay here with them. They'll come back to the house as soon as we leave the Legion. Arnold's lending us his car. I can't wait and I know Jack can't either.'

'And did you get yourself sorted at the doctor's? You know? Just in case Jack hasn't got anything prepared.'

Alice blew out her cheeks. 'Yes, it's packed away in my case. Fingers crossed it works.'

'Well, you've been lucky up to now, so good luck for the future.'

Alice laughed. 'Thanks. We'll need it, I'm sure.'

'Right.' Sadie took charge. 'Let's go downstairs and sort the flowers and the kids out before Jimmy and Millie's dad arrive with the cars.'

*

Alice was relieved to see Jack's eyes light up as she walked into the reception area of Mount Pleasant registry office. He was waiting with Arnold and Winnie, all dolled up in their best. Jack's new navy pinstripe suit looked smart and Winnie straightened his navy tie and fussed with his collar. She took the white buttonhole flower from Sadie and pinned it to Jack's lapel.

'There,' she said, brushing imaginary fluff from his front. 'You look proper bonny now, my boy.' Winnie smiled as Jack bent to drop a kiss on her cheek. She pinned on Arnold's buttonhole and her own. 'That's it, we're done. Don't you all look grand?'

Cathy was hopping from foot to foot with Gianni, and Brian grabbed her hand to get her to stand still as Freddie and his wife and Marlene and Stan crowded into the reception area alongside Millie and her family.

After thinking they'd got no one to invite, Alice was pleased to see such a good turn-out. More than there had been for her and Terry's wedding in fact. She felt a little tug of sadness wash over her as she thought of Terry but pushed it to one side. It was time to move on and become Jack's wife. And she felt more than ready. She took a deep breath and smiled as the registrar beckoned them all into the room where the wedding ceremonies took place. Standing beside Jack, who looked at her and squeezed her hand, Alice smiled and let go of the past.

*

After the sumptuous buffet and a toast to the happy couple, led by Arnold as best man, Millie got up on stage to sing Judy Garland and Gene Kelly's 'For Me and My Gal'. She was accompanied by the pianist, and everyone joined in.

'Go on,' Arnold encouraged, giving Jack a gentle push. 'Get out there and have the first dance with your new wife.'

Jack turned to Alice and smiled. 'May I, Mrs Dawson?'

Alice grinned. 'You may.' Her new name, and the first time anyone, apart from the registrar, had used it. She slipped off her jacket and took Jack's outstretched hand as he led her onto the dance floor, to loud cheers from their guests.

'You happy?' Jack asked as he waltzed her round.

'Very. Are you?'

'I am,' he replied, looking into her eyes. 'You're all mine now, and, er, I love you, gel.'

'Do you? Really?'

He nodded, smiling. 'I do, Alice. Do you honestly think I'd put myself through all this wearing a suit malarkey and bloody buttonholes if I didn't?'

She grinned. 'I guess not. And Jack, I love you too.' If he never said it to her again she could live with that. He'd said it at just the right time and that meant the world to her.

*

Alice waved goodbye to a weeping Cathy, who clung to her waist; she didn't want Mammy to go away with Jack. Alice gave Brian a hug.

'Look after her and make sure you both do everything Marlene tells you to,' she said. Jack was calling her name and she lowered her voice so that he wouldn't hear her. 'And tomorrow, take her round to see Granny Lomax. Hopefully she'll be in and Cathy will enjoy that. I'll see you on Monday when we get back. I have to go now,' she finished as Jack called her name again from beside the car that someone had put a home-made 'Just Married' banner on. She clambered into the passenger seat and breathed a sigh of relief. As the car drove away to rousing cheers, from the corner of her eye Alice saw Cathy pull away from Brian's grip and run towards a figure standing back from everyone else; Granny Lomax. When had she arrived? Alice just hoped that Jack wouldn't spot her too; otherwise his good mood would evaporate faster than the

Mersey mist on a fine day. She glanced across at him, but he was smiling, oblivious.

'We'll just nip to yours and pick up your case and then we'll be off,' he said. 'Mine's already in the boot because I stayed at the Legion last night. Winnie insisted on it so she could help me to get ready! Tell you what, gel: it's so quiet first thing up there. All I could hear were birds singing and pigeons cooing. Bliss. No nosy neighbours to disturb us or hear what we're doing. Very private and I like that. It's perfect, in fact.'

Alice smiled, relaxing back in her seat. Although she liked all her neighbours on Lucerne Street, it was the sort of place you could keep nothing to yourself. It would be lovely to enjoy some privacy for a change. She dashed into the house as Jack pulled up outside and picked up her case from the hall floor. This was it. She would be coming back here on Monday a new woman, ready to share the future with Jack and the kids.

*

The room on the second floor of the Clifton Hotel on Talbot Road in Blackpool was quite spacious, clean and nicely furnished. Alice ran her hand over the pink candlewick bedspread that toned with the pink brocade curtains at the window, and matched the lampshades on the bedside table lamps. There was a sink in the corner with a cold tap and a large enamel jug sitting underneath. A wardrobe stood in one alcove of the chimney breast and a chest with six drawers in the other.

'It's a lovely room,' Alice said to the tall, chubby-faced landlady, Mrs Swann.

'Thank you, dear. I'm sure you'll be very comfortable, Mr and Mrs Dawson. Hot water for washing is down the landing in the bathroom where you will also find the toilet for this floor. Baths can be taken in the evening but you will need to book first thing in the morning and it's an extra shilling a time. Breakfast is at nine o'clock prompt and your evening meal will be served at six thirty. All rooms are to be vacated by ten am and no returns before four. Now, I'll leave you to unpack and will see you shortly in the dining room.'

'Thank you,' Jack said, seeing her out and locking the door behind her. He raised an eyebrow in Alice's direction. 'Wouldn't like to meet that one down a dark alley.'

Alice grinned. 'She's a bit stern. We'd better get a move on and unpack our bits and bobs and get ready for tea. Can you get some hot water in that jug then we can freshen up a bit.'

Jack took off his suit jacket and dropped it on the bed. He bent to pick up the jug and winced.

'What's wrong?'

'My foot's giving me gyp. Been on my feet most of the day and then dancing and driving, it's set the nerves off tingling. I'll take a couple of Anadin with a drink of whisky later. That'll take the edge off.'

Alice frowned. 'Should you take painkillers with alcohol?'

He shrugged. 'It's the only thing that helps ease the pain. You want a nice wedding night, don't you? One to remember.'

She nodded. 'Of course.'

'Then I've got no choice.'

He limped from the room carrying the jug, leaving Alice staring after him. Perhaps it was time he went to see a doctor again about that foot, she thought. Get some proper painkillers that worked better than Anadin and whisky. That combination couldn't possibly be good for him. She'd suggest it when they got home, see what he thought. She unpacked her case and put the diaphragm in her handbag. Depending on his mood later, she might well need it tonight.

*

Granny Lomax walked back from St Michael's Sunday morning service with a feeling of deep shock in her gut. The after-service coffee morning had proved to be a source of information she hadn't expected to hear. Not that she liked to gossip, but when she'd overheard two women talking, and her ex-daughter-in-law's name crop up in conversation, she'd tuned in to what they were saying.

'Well, personally I think she was mad to marry him, a nice girl like Alice, and after everything she's been through and losing her husband like that,' one woman said. 'He's nothing but trouble. And I believe she's sold her house as well so that he can take on the Legion when Winnie and Arnold retire. All that money she'll be handing over and it'll soon be wasted knowing him. Everyone down our street knows what a boozer he is. He's just like his father was; handy with his fists and all. Harry Dawson was always knocking their mother about when he couldn't get his own way. We used to hear her begging for mercy on a Friday night when he'd come home from the pub kaylied. I know the walls were thin, but not that thin. She'd be screaming, poor woman. And there was nothing we could do. Always had black eyes and bruises everywhere. It was a blessing when he corked it. At least she had a bit of peace then until *she* died as well. The oldest boy was never any bother, but that Jack was always a cheeky little sod; and cocky as hell at giving lip. His father used to tan his backside but it made no difference.'

Granny Lomax had sipped her tea as the other woman began. 'Yes, I feel sorry for poor Alice. She's no idea what she's letting herself in for. And she's got that lovely little girl as well *and* her brother that she looks after. I wonder if Jack's told her about his own kiddie that he abandoned during the war. She'd be about four now. Poor little mite. He didn't want to know and left that poor Susan girl high and dry. Swore blind it wasn't his. Susan's mam's done a good job of bringing the kiddie up as her own though. They're all better off without Jack Dawson in their lives. If he hadn't shot himself he'd never have got involved with Susan and put her in the family way. He should have been in bloody Germany like all our lads were. Flaming coward, he was. Made sure he didn't do too much damage, but just enough to get him off the hook. He wants locking up.'

Granny Lomax had got to her feet and put down her empty cup and saucer. She'd heard enough and felt sick to her stomach at what she'd just learned. She herself had heard rumours about Jack, but these two women appeared to have been close neighbours in the street he'd grown up in, and knew the family in fact.

She'd hurried outside and taken several deep breaths to calm herself. Before she said anything to Alice she'd need to prove everything was true and for that she'd have to find evidence. As she'd stood there, her head whirling, the two gossiping women had come out of church and walked past her. She'd decided to take a chance.

'Excuse me,' she called. The women turned around.

'Yes, love?' one of them said. 'Are you okay? You look a bit pale. Do you want me to fetch a chair out for you?'

'Er, no, that won't be necessary, thank you.' Granny Lomax apologised for being nosy and told them what she'd overheard them discussing and how it had distressed her. Both their faces lit up. They nodded when she asked if they could help her and she told them that she was Alice's ex-mother-in-law and was extremely worried about her family. After a lengthy conversation they had written down the address of Susan and her mother and told her that Jack had lived in the same street. They'd wished her well and gone on their way.

Now, Granny hurried back home and let herself in. She'd left a small chicken cooking that her farmer friend had brought round yesterday, and the good smell that met her in the hall was appetising. Maybe Cathy and Brian would call in today while Alice was away. She'd bet that Marlene, who she'd seen take the children under her wing when she'd sneaked into the Legion grounds yesterday for a quick peek at her granddaughter, would be at home cooking Sunday dinner for her own big family.

She set to and peeled enough potatoes just in case. She could walk round and invite them if they were at home. She pulled the chicken out of the oven and put it on a plate to cool. Deciding to hurry round to Alice's before she prepared any more veg, she picked up her handbag and keys and locked up. As she rounded the corner she saw Brian and Cathy walking down the road and her heart swelled. Cathy let go of Brian's hand and ran towards her, her little face alight with joy.

'I was just on my way to see if you wanted to have your Sunday dinner with me,' Granny said, enfolding Cathy in a hug.

Brian beamed. 'Oh, yes please. I'm starving. So is Cathy. Marlene cooked us a nice breakfast but she's had to go home for a few hours. She made us some jam sarnies, but we've eaten them already.'

Granny laughed. 'That's my boy. Come on then. It's roast chicken with all the trimmings.' The way to Brian's heart had always been through his stomach. She was going to enjoy the afternoon with the children and then tonight she would sit quietly and work out a plan to put together as much information about Jack Dawson as she could. Now Alice was married to the man, there wasn't much she could do about that. Alice had made her bed, but she would make sure her granddaughter was protected if it was the last thing she did.

Chapter Eighteen

Alice sighed when Jack cried out in pain as he removed his boot. He hadn't been very happy to begin with, as they'd had to walk around in the rain that had started not long after breakfast. They'd walked the length of the promenade and strolled up the South Pier. They'd had a bite to eat in a pub at dinnertime and a couple of drinks and then wandered aimlessly around the Pleasure Beach until they were allowed back in their room again to dry off and get ready for the evening meal. Jack had been on his feet all day now and he'd told her he was in agony as they climbed the two flights of stairs up to their room. He lay back on the bed and Alice got him two Anadins from the packet in her handbag. He washed them down with a swig from the half bottle of whisky he'd bought earlier from an outdoor licence up the road.

'I'll just shut my eyes for ten minutes while they kick in,' he said.

'Okay. I'll use the bathroom and get changed ready for our meal.' She hurried down the corridor, shaking her head and wishing they'd gone home today. One day away was enough really when they had so much to do back in Liverpool. Mind you, if the weather had been nice they could have sat on deckchairs on the sands and relaxed. Nothing worse than wandering around in that fine rain that wets you through. She wondered what Brian and Cathy were doing right now and hoped they'd had a nice time with Marlene, who would no doubt have spoiled them. There was a queue for the bathroom, with a woman and two small boys in front of her.

'Mam, I wish that fat man would hurry up,' the eldest said, fidgeting from foot to foot. 'He's been in there for ages. I'm gonna wet meself in a minute.'

'Shh,' his embarrassed mother said. 'He'll hear you.'

'Mammy, I need a wee-wee,' the little one said, 'and I can't wait.'

The young woman turned to Alice and whispered, 'Do you think the landlady would mind if we used the bathroom on the floor below? I mean, it is a bit ridiculous, all these rooms up here and only one toilet.'

'I don't see why she should,' Alice replied. 'He's going to have an accident if you don't get him in soon.'

'Me dad said the landlady reminds him of Eva Braun,' the older boy piped up.

Alice stifled a giggle. 'Shh, she might hear you. I'd take a chance and go downstairs,' she said to the young woman.

She rolled her eyes and dragged the little boy down the stairs and the other one followed her. Alice strained her ear to the locked door. She couldn't hear a thing and knocked gently.

'Hello, are you okay in there?' No reply. She chewed her lip and knocked again. A faint sound reached her ears. It sounded like someone calling for help. 'Oh lord,' she muttered. 'Hang on a minute,' she called. 'I'll go and fetch help.' She ran down the stairs, past the woman and her two little boys and into the reception area.

'I think someone is in trouble in the top-floor bathroom,' she gasped to Mrs Swann, who was busy booking in a family at the welcome desk. 'A man went in ages ago and he's still in there calling for help.'

'Albert,' Mrs Swann called out to her husband. 'Top-floor bathroom. It sounds like someone's collapsed in there. Can you go and see? I'll be up when I've finished here.'

Alice followed Albert up the stairs and waited while he banged on the bathroom door. A faint cry for help sounded again. He tried the door but it was locked.

'He's put the bolt on. I'll have to break the door down. Just hope he's not behind it. Can you go and ask the wife to phone for an ambulance, love, just in case.'

Alice nodded and ran back downstairs, where Mrs Swann was handing over a key and pointing out the stairs to her new arrivals.

'Room five is facing the top of the stairs. Right dear,' she turned to Alice, 'what's happening?'

'Mr Swann said can you phone for an ambulance please,' Alice gasped. 'He's breaking the door down.'

'Oh dear. So whoever is in there has taken poorly?'

'It looks that way.'

'I bet it's Mr Simpson, one of our regulars. Can you go back and help my husband and I'll make the call right away. I'll be with you as soon as I can.'

Alice shot back up the stairs to find Mr Swann bending over a portly man. The man's face was grey and clammy and he was moaning in pain and clutching his stomach.

'Ambulance won't be long,' she said, kneeling beside Mr Swann. 'Shall I get a pillow and blanket?'

'In the cupboard behind you,' Mr Swann said, pointing.

Alice made the man comfortable. 'Is there anyone with you?' she asked.

He shook his head. 'On my own,' he whispered. 'Wife died last year.'

'Can we get in touch with any family?' she asked as Mrs Swann came rushing up the stairs.

'No one,' he said, licking dry lips.

'Five minutes,' Mrs Swann said. 'Won't be long, Mr Simpson. Are you in a lot of pain?'

'My stomach,' he said. 'Think I've got another blockage.'

Alice looked at Mrs Swann, who patted the man's arm comfortingly. 'Bowel cancer,' she muttered to Alice. 'I used to be a nurse. I know he's got it. Has had for some time.'

Alice chewed her lip. Poor man. No wonder he was in such pain. She still needed to use the toilet though and excused herself.

'I'm going to have to pop to the first-floor bathroom,' she whispered. She'd been ages. Jack would wonder where she was. She didn't want to antagonise him when he was on a short fuse with pain.

'Yes, love, you get on. We'll see to the evening meals when the ambulance has been,' Mrs Swann said. 'Everything's ready.'

Back in the room, Jack was sitting on the edge of the bed, face like thunder. 'Where the hell have you been?' he demanded.

Alice explained what had happened and went to sit beside him, but he pushed her away. The whisky bottle on the bedside table was now empty and she realised that, between the whisky and the two pints he'd had at dinnertime, he was now very drunk. And he'd been taking painkillers.

He got up, hobbled to the door and locked it. 'Bet you're making that up,' he snarled. 'Have you been up to something? Your face is all flushed.'

Alice gasped. 'Don't be so stupid. Jack. Of course I haven't.'

He crossed the room and lashed out at her, catching her on the chin. Stunned, she put her hand up to her face.

He bent and yelled in her face, 'Don't you ever call me stupid again. Do you hear me? Now you apologise.'

'I… I'm sorry,' she mumbled, feeling his spittle on her cheeks and shocked by his outburst. His eyes looked wild and an angry red circle had appeared high on each cheek. He didn't seem to be in pain any more though.

'And so you should be. Now get ready to go down for our evening meal.'

He swilled his face at the sink and ran a comb through his hair while Alice remained seated, still shocked and holding her chin. She reached for her handbag, got out her comb and lippy and tidied herself up. She could see a red mark on her chin in her compact mirror and dabbed on a bit of crème puff powder to cover it. She hoped it wouldn't bruise.

The dining room was buzzing with talk of how Mr Simpson had been taken away in an ambulance. Mrs Swann came over to thank Alice for her help. Jack ignored the landlady and Alice waited for him to tell her he was sorry for not believing her, but he was busy gazing around at each table, frowning as he studied the guests.

'So which one was it?' he slurred. 'Which one had his tongue down your throat while I was lying on our bed in agony?'

Alice chewed her lip and looked down at her plate of sausage and mash. She ignored his comment, which only seemed to rile him more, but she didn't want to cause an argument in front of all these people. They finished their meal in silence.

Back in their room Jack pulled on his jacket and made for the door.

'Where are you going?' Alice asked. 'Aren't you waiting for me?'

Jack turned, his lip curled in a sneer. 'Out,' he announced. 'Two can play at your game.' And with that he was gone, slamming the door behind him.

Alice sat on the bed, tears filling her eyes. Should she go after him? Would it make things worse? He'd had far too much to drink and with the painkillers on top it was a bad mix. The nice Jack she'd married only yesterday had vanished along with the sunshine. One day into their marriage and he'd walked off, threatening to find another woman. What had she let herself in for? She hoped he remembered that Mrs Swann locked the front door at ten thirty.

*

Stretched out on the bed fully clothed, Alice lay awake, waiting for Jack to come home. It was ten fifteen according to her watch. Mrs Swann had popped up earlier to let her know that Mr Simpson was comfortable in hospital and to thank her for the help. Not that she'd really known what to do, Alice thought, but her being quick to respond had been better than nothing. She didn't dare let her thoughts dwell on what might have happened if she'd done nothing.

She sat upright as the door handle turned and Jack stumbled into the room. He smiled lopsidedly and said, 'Hiya, gel,' as though nothing had happened earlier. Alice watched him take off his clothes, drop them on the floor and flop down beside her naked. Within seconds he was flat out and snoring. She slid off the bed, folded his discarded clothes and placed them on a chair. She couldn't detect any scents of other women or strange perfume on them and hoped he'd just been drowning his imagined sorrows in a few pints. At least with him sleeping she could relax and not have to worry about him being rough with her. So much for their honeymoon. She hoped this was a one-off and not a sign of how things were going to be for the rest of her life. The thought that she'd made a huge mistake filled her with panic at what might be to come.

*

The following afternoon, Alice and Jack arrived home before the kids were due back. It was still the school holidays and Brian had previously told Alice he would be spending the Monday with friends. Marlene had offered to take Cathy shopping and was due to bring her back at tea time. Jack dropped Alice and their cases off and returned Arnold's car to the Legion, telling Alice he'd just have a quick pint with Arnold and then come straight back.

Alice took the cases up to the room she would now be sharing with Jack. Nothing had been said about last night's episode on the way home. He had woken in a good mood and made love to her in a gentle manner with no sign of the manic Jack from last night. Alice had succumbed to his advances, afraid that saying no would end up causing another argument. He'd even taken precautions, so it was best to keep her mouth shut and go along with him. She would need to talk to him about taking painkillers with alcohol though, because she was sure that had been the cause of his mood swing. But she would have to choose the right time.

Alice unpacked their clothes and found a white paper bag tucked into Jack's case along with the newspaper he'd popped out to buy that morning. Two sticks of pink peppermint rock fell out of the bag. She smiled. He must have bought them for Cathy and Brian. She shook her head. Her new husband wasn't all bad. There was a caring Jack in there, the one Winnie looked on as a son, and Alice planned to make sure he was more prominent in her life than the Jack from last night. It would take time and patience to change him to the sort of husband Terry had been, but she was in it for life and would need to find that time.

*

Alice stared out of the tram window, her thoughts miles away. It was Tuesday morning and she and Sadie were on their way into work.

'So, how did it go?' Sadie asked, nudging Alice's arm. 'You're very quiet. Thought you'd be all bubbling over with happiness.'

Alice sighed and shook her head. 'It was very nice, for the most part.'

'But?' Sadie probed and looked closer. 'Alice, your chin. What happened?'

'Er.' She looked around to make sure no one was listening but the tram was fairly quiet and people were engaged in their own conversations. 'My chin had an argument with Jack's fist,' she whispered, her eyes filling as she remembered how and why. She hadn't planned to tell anyone, but Sadie had caught her off-guard and she was feeling a bit low this morning and needed a confidante. She'd blocked her mind last night while they were all at home together and Jack and Brian were talking while she put Cathy in the bath and to bed. When she came back downstairs and joined them in the front room Brian had also noticed her chin. Jack had laughed it off, looked at her meaningfully and told her brother she'd walked into the open wardrobe door. Alice had left the room and gone into the kitchen. She'd stood by the sink and sipped a glass of water to compose herself. Would life always feel like she was walking on eggshells from now on? In bed later she'd asked Jack why he'd lied to Brian and he'd looked puzzled.

'It was a white lie,' he'd said. 'No point in Brian thinking badly of me, is there? Bad enough that his sister does now. It was one mistake, and only because I had to take painkillers after walking around all day. I hope you'll let it drop now.'

And that had been it. Turning his back on her, he'd fallen asleep within minutes. This morning he'd left the house early, telling her he was going back to his old digs to pick up the rest of his stuff and then on to the Legion to help Arnold start his packing.

Sadie's jaw dropped and she clapped her hand to her mouth. 'He hit you? Oh no, Alice, why?'

'I'll tell you at break time,' Alice whispered as the conductor announced their stop. 'It'll be a bit quieter then. But if anyone else notices, the official story is that I walked into the open wardrobe door in Blackpool!'

*

Granny Lomax walked back to her bungalow, satisfied that she had the information she needed. She'd found Jack's ex-girlfriend Susan, the mother of his child, easily enough. She lived in a street of neat and tidy terraced houses over the other side of the church. Getting her to talk had been the difficult bit as Susan had clammed up as soon as she'd heard why Granny was visiting her mother. She'd been out at the shops with her little girl when her mother answered the door. A brief explanation was all it took for the woman to allow her inside. Jack's name was mud in that household.

'So your ex-daughter-in-law has married him then?' Margaret Law, Susan's mother, had asked, shaking her head sorrowfully.

'I'm afraid so,' Granny Lomax replied.

'Oh dear, well God help her, that's all I can say.'

'Exactly. I just needed something I can pass on to Alice, as I'm sure things will go downhill very quickly.' She'd gone on to explain how Alice had sold her house and that she was helping Jack to obtain the licence of the Legion with her money. And how she was worried to death about her young granddaughter living under the same roof.

'Tell her, Susan, tell her what he said and did when you told him our Lizzie was on the way,' Margaret had said to her daughter and granddaughter who arrived back from the shops.

Susan had nodded, giving the child a biscuit and telling her to go and play in the back yard for a while. Jack's daughter was the image of him and a sweet little thing called Elizabeth.

The little girl ran off and Susan sat down on an armchair by the window and looked at the floor. Granny was shocked to see how young she looked. The sunlight streaming through the window highlighted her fresh, clear complexion and glossy dark hair. She was a pretty girl, but with the dark shadows of worry beneath her eyes.

'He told me to get rid of it,' Susan began, wringing her hands, her voice breaking. 'He gave me a bottle of gin and said I had to drink it sitting in a hot bath. It didn't work, of course,' she said as her mother snorted. 'Then he said he'd push me downstairs if I didn't do something soon.' She shrugged. 'I didn't know *what* to do. I was scared of him, so I just went along with his suggestion to save argument.'

Granny Lomax gasped. 'It must have been very frightening for you if you were scared of him, Susan.'

'It was,' her mother said. 'She wouldn't tell me what was wrong the night she came home upset. She'd told us she was off to the Mayfair with her pals. That's where she'd met up with Jack a few weeks earlier. Of course we knew of his family as he didn't live far from here and I'd never have agreed to him taking her out if I'd known. He has a bad reputation. He pursued her and she went out with him a couple of times, and then once more on the night when he put her in the family way. She was only just eighteen when Elizabeth arrived. I confronted him but he laughed in my face, said he'd not touched her and the baby couldn't be his.

'He said he was incapable since his shooting injury, as the pain overrode every feeling in his body. He even said to consult his army medical officer for proof. He denied giving Susan gin and threatening to push her down the stairs; swore blind that she'd made it all up. I didn't know what to do. I lost my husband a few years ago and my two sons were away fighting. They'd have killed him, but sadly they never came home from the war. We just had to get on with things on our own. Elizabeth is the spit of him, but he still won't have anything to do with her or Susan. We haven't had a penny from him. He told Susan that he hates kids anyway and would never bring one into the world for that reason. Hah, famous last words. There's not many folks round here know he fathered Elizabeth; just the couple of ladies you met as they helped us out when she was born. Most folk were too busy with the war and their own problems to take much notice at the time. We pretend her father was a soldier that got killed. It's easier that way.'

After a cup of tea, Granny had left and felt more worried now with her new-found knowledge and the thoughts that her granddaughter was under the same roof as a man who claimed to hate kids. But would Alice believe her? She doubted it. She was smitten with Jack and seemed to think the sun shone out of his backside. Brian seemed to like him too. It was going to be difficult to be patient and see how things played out. But at least she now knew far more about him than Alice did, or any of his friends and supporters.

Chapter Nineteen

December 1947

With just one week to go before Christmas, Alice placed her hands in her lap as Dolores Redfern, supervisor of the cosmetics department, cast an eye over her application form. Alice crossed her fingers and curled them inwards, her nails digging into her palm. She'd been waiting ages for a vacancy to arise and as soon as a girl she knew on the Max Factor counter had let her know last week that her colleague was leaving in January to have a baby, Alice had applied. She looked up from gazing at her hands as Miss Redfern cleared her throat and glanced at her over the top of her steel-framed glasses.

'Well, Mrs Lomax, this all seems to be in very good order. As we've already discussed, you have plenty of experience in serving the general public and of course as a Lewis's employee, you are quite used to the fact that the store is undergoing major rebuilding works and all the inconvenience and disruption this entails. I do have one other interview to conduct today and I will be making a decision early in the New Year. I will be in touch with you as soon as the store reopens following the New Year bank holiday closure. If you are the successful applicant, there will be a two-week training period when you will be taught how to demonstrate the application of the products, but that will all be done in the department and this vacancy carries supervisory responsibilities after a few months. So there's plenty of room to further your career with us. Thank you for attending and I bid you a happy festive season with your family.' Miss Redfern got to her feet and gathered up her paperwork from the desk.

Alice jumped up and shook Miss Redfern's outstretched hand, feeling hopeful that this interview would lead somewhere eventually. She looked at her watch as she made her way back up to haberdashery. The store was busy with shoppers and an excited queue of small children, clutching the hands of their mothers, were waiting by the temporary grotto – half the size it used to be before the war, due to lack of space – to see Father Christmas. Marlene had promised to bring Cathy down to see him later this afternoon and then they were going to wait in the café for Alice to finish work.

*

Alice dashed back up the stairs and took her place behind the haberdashery counter.

'How did it go?' Sadie asked, wafting a cloth over the ever-present film of dust on the glass tops. She had decided to stay put in haberdashery for now and keep applying for library vacancies.

'Okay, I think,' Alice replied. 'Fingers crossed now. Miss Redfern has got another interview to do later and then she will let me know in the New Year. She told me the post carries a supervisory position eventually, so that will mean more money and the hours are full time. Just as long as Marlene can still help with Cathy, it should all be good.'

'I'm sure she will. Marlene enjoys looking after her. Oh look.' Sadie pointed to a small woman hurrying towards them. 'Here's my mam. Wonder what she wants? She didn't say she was coming into town today. Hiya, Mam. What's up? You look a bit mithered.'

Sadie's mother thrust an envelope towards her. 'This came earlier. But it was addressed to me so I opened it to read. It's from Luca. He wants to see Gianni before he goes back to Italy for the winter months.'

Sadie's face drained as she read the letter. Luca Romano, her estranged husband, didn't want to cause any problems, he said, but he felt it was time that Sadie let him have some sort of contact with his son. He'd let Sadie do as she thought best during the war as he'd had no choice other than to go back to Italy with his family. But now the war was over and the fair would spend a lot of time in Britain over the next few years, he felt he had the right to get to know Gianni. Sadie chewed her lip and passed the letter to Alice. Luca was planning to come to the house on Christmas Eve for a short visit and hoped he'd be welcome. The following week they would be going back to Italy until the spring.

Alice read the letter and handed it back to Sadie. 'I don't know what to say. But surely it can't do any harm just to let him have a short visit?'

'What if he insists on taking him away?' Sadie said, her eyes filling. She dashed away her tears with the back of her hand. 'I might never see him again if he takes him to Italy.'

'How can he?' her mam said. 'Your dad and me and your two brothers will all be there. He won't take him away with us lot on your side. But I can't see the harm it will do, to be honest. A quick visit and then, like he says, he's going back abroad. Gianni should really get to know his dad, love. After all, he wasn't a bad man, was he? It's just the lifestyle you didn't like. But Luca's a hard worker and he might want to give you a bit towards Gianni's keep. Let him come, and see what happens.'

Sadie sighed. 'Seems like I haven't got much choice as he's arriving on Christmas Eve and there's no address for me to write back and say don't bother. But this is it. One visit and then no more. I will make sure I'm out of Liverpool each time that fair comes to visit, like I did last year. I'll take Gianni to my aunt's in Chester.'

'That's up to you, chuck,' Sadie's mam said. 'Get this first visit out of the way and see how you feel. Right, I'd better get back. That tram was swaying all over the show coming down here. Packed to the roof it was. It's really busy out there. Nice to see, mind, after the last few years when no one ventured too far from home. I'll see you later, Sadie.'

Alice served a customer who wanted red wool and knitting needles to make some last-minute gloves for a present and then turned to Sadie, who still looked pale and worried.

'It'll be okay, you know. At least Gianni has still got a dad that cares for him. My poor Cathy hasn't.'

'Yes, and look how Terry died. That's exactly what I'm terrified of. I hate motorbikes, like you do. If Gianni gets wind of the fact his dad rides one, he's bound to want to try it when he's older. It doesn't even bear thinking about. But like I say, one visit and that's it. Luca can write to Gianni, send him birthday cards, whatever, but Gianni is not going anywhere near that fairground while I still make the decisions about his upbringing.'

*

Alice put the finishing touches to her makeup, brushed her brown hair until it fell into shiny curls onto her shoulders and did a twirl in front of the mirror. She smoothed the full skirt of her new red woollen dress that Jack had bought her for Christmas, swaying from side to side and imagining his arms around her. She hoped they'd get the chance of a dance together tonight when he took a break. She was really looking forward to the New Year's Eve party they were throwing downstairs in the concert room. Cathy was staying over at Granny Lomax's until tomorrow and Brian had gone out with his friends to celebrate the New Year and would be sleeping over at one of their houses. For the first time since the honeymoon, she and Jack had a night to themselves. Christmas had been so busy, both at Lewis's and here at the club. She'd not had a minute to think for weeks now, what with the move and getting settled in at the new flat and Jack bringing in workmen to change a few things around. The concert room was looking lovely and they were busy nearly every night of the week. Better than he'd hoped, Jack had told her. Alice felt proud of him, the way he was managing the club and looking after the money she'd handed over. Her half of the house sale was now invested in the club and Brian's had been put into a separate bank account for his future. He wasn't allowed to draw any out without Alice's co-signature, but he didn't need to touch it yet, not until he went on to college and hopefully university in time. She couldn't wait to find out next week if her interview to work in the cosmetics department had been successful. Life was certainly good at the moment, and after so many lean years of scrimping and scraping Alice knew for certain that marrying Jack had been the best decision she'd made since losing Terry.

Since the episode in Blackpool, which they never spoke about, Jack had been okay. He'd been to see a doctor about getting some help to relieve the pain in his foot. After a day of working and rushing around it was at its worst and it made him short-tempered. His doctor had prescribed a drug called Meperidine, which he'd been taking for a few weeks now. He still wasn't supposed to wash it down with alcohol but he did, though it didn't have as much of an effect on him as the previous drug he'd had.

Alice had hardly worked on the bar with him since the move. He worked alongside Sheila, the new barmaid, and another woman called Polly who just came in for the odd night, and if they had anything special on. He'd told Alice he preferred it if she just left them to it. With all the extra hours she was now doing, she was tired by the time she got home from work, cooked a meal and sorted out Cathy and Brian and homework, so it hadn't bothered her too much and she'd do anything to keep him happy. He was worn out by the time he'd finished off and seen Sheila out and fell asleep pretty much right away. Alice was glad he did as he was always worse the wear for drink and she knew he might handle her roughly. He was gentle and loving when sober, but it was still not quite what she'd expected from a husband. He was nothing like Terry had been. But, then, no two people were alike and she did love him.

Jack wouldn't allow Granny Lomax on the premises but had no objection to Brian and Cathy going to see her. Alice usually went with them but didn't stay long. Granny always seemed to want to talk about Jack, about how he was spending her money, and she said she had something else to tell Alice, but Alice had told her that she hadn't got the time to listen to idle gossip so whatever it was had remained unspoken. Alice didn't feel it was appropriate to discuss their private life with her. Jack would go mad if she told him. She always left the children there and went home after half an hour. Brian brought Cathy back later for tea.

None of it was quite how Alice had envisaged married life would be, but it seemed to be working. They were all rubbing along together, the flat was lovely and spacious and she'd made it nice and comfortable for them. Jack had instructed a decorator to paint right through in fresh light colours and they'd chosen new carpets and curtains. They'd brought Alice's furniture from Lucerne Street and bought a few new bits and pieces to go with it. Brian loved his spacious bedroom, which doubled as his study, and to Alice's surprise, Jack had said Cathy could have a doll's house for Christmas, while they'd got a bit of spare cash from having a good month in November. It was now in pride of place in her pink and white bedroom.

Cathy had been delighted with the house, but still seemed wary of Jack and kept mainly out of his way, although he did try to win her round and read her the occasional bedtime story while Alice took a long soak in the bath. There was the odd night that Cathy had woken from a nightmare. Fortunately, her screaming hadn't disturbed Jack's alcohol-induced slumbers. Alice couldn't get to the bottom of the nightmares as Cathy couldn't, or wouldn't, tell her why she had bad dreams. Occasional bed-wetting was also a problem and Alice did her best to hide the evidence in the laundry basket, doing the washing at night while Jack was down in the bar.

Tonight, the wartime band that Millie had sung with was performing in the concert room and Millie was going to sing with them. Although heavily pregnant now, with her baby due in February, she had insisted she was getting up on stage tonight. Alice couldn't wait to spend some time with her friends. With Jack not needing her on the bar, she'd be able to have a drink and relax and enjoy herself.

She closed the door to the flat and strolled down the stairs. She could hear the low murmur of voices coming from the kitchen, one of them Jack's, the other Sheila's. She couldn't make out what they were saying, but Jack's voice sounded low and suggestive and Sheila giggled loudly and said, 'Ooh, Jack!'

Alice stopped herself from pushing down the handle on the hall side of the kitchen just in time. The door was usually kept locked, as they always used the door from the bar into the kitchen, but had been unlocked over the festive season. A little chill ran down her spine as Alice realised that Jack and Sheila seemed to be even more friendly than she'd first thought. Alice felt consumed with anger; not only was Jack violent on occasion, but he seemed to think it was okay to play away right under her nose. Well, she'd see about that. She gritted her teeth and marched into the concert room. Polly was on her own behind the bar. The girl looked flustered and the queue was long. Seething inside, Alice joined Polly, pulled a few pints and poured a number of gin and tonics, with still no sign of her husband and Sheila.

'Where's Sheila?' she asked when they had a lull, knowing full well where she was, but wanting to see if Polly said anything to confirm her suspicions.

'Er, she's helping Jack plate up the buffet,' Polly replied, pushing a straying blonde curl out of her eyes. 'Thanks for helping out then, Mrs Dawson. It's a bit of a mad rush when they all come in at once.'

'No problem, Polly. But you shouldn't be on your own on a busy night like tonight. I'll go and get Sheila out here.'

She steeled herself and barged into the kitchen, where Sheila was looking flushed and gooey-eyed at her husband.

'Jack, what's going on?' she asked him, who was leaning with his back against the wall. 'It was crazy out there when I just came down and poor Polly was rushed off her feet. Sheila, you need to be on the bar. I'll help Jack in here.'

Jack nodded and caught Alice by the waist. 'Of course you will, gel. Sheila, you go and help Polly. Alice will help me now she's finished prettying herself up.'

Alice frowned when his smile didn't quite reach his eyes and she moved away from him. Sheila excused herself and waltzed out of the kitchen, high heels clicking on the floor, throwing a last knowing look in Jack's direction.

As the door closed, Jack grabbed hold of Alice's arm above the elbow and dug his fingers in. 'Don't you *ever* undermine me in front of my staff again. Do you hear me? *I* give the orders around here, not you.'

Alice took a deep breath. His eyes were glazed; he stank of whisky already, not to mention cheap perfume that smelled of cat pee, the sort Sheila drowned herself in each night.

'Now get them plates of sarnies wrapped in greaseproof paper,' he ordered. 'Put them on the back table over there when you've finished. I'll go out and help my staff. I'll see *you* later.'

Alice rubbed her arm where he'd dug his fingers in. No doubt she'd bruise there now. Good job her dress sleeves were three-quarter length. She wondered if Jack had been kissing Sheila; they'd certainly looked as though a degree of intimacy had passed between them and the barmaid's usually glossy lipstick had looked a bit faded. Maybe it happened regularly while Alice was up in the flat at night. Maybe they did more than kiss and that's why he was always tired when he came to bed and only bothered her for sex on the odd occasion. How would she know? She should have felt jealous, after only four months of marriage, but strangely she didn't. She felt more hurt if anything. Perhaps this marriage was a mistake after all. But, she reminded herself, Brian's money was in a secure account for his future, they all had a decent roof over their heads, good food on the table after years of rationing and money coming in regularly from the club and her wages. It was a lot to be thankful for and, even if she'd chosen to accept a bit of help from Granny and remain single, the lifestyle they had now was far superior to the one she could have given Brian and Cathy on her own.

*

After taking a few minutes to recover from the discovery of her husband and Sheila together, Alice helped herself to a sherry and made a beeline for the table where Freddie and his wife, and Marlene and her husband, were seated, along with Millie and Jimmy, and Sadie and her friend Jenny. After much hugging and kissing, Jimmy introduced a young man who was sitting beside Millie as his older brother Johnny, who had been staying with them for the festive season. He shook Alice warmly by the hand and pulled up a stool next to him.

Alice took a seat and smiled happily around at all her closest friends. At least she had them to support her, even if her marriage wasn't quite what she'd hoped for. She raised her glass. 'Cheers, everybody. Here's to a happy future.'

'Hear, hear,' Freddie agreed. 'How's it going, chuck? His lordship running this place and married life, I mean? Seems to be making a success of it so far.'

'Yes, he is. It's all right, thanks, Freddie,' she replied. 'Still early days on both counts and it's hard work, but you know.'

Freddie nodded. 'Takes a while to adjust and it's a big change for you all.' He frowned, looking over at Jack. 'He looks a bit worse for wear and it's not even nine o'clock yet.'

Alice sighed. 'His foot isn't too clever at the moment. He's on new tablets. But a bit of whisky takes the edge off the pain.' She caught Sadie's raised eyebrow and shook her head slightly.

'How did Christmas Eve go?' Alice hadn't seen Sadie since Luca's visit as Sadie had taken the week off as part of her annual holiday.

Sadie shrugged. 'Okay, I suppose. Luca won Gianni over as I knew he would. Brought him loads of presents from his family, including a model plane that Gianni just loves. He gave me an envelope with a small fortune in it to make up for all the years he's missed supporting us. And he asked to speak to me alone, so we went into the back room for ten minutes. He asked me to go back to him as he still loves me.' Sadie's eyes filled as she spoke and her voice cracked. 'But I can't do that. He won't give up the fair for us, so that's that. End of the matter.'

'Oh, Sadie.' Alice rubbed her arm gently. 'You still love him, don't you?'

Sadie nodded. 'But not enough to go back to the fair, I'm afraid. I'm going to use some of the money he's given me to do a course that will give me the qualifications to get a better library position than I've been applying for. That way I can give Gianni a secure future. So, in a roundabout sort of way, he's helping us. He said he'd write when he could.'

Alice nodded and took a sip of sherry. Why was life so flipping complicated for them all?

She grinned as Millie squealed and got slowly to her feet. She pointed to the doors, where Jack was letting in her old band. Millie waddled over to meet them and was met with embrace after embrace. The band members put their instruments down on the stage and accepted the pints Jack was busy pulling for them. Millie came back with a sheaf of song lyrics for the night's playlist and she and Alice leafed through them.

'There's some great new songs in here,' Millie enthused. 'Good job I've got the wireless at home to practise my singing to. Jimmy said he's getting us a gramophone this year, so I'll be able to keep a bit more up to date. Oh, look, "Tennessee Waltz", I just love it. You can't even buy that song here yet. And "You Belong to Me". Oh and, Alice look, two Andrews Sisters songs. You have to get up with me and sing them. "Near You" and "Rum and Coca-Cola".'

Alice chewed her lip, remembering the last time she'd sung with Millie and Jack's unreasonable reaction to her performance. He was already annoyed with her, and she didn't want to rile him further. 'Er, I'm not sure I can tonight.'

'Oh, come on, Alice. Course you can. You know you want to,' Millie cajoled. 'We're good together.'

'Yeah, go on, Alice,' Johnny said, grinning. 'I've heard all about you and my lovely sister-in-law's duets. You can't let me down now I've come all the way from Blackpool to see you.'

Alice smiled. Johnny was so like his brother with the ginger hair and warm, friendly eyes.

'Oh, go on then.' She knew it would cause trouble later, but at the end of the day, she told herself, Jack wouldn't be running this place if it wasn't for her selling her house. It was time she started to have a say in things and she was going to start now by singing with Millie, whether he liked it or not. She thought back to walking into the kitchen on him and Sheila earlier. If he said anything out of place tonight she would insist he sack Sheila. The Legion was *her* business as well. Another couple of sherries and she'd be feeling a bit braver. New Year, new beginnings, and all that.

*

After Alice and Polly had cleared away the buffet plates and cutlery, with not a crumb left on the table, the band tuned up on stage. Alice helped herself to another sherry, aware of Jack's stare burning into her back.

'Don't have too many, gel,' he said, coming to stand beside her. 'I want a waltz later with my wife and I'd prefer it if she could at least stand upright.'

'It's only my second,' Alice said. 'And if we're counting, how many have *you* had tonight?'

She saw his jaw tighten and he grabbed her arm; then, seeming to remember they were in view of a club full of people, squeezed it hard as if in warning and let go, half-smiling.

'Not enough,' he muttered. 'Now get from behind this bar while we serve our customers. Some of us have to work tonight.'

'I did offer—' Alice began, but he'd already turned his back and started pulling a pint. She took her drink across to Freddie's table and then made her way to the ladies'. Thankfully it was empty and she leant against the sink and took a deep breath. She rolled up the sleeve of her dress and looked at her arm, where Jack's fingerprints from earlier were already starting to show. She jumped as the door flew back and Sadie hurried in.

'Alice,' she began as Alice quickly pulled her sleeve down. 'I've been observing him all night so you don't need to hide that from me. Also, you don't seem yourself. What's going on?'

Alice blinked rapidly. 'Nothing. He's, er, he's in pain with his foot. He just gets snappy, that's all.'

Sadie shook her head. 'He's not snappy with Sheila and Polly though, is he?'

'Leave it, Sadie. I can deal with him. I'll just keep out of his way.'

Sadie raised an eyebrow. 'I think you'd better. But it shouldn't be like this. He should be worshipping the ground you walk on, with all that you've done for him.'

Alice stared up at the ceiling. 'He does, when he's feeling okay. Anyway, come on back to our seats, the band are getting ready to play. It'll be Millie's last performance before the baby arrives. Let's go and cheer her on.'

*

Jack smiled proudly as Millie's beautiful voice soared to the rafters, singing one of the club members' favourites, 'White Cliffs of Dover'. It had been a good idea to get the band and Millie in tonight. When she announced that she was going to perform a song that not many would be familiar with yet, Pee Wee King's 'Tennessee Waltz', the cheers and whistling and shouts of 'Oh yes we are!' drowned her out. Millie smiled and began to sing the lovely ballad.

As the chorus got underway, Jack came and claimed his wife for a dance. He looked into Alice's eyes as he waltzed her around the dance floor, along with several other couples who'd got up to join them.

'Don't forget whose sweetheart *you* are tonight, gel,' he whispered, echoing words from the song, as she drew her head back and looked at him. She nodded and laid her head on his chest. He dropped a kiss on top of her head as he led her to her seat and then limped back behind the bar while the crowd went mad for more from Millie.

Jack saw Millie beckoning for Alice to join her on stage. She wouldn't dare, would she? He'd told her not to do it again. But Alice shot him a defiant look and got up to stand beside Millie. There was nothing he could do now without showing himself up. The band struck up with an Andrews Sisters song and Alice and Millie began to sing 'Near You', Millie carrying the song with Alice harmonising. She looked happy, but wasn't even looking in his direction. Jack followed her gaze to Millie's husband Jimmy and a man who looked very like him. Jimmy's brother? He clenched his fists. She'd better not make a fool of him in front of his friends and customers.

While the bar was quiet as the customers were all entranced with Millie and Alice, he grabbed hold of Sheila's hand and pulled her into the kitchen, pushing the door shut behind them. He wedged a chair beneath the handle. Millie and Alice usually finished with two or three songs, just enough time for a quickie with Sheila. He pushed her into the pantry and up against the wall, hitching up the skirt of her dress and grinding against her. Sheila never refused him and tonight was no exception as she gave herself freely while the band played on, drowning out her squeals as he manhandled her. She liked it rough and the more excited she got the more Jack obliged. By the time 'Rum and Coca-Cola' was coming to an end, so was Jack, and he pushed Sheila away, zipped himself up and limped back to the bar. He was just in time to see Alice and Millie taking a bow and Jimmy, and the man with him, jump to their feet whistling at the girls, who were laughing with their arms around each other.

Jack took a deep breath and helped himself to a double whisky that he knocked back in seconds along with another painkiller for his foot. In spite of feeling euphoric only seconds ago, he was now consumed with anger. How dare Alice make a fool of herself, and him, like that? She had men whistling at her, and now he could see Freddie and all the people at his table giving both girls a hug and a kiss and then Jimmy's mate, brother, or whoever he was, had pulled Alice into his arms and dropped a kiss on her cheek. He saw Sheila slink out of the kitchen, her cheeks flushed and her hair mussed up. She smiled at him but he turned away, keeping his eyes on his wife. Sheila had served her purpose for tonight.

Jack sucked air through his teeth, fighting down his anger as he made his way to the stage to thank the band and Millie for their fantastic performance. He didn't mention Alice, and although a few people called out, 'Don't forget your wife,' he pointedly ignored them. It was fifteen minutes to midnight and he announced last orders and to be quick so they could all toast in the New Year. He called for Alice to come and help as the mad rush to refill began. With one minute to go, Jack timed the countdown with everyone joining in. The band played 'Auld Lang Syne' and everyone sang along.

As the band packed away and people began leaving, congratulating him and Alice on the best New Year's Eve party they'd ever been to, he felt proud of his business and his club. Polly and Sheila had collected the glasses in and were busy washing them. Jack told the girls to leave them and go home. He and Alice would finish off. She was busy saying goodbye to Millie, Jimmy and the man they were with. He heard her telling Millie she would call in to see them tomorrow afternoon when she picked up Cathy from Granny Lomax's.

'Like hell she will,' he muttered under his breath. Brian could go and get the brat when he came home. He locked the doors after the band had loaded their van and went to join Alice behind the bar.

*

Washing glasses at the sink, Alice shuddered as she felt Jack's breath on her neck and his hands snaking tightly around her waist. She inclined her head to one side to avoid the stale alcohol smell that made her feel like gagging.

'Would you rather it was him holding you?' he snarled, swinging her round to face him. 'That mate of Jimmy's, would you rather it was him?'

'That was Jimmy's brother, and no I wouldn't. Why are you saying that?'

'Because I think you would. I could see it in your eyes when you were looking at him.'

'Don't be so ridiculous.' She tried to pull away but he pushed her up against the kitchen door, which wasn't properly closed. It flew open and the pair of them fell backwards, Jack on top of her.

Alice gasped as her back smacked against the cold kitchen floor. She felt winded as Jack pulled himself up and tore at her dress.

'Jack, stop it. You're drunk, leave me alone.' Her pleas were in vain as Jack ignored her and continued to rip off her clothes. Alice closed her eyes and gritted her teeth as he banged her head against the floor, telling her to look at him. The last things she remembered were his angry eyes and his fist smashing into her face, before she passed out.

Chapter Twenty

January 1948

Alice opened her eyes and tried to move. She felt chilled to the bone and whatever she was lying on was cold and hard and certainly wasn't her comfortable bed. She tried to sit up but a flash of pain shot through her head and she groaned and closed her eyes again, wondering where she was. As she lay there trying to work it out, little fragments of memory came back to her: singing with Millie and the band, helping behind the bar, the New Year's Eve celebrations, and Jack, grabbing hold of her before everything went black.

She forced her eyes open again and looked around. The light above her was bright and she shielded the glare with her hand. She inched herself into a sitting position, wincing at the aches and pains in every part of her body. She was in the kitchen, on the hard red quarry-tiled floor, and she was naked. No wonder she was cold. She could see the dress she'd been wearing earlier, tossed to one side. She reached for it to cover herself and pulled it back on. Her feet were bare of shoes, her stockings in shreds and her underwear nowhere to be seen. Where was Jack? Her face felt wet and she ran a hand over it. Blood; and it was dripping from her nose. Slowly she got to her knees and used the edge of the table to pull herself up. She flinched at the stickiness and pain between her legs.

'Oh, Jack,' she whimpered. 'What have you done to me?' She groaned as she limped towards the door and pulled it open. She stifled a scream as Jack turned towards her from his position on a bar stool, where he was smoking a cigarette and raising a glass to his lips.

'Ah, Alice,' he said, a smirk on his face. 'You've decided to wake up at last, eh gel? Fancy drinking more than you can cope with. You fell over after trying to get me to make love to you in the kitchen.'

He laughed as she stared at him, hardly believing her ears at what he was saying.

'You banged your head on the floor as you went face down and then asked me to leave you there to sleep. I was going to nip upstairs and get you a pillow and blanket when I've finished my fag. Oh see, you've banged your nose. You'll have two lovely black eyes tomorrow, gel. You need to control that drinking of yours. Want me to help you up to bed now?'

'You lying bastard,' Alice screamed at him. 'You attacked me and then took me by force. Look at the state I'm in. I'm going to the police when it gets lighter.'

'And tell 'em what? Everyone saw you swanning around the club knocking back the sherries. No one will believe you. And we're newly-weds so it's quite natural that we'd want to do it in places older married couples wouldn't bother. I'll just tell them you couldn't wait to get me up the stairs and that everything we did was because you wanted it. I was only having my conjugal rights. You'll be embarrassing us both if you get the police involved. You'll make a right holy show of yourself, just because you can't remember what you did.'

Alice shook her head in disbelief. 'You're lying. I can't believe you've done this to me, Jack.'

'Can't you, gel. And you don't think *you* did anything wrong tonight, eh? Making eyes at Jimmy's brother, and getting up to sing with Millie when I told you that was not going to happen again.

And undermining me in front of my staff as well. All I've done is have my way with my wife after she fell over from being drunk. Report me then. See what will happen if I get locked up. We'll lose this place. You'll have to find somewhere for you and the kids to live and then you'd have to use Brian's money to pay for it all. No college education for him if you do that. Isn't that what this is all about? That you have a decent place to live and Brian can go on to further studies. This isn't easy for me, you know. I have to live with your brat and you have no idea how much I hate her. I can't stand kids, but I put up with her so your brother can have the best chances in life. Just you remember that when you're bad-mouthing me to all and sundry. And I haven't got over that old cow keeping going on at me being responsible for Terry's death either. Do you have any idea what that does to my mind? No, you don't, because it's all about you and them kids and what you all want. I've given up my freedom to marry you. You need to show some respect and appreciation, lady, and be grateful to have a roof over your head. Now get out of my sight before I decide I want more of my rights tonight. I'll join you later.'

Alice crept out of the concert room and fled up the stairs, clutching her torn dress around her body. She'd caught a glimpse of the clock in the bar as she'd been talking to Jack. It was only two thirty, so she hadn't been out cold for that long. She locked herself in the bathroom and turned on the bath taps, pouring in a few drops of lavender-scented bubble bath. She needed a hot bath as soon as possible to wash the disgusting smell of Jack from her body. He'd definitely not used anything and she was bang in the middle of her monthly cycle too.

She turned to look at herself in the mirror and gasped. Her face was a mess. She picked up the flannel from the sink and dunked it in the bath water, flinching as she gently patted the dried blood from her face. It was caked on her chin where it had dripped down from her throbbing nose. Alice was surprised it wasn't broken. She remembered now seeing Jack's fist coming towards her before she passed out. She shuddered to think of him using her body while she was unable to protest or fight him off.

She got into the bath, lowering herself gently down. Her back and buttocks were hurting, and she'd bet she was full of bruises in areas she couldn't see. She'd check in the full-length wardrobe mirror later. Although she'd shot the bolt home on the bathroom door it didn't stop her listening out for the creak of the stairs as Jack came up to bed. She wished the kids were here, although she wouldn't have wanted them to witness Jack attacking her. She didn't feel safe but she knew he wouldn't let her out of his sight tonight now. She was trapped. No one would hear her scream here. Hadn't he said only a few months ago how quiet and isolated it was with no immediate neighbours to shout out to? And what sort of state was her face going to be in by the morning? There was no way she could go and pick Cathy up or visit Millie like this. She hoped Brian wouldn't be too late back. He would have to do it. Tell Granny she had a stomach upset or something. And she was due back in work on Friday January 2nd. Next week she would hear news of her possible new job in cosmetics, with a bit of luck. But she couldn't face anyone at work with her face a mass of bruises.

She should leave Jack, reluctant as she was to give up on her marriage after only four months. But where would she go? Not back to Granny's and all the 'I told you so's' she knew she'd get. Plus, no matter what Granny had said about helping them out financially, she wasn't a bottomless money pit and Alice couldn't keep taking. If she left now she would lose all the money she'd put into the Legion and have no choice but to dip into Brian's. It wasn't right. She had to stand on her own two feet.

She gently soaped her arms and legs and the rest of her body, her mind working overtime. She didn't want to touch Brian's money after everything they'd gone through to get here. That would stay where it was until he needed it. There really was no choice but to stick it out until Brian had finished his education and Cathy had left primary school. If they stayed here Cathy might get in at the grammar school as well. She could become a nurse with all the right exams under her belt. Alice would just keep out of Jack's way; do her best to keep him sweet, put up with whatever he was doing with Sheila and whoever else he was messing about with and get on with her life, working hard and saving as much as she could, until she could finally escape.

*

Jack was in the bar finishing the clearing up when Brian arrived home at midday.

'Happy New Year, son,' he greeted Brian. 'Can you go and pick Cathy up from her granny's? Your sister isn't feeling too good. She's lying down with a bad headache. And while you're out call in at Millie's and apologise that she's not coming over today. She'll catch up with her later in the week. I'll get some scran ready for when you get back. There's some turkey left over from last night's buffet, so you can both have sarnies, and I've saved you some cake.'

Brian's face lit up at the mention of food. He dumped his bag of clothes in the hall. 'Did she have a bit too much to drink?' He grinned.

'Way too much,' Jack said. 'She could hardly stand up.'

Brian grinned. 'I know the feeling. I did the same at my mate's party. But we had a great time. I met a girl.' He blushed slightly.

'Did you, lad?' Jack laughed. 'A word of advice from one who knows. Remember what I told you about girls. Don't get too involved; they're more trouble than they're worth.'

Brian frowned. 'You don't think that about our Alice though, do you?'

'No, mate. She's one of the best. Anyway, your Alice is a woman, not a bit of a kid. And watch your step because some girls will try and trap you given half a chance. Never take a bath without wearing wellies. You get my drift, Brian?'

'I do,' Brian replied. 'I've too much at stake to get tied down.'

'You have, mate. Any problems, you know you can always come and talk to me. Right, go and get the little 'un while I finish off here. And don't forget to call at Millie's.'

Jack saw Brian out and went upstairs to see to Alice. She was lying fully dressed on the bed and she jumped up as he entered the room.

'It's okay, gel. Just coming to see if I can get you a cuppa? I've sent Brian to Ma Lomax's to get Cathy and to call into Millie's to tell them you won't be visiting. Don't want them popping round here, wondering why you didn't call, do we?'

Alice shook her head. 'I can't see anyone while I look like this. You used me as a punch bag last night and I didn't deserve it.'

'Don't push me, Alice. I admit I had too much to drink, and on top of double painkillers to help with being on my feet all day, it just sent me doolally. It won't happen again. I'll make you that brew. Just keep out of the way for today.'

'Cathy will want to see me when she comes home.'

'Well she can't, can she? She'll just have to do as she's told for once. We'll tell her you're poorly and she has to keep away in case she catches something.'

'And what about work tomorrow?' Alice sobbed. 'I can't go in looking like this. I've got two black eyes, a swollen nose and a fat lip. Not to mention all the bruises on my body.'

'I'll phone them and make excuses for you, tell them you need a day or two resting. You'll feel better by Monday.'

He'd left her staring after him, a look of hatred on her face. He'd fucked it up big time now. He couldn't even remember half of what had happened last night. It was all so hazy. But he must have knocked her about badly, because she looked a right bloody mess this morning. And he knew he'd had his way with her because he'd found her torn underwear in the kitchen. She'd get over it though; she didn't have a choice, because he had every penny that was left over from the sale of her house stashed safely away in the Legion account and the bank would only accept his signature to draw on it. Brian's money was in another account that Jack had no rights to and, if he knew Alice, no matter how much she might want to leave him after last night, there was no way she would take a penny from her brother after waiting so long to make sure his future was secure.

*

'Has she been a good girl, Granny?' Brian asked as Cathy pulled a face when she saw that Alice wasn't with him. He accepted the mug of tea and mince pie from Granny Lomax and sat down on the sofa to enjoy it.

'She always is,' Granny replied. 'Let's get your shoes on and then you can pack all your things away in a bag while I talk to Brian.'

Cathy ran into the bedroom to get her dollies and books together and Granny looked at Brian over the rim of her mug. 'So what's wrong with Alice that she couldn't come to pick Cathy up? I wanted to wish her a Happy New Year.'

Brian shrugged. 'Jack said she was still in bed as she'd had too much to drink and didn't feel well.'

'Hmm, that doesn't sound like Alice. She rarely drinks more than a couple of small sherries. I hope his bad boozing habits aren't rubbing off on her or they'll run that place into the ground between them in no time.'

Brian frowned. 'Alice wouldn't let that happen. She'd probably just had one too many. It was New Year's Eve, after all.' He stopped as Cathy came back into the room. 'Ready, Cathy? We need to pop into Millie's on the way and tell them Mammy isn't well.'

'I want to go home and see Mammy,' Cathy said.

'And you can. But we have to call at Millie's first.'

Granny frowned. 'Why don't you leave Cathy here and I'll bring her back to the Legion later? If Alice is feeling unwell, she won't want to be dealing with the little one. And Jack's not good around children, as we know.'

Brian shook his head. He knew that Jack wouldn't like that, and he was quite capable of seeing to his niece's needs if Alice couldn't.

'Thank you, but we'll manage.' He got to his feet and took the bag of toys from Cathy's hands. 'Come on, let's go.'

Brian held Cathy's hand as they hurried down Linnet Lane. Granny was good to them in her own way, but sometimes she asked awkward questions about his sister and Jack that Brian felt were inappropriate. Jack called her nosy, and he was right. Brian liked Jack. He'd always got on well with him and when Brian did a bit of glass collecting in between studying, he paid him well. He gave him cigarettes too, and the odd half pint of ale with strict instructions not to tell his sister. Alice seemed to nag him at times for no reason that Brian could see. Jack said it was often the way with women and when they were in that sort of mood it was best to keep out of their way. It was good to sit and talk man-to-man after the bar closed and Alice thought he was in bed. What she didn't know wouldn't hurt.

*

Millie frowned as she saw Brian and Cathy out and closed the door behind them.

'That's really odd, because Alice only had a couple of small sherries last night,' she told Jimmy. 'She said she didn't want too much to drink, just enough to make her happy. Yet Brian says that Jack told him she was so drunk she could hardly stand up.'

'Maybe she had a few more after the bar closed when her and Jack relaxed upstairs.'

'Oh, maybe. Didn't you notice that she was a bit on edge last night though? I've known Alice for years and she's not as happy as a newly-wed should be. Something's changed. But I don't know what.'

Jimmy shrugged. 'Probably just tired. She works hard and they've had a lot on lately with the move and getting the club sorted out. She got a bit of a break last night with Jack having the two new barmaids though.'

'Hmm,' Millie said. 'He used to have a thing going with that red-headed Sheila one and she's still sweet on him. I can tell by the way she looks at him.'

Jimmy laughed and put his arms around her the best he could. 'Well, it's not your problem, so let it drop. You've got enough to concentrate on now with this little fella coming into the world.'

'Don't you mean little lady?' Millie teased. Jimmy wanted a son badly, but a girl would be lovely too. Whatever they were blessed with would be loved and cherished by them both.

Chapter Twenty-One

Alice held her breath as Miss Redfern handed her an envelope at the end of the first week of the New Year.

'Congratulations, Mrs Dawson. I'm delighted you will be joining us in the cosmetics department. Your contract and hours to be worked are in the envelope. I hope you will be very happy working with us on the Max Factor counter.'

Alice thanked her profusely and floated back upstairs to haberdashery and Sadie in a dream. Full-time hours meant more money that she could save towards an escape plan, should it ever be necessary, and working on cosmetics was her dream come true.

Sadie insisted on buying the tea and buns at break as a way of celebrating the good news.

'How do you feel now?' she asked, picking the cherry off the top of her bun and popping it into her mouth.

'Thrilled to bits,' Alice said. 'And I'm sure Jack will be as well. Although the hours are longer so he's going to have to do more about the house than he does now and I can't see him liking that. But the extra money will be very handy. He wants to buy a car, so maybe in time we'll be able to afford one.'

'Make sure you keep some back for yourself, Alice. You work hard for your money.'

Alice nodded. Over the last few days she and Jack had settled back into a routine of her keeping out of the way, and he and his barmaids, along with help from Gloria the cleaner, running the club between them. She'd started to feel a bit more relaxed around him, and he hadn't been drinking quite as much. Although he was still taking his painkillers regularly, he wasn't doubling the dose as he'd done over the festive season. He was constantly apologising for his New Year's Eve behaviour, and although Alice wanted to believe him, she wasn't totally convinced he meant it. However, it was better than nothing. She'd managed to avoid seeing anyone for the first couple of days and had plastered on arnica and a lot of makeup when she went back to work to hide the worst of her bruises. Luckily, Brian and Cathy hadn't noticed anything was wrong.

*

By the time Millie's bouncing baby boy, Paul James, arrived at the beginning of March, a full two weeks after his expected due date, Alice knew for certain that she was pregnant. It couldn't be worse news and she felt in despair as she sat in front of the doctor when he gave her the result. She'd just been promoted at work to the supervisor's position in her new cosmetics job, much earlier than expected, and was really enjoying herself.

But nothing got past Sadie, who had questioned her constantly and in whom she'd confided when she realised her monthly was late. She'd confessed that Jack had taken her by force and she was certain she was pregnant as a result. Sadie had sympathised with her and told her to leave him, but Alice said it wasn't an option and she had no choice but to stay put for the foreseeable future.

Alice walked out of the surgery on legs of jelly. She needed to talk to one of her friends, but she couldn't go and burden Millie as she was in hospital for five more days. Sadie was still at work. Hardly anyone else would be home at this time in the afternoon, apart from Granny Lomax, and she couldn't possibly go there. But Marlene wouldn't be picking Cathy up from school until later, and even though Marlene wasn't her usual confidante, Alice needed a friendly shoulder to cry on. She set off towards Marlene's house, dragging leaden feet. Jack would go absolutely berserk when she told him her news. He hated kids and she'd have to give up work. They'd lose a chunk of their income and it would set them back months. He'd blame her for not taking precautions, even though it was his fault. He'd probably start drinking heavily again and she just didn't think she could cope with any more abuse.

Alice burst into tears when Marlene opened the door and let her in. Marlene simply enfolded her in her arms and let her sob on her shoulder. She led her through into the neat and tidy back sitting room, pushed her gently onto an armchair under the window and poured a mug of strong tea from the china tea pot sitting on the table.

'I must 'ave sensed you were coming,' she said. 'I've just made a fresh pot.' She handed the mug to Alice and poured one for herself. 'What's up, chuck? 'Ave you 'ad bad news? Oh, I 'ope nowt's 'appened to Terry's mam.'

Alice shook her head and wiped her eyes. She took a deep breath and a sip of the hot sweet tea. 'She's okay, as far as I know. But I'm pregnant. And Jack will go mad.'

Marlene frowned. 'Well what's wrong with that? It's good news, surely. And why will Jack go mad? Being a dad will be the making of 'im.'

'You don't understand,' Alice sobbed. 'He hates kids. He only tolerates Cathy because he's got no choice. He told me from the start that he didn't want any of our own.'

Marlene raised an eyebrow. 'Well that's too bad. 'E should have been more careful then, shouldn't 'e? But you mustn't get yourself all worked up like this, Alice. It's not good for you. These things 'appen. 'E'll be all right once 'e's over the shock.'

Alice took a deep breath. 'I don't think he will. He's going to be so angry.'

Marlene frowned and blew out her cheeks. 'Well it might be a shock, but 'e shouldn't be angry with you. Takes two to tango, chuck. Drink your tea before it goes cold and I'll 'ave a think.'

Alice did as she was told. She felt sick with fear and worry, dreading Jack's reaction later. Maybe she should wait a while and get used to the news herself first. She might feel a bit stronger about telling him then. But no matter how or when she told him, there was no getting away from the fact that this baby was the result of New Year's Eve. How would she be able to love it when each time she looked at it, there would be a reminder of that awful night?

'Right. You 'ave to talk to 'im, gel.' Marlene's voice broke her thoughts. 'Get 'im in a good mood before you say anything, and 'e might feel okay about it once 'e's got used to the idea. It's not something you can keep from 'im. 'Ow far are you?'

'Ten weeks,' Alice said. 'It happened at New Year. We, er, were a bit careless.' There was no chance it had been any other time as Jack had thankfully kept his distance from her since.

Marlene smiled. 'Too much alcohol, no doubt. Makes us throw caution to the wind and regret it for a lifetime afterwards. That's 'ow I copped for all my three. Not that I regret 'aving them of course. Just wish they'd been a bit more spaced out with chance to breathe. Well, like I say, you need to tell 'im. See what 'e says and if 'e's adamant 'e doesn't want to be a father, you've two choices. Either leave 'im and set up on your own, or get something done about it. There's a woman in Bootle. I can ask around for the address. But let's 'ope it won't come to that, chuck.'

'Well I can't leave him,' Alice said, choking on a sob. 'I've nowhere to go and all my money is tied up in the Legion. I'm not sure how I feel about having this baby. I mean, I always wanted another with Terry, but Jack and I didn't plan to have any. I don't even know if I want it myself.'

Marlene frowned. 'And what about, "I can't leave Jack because I love 'im"?'

Alice hesitated momentarily. 'Er, well, yes, of course I do.'

'Well,' Marlene paused for a minute. 'There you are then. Get yourself off 'ome and talk to 'im and I'll pick Cathy up and bring 'er back 'ere for 'er tea. Gives you two a bit of time to yourselves.'

*

Sheila was just leaving as Alice got back home to the Legion. There was a bloom to her cheeks and an air of something Alice couldn't quite put her finger on, but she was positive that, whatever it was, it was keeping Jack away from her. Not that she cared at the moment. If pawing Sheila was keeping him happy, it was also keeping Alice safe and she could live with that. It was also grounds for divorce should she ever need it in the future. But she pushed that thought to the back of her mind as she strolled upstairs while Jack locked the doors for a couple of hours until evening opening time.

'You okay, gel?' he asked, coming up behind her. 'You look a bit pale.'

Alice nodded. 'Is Brian home yet?'

'He told you before he left this morning that he was having his tea at his mate's.'

Alice kicked her shoes off and sank into an armchair in the spacious living room. 'Ah, so he did. I forgot.' That was good. She could get it over with now without the kids around, while she had the chance. She took a deep breath and looked at Jack, who had sprawled out on the sofa, his feet up on the coffee table. 'Jack, we need to talk, seriously.'

He stared at her and lit a ciggie. 'About what?' He narrowed his eyes and she saw a flash of guilt cross his face. 'Me and Sheila are just mates, you know. Nowt for you to worry about there, gel.'

'I'm not,' she said, but stored that away for another time. She still felt hurt by the fact Jack had changed so quickly. 'I never doubted you were anything else. No, we have to talk about the fact that I've just come from the doctor's surgery and he's told me

I'm pregnant.' She felt quite satisfied as she saw his jaw drop and a horrified expression cross his face.

'Well, who you have been with then?' he accused. 'Because I haven't touched you since, well, you know when.'

'Yes,' Alice said. 'I do know when. And that's when it happened. This baby I'm expecting is the result of what happened at New Year, Jack. I'm ten weeks. It fits the time exactly, wouldn't you say?'

He jumped to his feet, clenching his fists. 'Don't you get smart with me, or else…'

Alice flinched, waiting for the blow she was sure would come. But he marched to the door and then turned back to face her.

'Get rid of it. I don't want any kids. I told you that right at the start.' He left the room and slammed the door.

She heard him limping down the stairs and the door opening to the concert room. He'd be at the bar knocking back whisky now. But he wouldn't dare to hit her later with Brian and Cathy around, would he? At that moment, Alice really felt that she hated him.

*

Alice dropped Cathy at Marlene's at the last minute and dashed away to catch the tram before Marlene could question her.

'How did you get on at the doctor's?' Sadie asked as she and Alice took their seats on the top deck.

Alice sighed. 'It was positive,' she whispered. 'Nightmare. Jack is furious. I'll tell you more at break time.'

Sadie squeezed her arm. 'Oh God, I can just imagine. What a mess, Alice.'

Alice nodded. 'You have no idea.'

'Are we still going to see Millie tonight? Do you feel up to it?'

'Yes, I can't wait to see her and little Paul. Did you wrap the teddy bear we bought?'

'I did. We'll get Millie some flowers as well.'

At work, Alice kept herself busy, rearranging the Max Factor counter in between serving customers. She loved her new job, and being in charge; she took great pride in making sure she gave the best advice she could when asked for help by women from all walks of life. From a simple lipstick to a full-blown change of makeup, people went away praising her skills. She always made sure she looked her best, although this morning the shadows beneath her eyes had taken some careful covering. She couldn't believe that in just a few short months she'd have to give this up to look after the baby. Or would she? Her head had been in a spin all night. She'd hardly slept a wink. Jack had come back in time to open the club, accompanied by Sheila, who'd shot her a look that could kill given half a chance, leaving Alice to assume she'd been told.

After closing the club Jack had practically ignored her and slept on the sofa. When he'd come into the bedroom to get undressed his only words had been, 'I meant what I said. Get rid of it.' And this morning she might as well have been invisible. It had been a relief to get out and come to work.

At break time she and Sadie took the table nearest the window where it was always quiet. She brought Sadie up to speed and took a sip of tea while her friend digested the news.

'So what are you going to do?'

Alice shrugged. 'I just don't know. One minute I feel sure I'm going to have it and to hell with what Jack thinks, and the next my mind is all over the place and I think I should get rid of it just to keep the peace at home. I feel awful even thinking that, but do I have a choice?'

'Alice, of course you do. Jack can't force you to do anything you don't want to do. It's your baby too.'

'Shh.' Alice looked around to make sure they weren't being eavesdropped on. 'I don't know that I can afford to give up work. Jack's used most of my money on doing the club up.'

'Well, it must be making a few bob. It's always packed out. Who does the books?'

Alice drew a deep breath. 'Jack does. I offered but he told me I wouldn't know what I was doing. He gives Brian a set of figures and Brian works it all out for him. He's very clever at mathematics so he finds it easy. Jack just puts the figures in a book and I never get to see them.'

Sadie frowned. 'Well, if I'd handed over half the money from the sale of my house I'd want to see the books. Are you mad, Alice? You need to ask him if the business is making enough to support you all if you have to give up work. He should get rid of a barmaid and let you do it after the birth. That will save a wage. You've had six months in there now so he should know what profit he's turned in that time. All the fancy stuff he's bought hasn't come out of what the club is making. You've paid for it all.'

Alice chewed her lip. The financial side of things had been taken away from her right from the start. Maybe she should have insisted on taking more interest and being kept up to date with how things were going. On the surface it all looked well; the club was always busy, and so she'd let Jack take charge, spending the money as he'd seen fit. Deep down, she'd let herself believe that he felt he was making less work for her because he loved her and it was his way of showing her he cared and it was time for her to take life a bit easier. But now she realised that probably wasn't the case at all. She would have to bring up the finance subject at some point, because whether Jack wanted it or not, he was going to be a father later this year. If only she'd been a bit more wary, listened to what people had said about Jack years ago. But he'd always been kind and caring towards her, looked after her when her mam was ill and after Terry died, and she'd had no reason at all to believe he would ever be anything else.

*

Alice popped her head around Brian's bedroom door. 'I'm off out now with Sadie, love. We're going to see Millie and the baby. Can you listen out for Cathy? She was tired when I put her to bed, so I don't think she'll be long before she falls asleep.'

'I will.' Brian looked up from under his floppy fringe. 'I've nearly finished my homework and then I'll pop down and give Jack a hand with the glasses. It's bingo night so it gets a bit busy and I need to earn some pocket money. I'll keep popping up to see if she's okay.'

'Thanks, love, I'll see you later.'

'Give Millie my love.' He was quiet for a few seconds and then, 'Alice, can I ask you summat? Is everything okay with you and Jack? Why did he sleep on the sofa last night? I felt there was a bit of an atmosphere this morning before we all left for work and school. I thought you two were dead happy together.'

Alice sighed. 'We had a few words, that's all. Nothing for you to worry about. It's okay. See you in a bit.' She patted his head and left the room.

'Where are you off to?' Jack shouted as she walked past the bar to the front doors.

'I told you earlier where I'm going,' she said. 'Brian will listen out for Cathy.' Before he could say anything else she walked out of the building and onto the main road, where Sadie was hurrying towards her. They linked arms and made their way to the tram stop.

'Did you ask Jack about the books?' Sadie asked.

'Nope. Hardly spoken to him. It'll have to wait until the kids are out of the way. Brian already asked me why Jack slept on the sofa last night. I just told him we'd had words.'

Sadie nodded. 'I really don't envy you. Bringing another child into an unsettled home is not a good thing.'

Alice shrugged. 'I can't get my head around what to do for the best.' She lowered her voice as the tram screeched to a halt.

'Marlene said there's a woman in Bootle. But I don't know if I can even think of that.'

Sadie rubbed her arm as they settled on seats at the rear of the tram. 'Try and have another talk with him. Threaten to leave him and ask for all your money back. Hit him where it hurts most. He won't want to lose the Legion, so he needs to be a bit more reasonable about things. You can always threaten him with speaking to a solicitor.'

'I'll see. Let's just enjoy our visit with Millie for now. Don't say anything, not even about me being pregnant yet. I don't want her worrying about me. She's got enough to cope with right now.'

*

Jack poured himself a drink and sat down on a bar stool. He felt furious with Alice. The fact that she was pregnant was bad enough, but the way she'd told him, so cocky in her attitude. Like she held all the cards now and he had no say. He wasn't standing for that. She either got rid of it or he'd knock the little bastard out of her. He'd had enough of being messed about with that bloody Susan girl a few years ago. Trying to pin the blame on him. He'd seen her and the kid off and he wasn't about to go down that road again.

He looked up as Sheila spoke. 'Sorry, gel. I was miles away.'

'I just asked where Alice had gone, that's all,' Sheila said.

'No idea. And I don't bloody care either.'

'Jack, you need to sort yourself out. I know you were angry when you came to see me after she told you about the baby, but it's not the end of the world. Have you ever thought that it might be good for you, being a dad?'

Jack glared at her over the top of his glass. 'How do you work that one out? I don't like bloody kids. I don't want to be a father. I couldn't have made it clearer.'

'Well, she didn't do it on her own. It's your fault as much as hers, for God's sake. You men need to start taking responsibility for your actions. It's always the bloody same. If I hear one more fella tell me his girl's gone and got herself pregnant, I swear I'll smack their bloody face. Now buck up. We've got work to do.'

Jack half-smiled. 'Sorry, gel. It just spoils everything.'

'Only if you let it. How do you think poor Alice feels? She's just started her new job and finding her feet with it. I'd be fuming if you knocked me up. Bloody good job I do something about it in advance, because I can't trust you to sort it.'

Jack put his glass down and patted her on the backside. 'And thanks for doing it, gel. I couldn't handle that one. Alice and I need to talk, without arguing. And I'll do my best to see her point of view, but I still don't want this kid.'

*

Alice stroked the dimpled chin of Millie's beautiful baby boy. He stared unblinkingly up at her with bright blue eyes. His tufts of blond hair, fair eyebrows and lashes were more Millie's colouring than Jimmy's ginger.

'He's gorgeous,' she said, feeling tears springing to her eyes. Would her own baby ever look into her eyes?

'Alice, are you okay?' Millie asked, concern in her voice.

'I'm fine. Just thinking about when I first held Cathy in the air raid shelter and how lucky you both are that Jimmy isn't abroad like Terry was. At least you get to share these first precious days together.'

'We are, very lucky. Jimmy is over the moon. He wanted a boy, but deep down it wouldn't have mattered what it was.'

'As long as it was healthy,' Sadie finished for her, looking at Alice, who was blinking hard.

'I'm just glad it's over,' Millie said, fidgeting to get comfortable. 'And I can't wait to have my stitches out tomorrow. So painful. Don't think I want any more.'

'Me and you both,' Sadie said, raising an eyebrow at Alice, who chewed her lip.

Millie stared at the pair. 'Something's going on. I can feel it in my water. Alice, are you…?'

Millie's question hung in the air as tears ran freely down Alice's cheeks. She nodded her head.

'I wasn't going to bother you while you're laid up, but yes. Ten weeks. I just found out.'

'Oh, congratulations,' Millie squealed. 'I bet Jack's thrilled to bits, like Jimmy was.'

'Er, well that's the problem,' Alice said quietly. 'He doesn't want it. Told me to get rid.'

Millie's eyes widened. 'No. Oh my God. Why would he say that?'

'Because he hates kids.'

Millie shook her head. 'Even so. I can't believe he would want that. I'm so sorry. I don't know what else to say. But you're not going to, are you?' She lowered her voice. 'Get rid of it, I mean.'

Alice shrugged and handed Paul over to Sadie for a cuddle. 'I've no idea what to do. I need to talk to him again, when he'll speak to me.'

'Well good luck,' Millie said and leant over to give Alice a hug. 'Please keep me up to date with what's happening.'

'I will.' But after holding little Paul and feeling a rush of love for a child that wasn't even her own, Alice knew she couldn't get rid of her baby, no matter what Jack thought, said or did.

*

Cuddling Millie's baby boy had decided Alice's own baby's fate. He, or she, was entitled to a life, no matter how it was conceived or what its selfish father thought. Alice had come home from visiting Millie in the hospital with an air of determination and her mind made up. As soon as Jack locked up the bar she was ready to talk to him. She made herself a mug of cocoa and sat with her feet up until she heard him coming up the stairs.

'Thought you'd be in bed, gel,' he said as he flopped down on the sofa next to her.

'I'm going soon, but we need to talk, Jack.'

'Oh aye? How was Millie by the way?'

'Millie's fine and so is baby Paul.'

He sighed and tapped his fingers on the arm of the sofa. 'Look, I'm sorry for what I said, Alice. It was a shock and after we'd decided no kids, it was the last thing I was expecting.'

She nodded. 'It was a shock for me too, but I want this baby, Jack. It deserves a chance.'

She offered him an ultimatum. He either stuck by her decision or he gave her back the money she'd handed over to run the Legion, and she and the kids would move out. 'If you don't agree then I will go and see a solicitor. I've still got the paperwork from the house sale, proof that I put the money in.'

She knew full well Jack would never be able to pay her back. Taking some control over the situation was giving her strength. Her confidence was growing as she looked at his stricken face. If he wanted to keep the Legion, he had no choice but to agree to her ultimatum.

'Okay, gel. Whatever you want. I'll do my best, but you'll have to bear with me at times.'

She half-smiled in reply. That would do for now. She'd give him this chance and see how things worked out. As long as he accepted the baby and kept his anger under control, she could cope.

Chapter Twenty-Two

August 1948

Alice eased her aching back onto the sofa and Cathy brought her a padded footstool from under the window. She swung her feet up onto it and wiggled her toes. Her ankles were swollen, her legs throbbed and her head was banging. She closed her eyes and let her mind drift over the last few weeks. No one could ever accuse her of not pulling her weight. She'd worked her final day at Lewis's today and it was longer than she should have continued working.

Her thoughts turned back to the surprise tea party thrown in her honour today. Mid-afternoon, Sadie had placed a blindfold over her eyes and, linking her arm through Alice's, had led her to the canteen.

'Surprise,' everyone had shouted as Sadie removed the blindfold. Alice was surrounded by half the staff from cosmetics, who all gave her a hug and kiss and wished her well for the future and the baby's birth.

'The rest of the girls will be down later,' Sadie said. 'They've had to take their breaks in shifts. Now sit down and I'll bring you some goodies over.' She was soon back with a tray of tea cups, sandwiches and sausage rolls. 'Get stuck in.'

Alice was surprised to find she was hungrier than she felt and wolfed down her share.

'Eating for two, I see,' Sadie teased, taking a sip from her cup.

After Alice had finished her food, the supervisor called her over to a table that was decorated with bunting and laden with packages. In the middle sat a wicker basket packed with baby toiletries and clothes. Alice's eyes filled with tears as she was presented with a large bouquet of colourful flowers and a card that had been signed by all the girls she worked with.

'Just to thank you for all the help you've given us over the last few months, Alice. Keeping up morale with all the work going on around us and also for staying on longer than you should have done. Now it's time to put your feet up and enjoy a good rest, until the little one arrives to keep you busy,' Dolores Redfern said.

Alice thanked everyone for their kindness and told them she was coming back to work as soon as she could. She smiled as a cheer went up and people came forward to give her a hug.

Marlene had made a return to work possible by kindly offering to look after the new baby as well as taking Cathy to school and picking her up afterwards. They'd agreed a small minding fee and Marlene seemed happy with it.

As Alice and Sadie sank back into their seats in the taxi that had been provided to get Alice and her presents home safely, she smiled wearily. 'Oh, thank goodness for that. Just Cathy's birthday party to sort out this weekend now and then I can take it easy.'

'Well, the kids are back at school next week so you can unwind and get ready for the birth,' Sadie had said. 'Enjoy the peace while you can.'

*

Cathy's seventh birthday party was held in the concert room and was packed with excited children from her class, who had all been invited to the event. They played noisy games of pass the parcel and musical chairs, with Brian taking charge of the music. Sheila and Polly had prepared the buffet of beef paste sarnies, sausage rolls, iced buns and pink blancmange.

They and Sadie waited on the children, insisting that Alice took it easy and sat with her feet up.

Sadie brought her a cup of tea and a bun over. 'They're having a lovely time,' she said. 'It's great that you've got this huge room so they can run wild, although Brian has pretty much got them under control and doing as they're told. He'd make a fabulous teacher, you know. Bet Jack's enjoying himself up there listening to every squeal and popped balloon.' She raised her eyes to the ceiling and grinned. Jack was in the flat upstairs, keeping out of the way.

Alice laughed. 'Well, he *was* invited to join us but he said he'd rather stick pins in his eyes than go to a kids' party.'

'Ah, Polly's bringing out the cake with the candles lit,' Sadie said. 'We'd best go over and sing "Happy Birthday" to Cathy.'

Alice pulled her daughter close as everyone joined in and wished Cathy a happy birthday. Cathy blew out the candles to cheers, her cheeks flushed and her eyes shining.

'Did you make a wish and have you enjoyed yourself?' Alice asked.

Cathy nodded. 'But I can't tell you because then it won't come true.' She ran off to join Debbie and another little girl, who were showing Gianni how to dance.

On leaving, with a slice of birthday cake wrapped in a paper napkin and clutching a balloon on a string, every child declared it was the best party they'd ever been to. Alice smiled as she waved them all goodbye and thought of Jack sitting upstairs, listening to the happy sound of children enjoying themselves. It wasn't his idea of fun, but to give him his due, he'd earlier set the room out ready, arranging the tables so there was plenty of room to play and run around. He'd pinned some streamers on the ceiling, and he and Brian had blown up the balloons. His efforts were better than nothing.

She and Jack were getting along better, and he was trying his best to be a part of the family. He'd got what he wanted and so had she. She could handle it, for now. Alice was pretty certain he was still sleeping with Sheila, but while he was, he was keeping his distance from her and considering how fat and whale-like she looked – and felt – she couldn't blame him.

Now everyone had gone home and Brian had walked Cathy round to Granny's with some cake, she was planning to take Sadie's advice and ask to look at the accounts, before Jack went down to the bar to work.

She took him some food upstairs and made a pot of tea. She sat down next to him and bided her time until he'd finished eating before broaching the subject.

'Now I've finished working,' she began. 'I can probably take over doing the books here. I've been used to doing the tilling up and paperwork in my department, so it can't be that much more difficult to do ours.'

Jack frowned and shook his head. 'You've enough to be thinking about with that babby coming. You don't want to be mithered with book-keeping on top of everything else.'

'But I'd like to be mithered, Jack,' she said. 'It's our business. I should know how we're doing financially.'

'Take it from me, we're doing fine. Anyway, the books are with the accountant right now, so you'll have to wait.'

Whether he was telling the truth or not, Alice had no idea, but she knew she'd be too busy to worry about them for the next few weeks. She'd ask again when she'd had the baby and had the time to study them properly. Brian would help her to understand them. Keeping things as normal as possible for the kids was all Alice wanted right now. Brian had one more year of college and then he could apply for university. Her job of making sure he had the best education was almost done. If she could make the marriage work for at least another few years, Cathy might get into grammar school. She was clever, like Brian, and deserved the best too. Alice would have to see how much she could stash away from her wages to help with the costs of uniforms and books, but she knew that Granny Lomax would help with all that if needed, especially for her only grandchild.

Alice, Brian and Cathy were going to Granny Lomax's bungalow on Sunday for tea, along with Millie and Paul and Sadie and Gianni. It was to be an extra little birthday party for Cathy. Alice saw little of Granny Lomax these days, but Brian and Cathy still did a regular visit on Sunday afternoons. Alice walked with them and then went to Millie's for an hour or two rather than trudge back to the Legion on her own. Besides which, she also didn't want to walk in on Jack with Sheila. Leave them to it. If Sheila was willing to meet his needs with nothing promised in return, then more fool her. There was no way Jack would divorce Alice to be with Sheila, even if he wanted to. Alice held all the strings financially, as she still had the proof the bond for the Legion had been paid for with her money, and she rejoiced in feeling like she had some sort of control over her life until she could afford to move on.

Back in July the National Health Service had been formed, making care in hospital and from the doctor's free. Having her baby wouldn't cost a penny so Jack couldn't even moan about that now. He seemed to have accepted his lot, but Alice still didn't trust him completely.

*

'More tea, Alice?' Granny Lomax hovered with the tea pot as Alice opened her eyes and smiled.

'Oh sorry, I think I dropped off for a minute,' she said as Granny refilled her empty cup.

'An hour, dear. You've had an hour. You must have needed it. You look wiped out. You shouldn't have stayed on at work for so long. It's time to be resting. Everybody is out in the garden on the lawn.'

'Are they? I'll join them in a minute.' Alice shuffled upright on the sofa. 'And I will rest now. I wanted to make sure I had everything I needed before I finished work. I've nothing left from Cathy's baby days. Didn't think I'd need them any more.'

Granny's answering smile didn't reach her eyes. 'Yes, I did wonder about that. I thought you and Jack wouldn't be bothering to extend the family. Seems I was wrong. I, er, I got the impression he doesn't really like children.'

Alice raised an eyebrow. 'He's changed his mind.' There was no way she could ever admit to Terry's mother how she came to be pregnant again.

'Really?' Granny's tone was disbelieving. 'Ah, here's Sadie. Hello, dear, are you coming in to keep Alice company? I'll just go outside and see if anyone else wants a refill.'

Sadie sat down beside Alice. 'How are you doing?'

Alice shook her head. 'I'm so very tired.'

Sadie nodded. 'I'm sure you are. Was she giving you the third degree then? I caught the tail end of the conversation.'

'Sort of. Just being nosy, I think. Said she thought that Jack didn't like kids.'

'You still haven't told her what happened that night?'

'God no. Only you and Millie know that. I'd be mortified if she knew. I'd never hear the end of how right she was about Jack and how I should never have married him. And she's dead right, I shouldn't have. But it's too late now. I'm trying to make the best of it all for the sake of my family. There's good days and there's bad days.'

'Well, we all have them,' Sadie said. 'But you know something, for all his faults; Jack wasn't too bad a few years ago. You really liked him and he liked you. So what went wrong? Do you think it's something in his past? Maybe he was treated badly in his childhood and that's what's made him like he is today? I mean, what he did to you was, and still is, inexcusable. And it's not something I would ever have thought him capable of. So what's changed him?'

Alice shrugged. 'Taking pills and drinking makes him paranoid. But he says he needs to do it, otherwise he can't deal with the pain in his foot. But it changes his personality. He's not nice when he's downed that mix.'

'Best just keeping out of his way when he has then. You're going to have to be careful over the next couple of weeks though now you've finished work. Try and keep on his best side.'

'I will do. I'll stay in bed until he's gone down to the bar. Marlene will come and pick Cathy up for the next few weeks.'

Sadie shook her head. 'What a way to live though, Alice. It's not right.'

'No, it's not, but it's all I've got for now,' Alice said with a wry smile.

*

'Alice, before you go, I need to speak to you in private,' Granny Lomax said after seeing the other guests out. 'I've asked Brian to take Cathy round to Marlene's house with a bit of birthday cake for her. I didn't want them to hear what I have to say.'

Alice, who had just been to the bathroom, waddled back into the lounge and lowered herself onto the sofa. 'Okay, what's up?'

'It's a bit delicate and I don't want to upset you, but I'm worried about Cathy, very worried, in fact.'

Alice frowned. 'Why? She's okay.'

'No, she's not. She's asked me if she can come and live here when you have the baby.'

'What?' Alice's jaw dropped. 'But why?'

Granny cleared her throat. 'Now, I don't think she's making this up, because she got all upset when she told me. Apparently Jack said that if she ever told tales about what happens at home he'd send her to the naughty girls' home and you and he would have more babies to replace her. She's never told tales to me, but I know she's been a nervous wreck for a while now, the bed-wetting episodes tell me that. And now of course you are having a baby, so she thinks that Jack is getting ready to take her away. That's why she got in first and asked if she could come here. Alice, it breaks my heart to think things have gone on that he doesn't want me to know about, things that are bad enough to threaten a little girl with. I didn't want to have to tell you this but I've been doing a bit of detective work after something came to light at the church coffee morning a good few months ago.'

Alice sat bolt upright and shook her head. 'People tittle-tattle all the time, you know what it's like round here for gossip. For all his faults Jack's my husband, and we're trying to do the best we can. I'll speak to Cathy and get to the bottom of what she told you.'

'He doesn't like children. I know that for a fact.'

'How… how do you know that? You don't really know anything about him.'

Granny laughed. 'I know more than you do, Alice. Has he ever told you about his daughter, Elizabeth, and her mother, Susan?' She sat back as Alice's face blanched. 'No, judging by the look on your face he hasn't. I met the young lady and her little girl some months ago. He gave them a hard time. Told her he didn't want the baby. Made her try and get rid of it and even threatened to push her down the stairs if she didn't. Susan was only just eighteen when the baby was born. He's had nothing to do with either of them since, and Elizabeth is about five now. Your husband is a nasty piece of work, Alice. He's not a nice man and it makes my blood run cold to think that my young granddaughter is living with him. And now you are about to give birth to his baby. I hope for you and the child's sake he's changed, but I won't hold my breath. I wanted to tell you this a while ago, but I know you'd have accused me of interfering. I didn't want to risk being cut out of Cathy's life entirely, but she's upset and so I've made it my business to say something now.'

*

Alice felt numb as she walked back to the Legion with Brian and Cathy in tow. She wondered if Jack had taken Susan by force, and whether there were others? And yet he had a certain charm that ladies seemed to like, including herself at one time. So why did he have a split personality? The customers all loved him; he got on with everyone he met. His staff respected him, as did Arnold and Winnie. Even Brian got along really well with him. Was it a medical condition that had gone undiagnosed all his life? And how could she get to the bottom of it without causing World War Three? She just felt so confused at the moment and knew she had to keep herself calm for her baby's sake. Now wasn't the time for confrontations; it would all have to wait, except for her concerns about Cathy. She'd need to deal with that as soon as she could.

Jack was asleep on the bed and Alice closed the door on him. He'd been sleeping on the sofa for ages now and complained of neck and back pain from not being comfortable, so after a busy lunchtime and afternoon in the club he was probably worn out, especially if his foot was hurting. Brian went into his bedroom to do some studying and Alice told Cathy to come and sit beside her on the sofa.

She held Cathy in her arms and spoke gently to her, telling her what Granny Lomax had said.

A worried look crossed Cathy's face and she whispered, 'Don't tell Jack I told tales, Mammy, please.'

'I won't, don't worry. But did Jack really say those things to you, or do you think he may have been joking so that you would be a good girl?' She still couldn't believe that he would threaten to take Cathy away.

Cathy shrugged. 'He said he would take me away to the naughty girls' home and have lots of babies with you instead of keeping me.' Tears ran down Cathy's face and Alice hugged her close.

'Well, let me tell you this,' Alice began. 'You're my little girl and Jack can't take you anywhere without my say-so, and I would never give you away. So I don't want you to worry about it any more. Okay?'

Cathy sniffed loudly and wiped her nose on her cardigan sleeve.

'You are going to be a big sister very soon and I need you here to help me look after the baby, so you're going nowhere, my girl.'

Cathy smiled through her tears. 'Will it be a brother or a sister? Debbie wants a sister but her mammy said she can want, she's not getting one. I'm lucky, aren't I, Mammy?'

'You are, sweetheart, we're all lucky, and we'll love our new baby, whether it's a brother or a sister, as much as I love you. Now go and get changed ready for bed and I'll read you a story.'

Cathy nodded. 'I like you reading me a story, but I don't like Jack doing it.'

'Well don't worry because he won't be doing it again. Either Brian or I will do that from now on. But listen, Cathy, we have to live here, so just keep out from under Jack's feet and try and be a good girl, okay?'

Cathy nodded and ran off to her bedroom. Satisfied that her daughter felt reassured, Alice dropped her head back on the sofa and sighed. The lounge door creaked open and Jack slid into the room. He came and sat down on the chair opposite her and half-smiled, as though unsure of his reception.

'Can I get you a cuppa, gel?'

Surprised, Alice nodded. 'If you don't mind.'

She watched as he limped out to the kitchen, coming back a few minutes later with a tray, two mugs of tea and a plate of lemon puff biscuits, Alice's favourites. He put the tray down on the coffee table in front of the sofa and sat down beside her.

He cleared his throat. 'Er, I've been thinking, we can't go on like this. I feel like I'm walking on eggshells all the time. I know what happened is all my fault and I am really sorry for what I did. I didn't know what I was doing, I swear. It's like someone else takes over my mind when I've had my pills and alcohol. Like I'm two people. I know that's not an excuse, Alice. But it's the way it is. After everything you've done for me I should be kissing the bloody ground you walk on. Instead I treat you badly and then knock you up. I'm so sorry, gel. Can you forgive me?'

Alice blew out her cheeks. She hadn't been expecting this. She had been ready to have a go at him for terrifying Cathy. Should she say something or just keep quiet and hope that her daughter felt reassured enough to put things behind her? Cathy might have misunderstood him, or Jack's threats might also be linked to his pill intake and drinking. Hopefully it would all get better now. Jack took her hand and she didn't pull away. Today he looked more like the Jack who had taken care of her when her mam died and supported her after Terry's death. He too had shadows showing under eyes that looked unhappy.

One half of her wanted to believe he was genuinely sorry while the other half wasn't quite sure. Did he care, or was he frightened of losing his home and his precious Legion? Would Sadie or Millie have given him another chance if they'd been in her place? They liked Jack after all, so maybe they would. Her confusion was growing out of all proportion now. Whatever she decided, she and Jack had no choice but to stay together and make it work.

'What about the baby?' she whispered.

'What about it? It's gonna be here in a few weeks. I'm just gonna have to get used to the idea that I'll be a dad, aren't I?'

Alice drew a deep breath and thought about the daughter he'd supposedly fathered and wanted nothing to do with. But this wasn't the time to bring that up. Perhaps the girl, Susan, had led him on, or the gossipmongers might even have made it all up.

She only had Granny Lomax's word on it. Whatever, she wasn't going to mention it just now. With a bit of effort on both sides they could make things work. It had to be better than her living alone with the children and deep down she still had feelings for the nicer side of him.

'Okay.' She nodded. 'But on one condition. Stop making a fool of me with Sheila. I'm not sharing you, Jack. People are starting to talk. Either she goes or I do, and I want my money back if that happens.'

He smiled. 'I fired her earlier. The last couple of nights I've done nothing but think about things. I wanted to make some changes. Sheila going was the first one, before I spoke to you. And I'm gonna get help, Alice, to get my head sorted out good and proper. I don't want to lose you, the kids or the business.'

Alice couldn't believe her ears and breathed a sigh of relief. 'You've really fired Sheila? Then yes, Jack. I need a peaceful life for the next few weeks at least. I'll help you to get yourself sorted out. Let's work together and look forward to a better future, for all of us.'

*

Alice slid out of bed as quietly as she could so as not to disturb Jack. She needed to use the toilet again. It was never-ending. It was the last Sunday of September, and the club had been so busy all weekend that she'd ended up helping Brian to collect the glasses, even though Jack had told her off for not resting. She was fed up, stuck upstairs, and had sneaked down once Cathy was asleep to see who was in the concert room. She'd spent some of the night talking to Marlene, Freddie and Sadie and had enjoyed their company. Sadie had told her that Luca wanted to see Gianni again before the end of the year, when he would be going back to Italy. She'd agreed he could come to the house, and as before, her family would be with her. Once a year wasn't a lot of time to spend with a parent, but as Sadie said, it was the best of a bad job and was better than nothing.

Sheila's replacement on the bar was a stocky, dark-haired girl with glasses called Valerie, who thankfully wasn't Jack's type. She wasn't as on the ball as Sheila, but she was learning fast and was perfectly pleasant to the customers, who seemed to like her.

At ten thirty Brian and Alice had come back upstairs and Brian had gone straight to bed as he had school in the morning. Alice's back was killing her and she'd run a bath and had a quick soak to ease her aching bones. She'd been asleep by the time Jack had come to bed, only to be woken by the demands of her flipping bladder again.

She waddled slowly towards the bathroom, gasping as a wave of pain shot around her middle. She doubled over and chewed her lip, recognising the pain as a contraction. Damn it, the baby wasn't due until next week, according to her midwife, but being conceived on New Year's Eve, it was probably bang on time. Her small case was packed and stood by the bedroom door in readiness. She used the toilet, put some soap, talc and her toothbrush in a small wash bag and was making her way back to the bedroom to wake up Jack when her waters burst and splashed onto her bare feet and the varnished floorboards in the hall, missing the rug by inches.

'Oh no!' She doubled over again as another pain shot through her. 'Jack,' she called, but there was no response. She called again and Brian came out of his bedroom.

'Alice, what's up?'

'The baby's coming and I can't get Jack's attention. Try and wake him up for me and then we need to phone for an ambulance. The number is fastened up on the kitchen cupboard. Grab a towel out of the bathroom and I'll sit on this chair out here, but I don't want to wet it.'

Brian ran into the bathroom and placed a folded towel on the hall chair and Alice gingerly lowered herself onto it. He dashed into the bedroom and came back out shaking his head.

'He's out cold. Must have been drinking after we left him downstairs.'

Alice sighed. That was all she needed. Jack had been making an effort to cut down on his drinking, just in case this sort of scenario presented itself. Typical that he'd decided to have a few on the one night she needed him.

'Never mind,' she said. 'Leave him be. He'll be no use to me now anyway like that. Run down and phone for the ambulance and I'll go with them. You can stay here and look after Cathy for me. Get her up for school and help her with her breakfast and uniform. Marlene will pick her up. Let's hope Jack is awake by then. I'll ask the hospital to ring here as soon as there's any news. And don't worry about me,' she said, looking at Brian's anxious face. 'I've done it before and this time there'll be no air raid warnings to contend with.'

*

Sandra Mary Dawson arrived kicking and screaming at six am on Monday morning, September 27th. Her exhausted mother gave a sigh of relief as both baby and afterbirth were delivered with ease. No emergency surgery for this one like there'd been after Cathy's birth, when the placenta had to be removed surgically at the hospital.

'She's got a good pair of lungs,' the midwife said, wrapping the screaming baby in a nappy and slipping the hook of the scales through the pointed ends. Sandra swung in the air, quieter now as the midwife stared at the dial. 'Seven pounds and three ounces. A good weight. Right, young lady, a quick cuddle from your mum and then we'll get her cleaned up while you have a little nap in the nursery.' She wrapped the baby in a white sheet and handed her to Alice.

Alice stared down at the frowning little face that studied her intently and smiled, feeling that familiar rush of love she'd had for Cathy and for Millie's baby boy when she held him. Relief washed over her. Sandra's conception thankfully didn't overshadow her feelings as she'd worried it might do. She looked nothing like Cathy did at birth. Sandra had dark hair and the same button nose, but that was the only real resemblance. With her chubby fists pushed into each cheek, her eyes were blue like Jack's, her rosebud lips the same shape as his and her eyebrows as dark as her hair, just like his. The name Sandra for a girl had been agreed by the pair of them just the other night, and Mary was Jack's late mother's name. Alice traced her finger around the tiny dimple in her chin and Sandra opened her mouth, seeking out the finger. Her gums clamped around it and she sucked hard, looking puzzled when nothing came out. Alice marvelled at how babies knew exactly what to do from the minute they arrived.

'I think she's hungry,' she said to the midwife. 'Shall I try and feed her? And will you ring my home and let my husband know he's got a daughter, please?' She hoped he'd be pleased, or at least try to seem pleased that he was. The thoughts of his rejected daughter popped briefly into her mind, but she quickly let them go. If the midwife rang now, Brian and Cathy would still be there, and maybe Jack could pop in for afternoon visiting to see her.

*

Alice opened her eyes as someone dropped a kiss on her forehead. Jack was standing awkwardly by the bed with a bunch of red roses.

'Hello,' she croaked, her mouth dry. She couldn't believe it was two o'clock already. She'd slept since giving birth, but she must have needed it. She shuffled up the bed and Jack moved to help her, putting the roses down on the bedside trolley.

'How you doing, gel?' he asked, taking her hand and squeezing it gently. He looked around the room. 'Where is it then?'

'Sandra is in the nursery, while I had a rest,' Alice replied, trying not to feel annoyed that he'd called their new daughter 'it'. He was here, he wasn't drunk or even smelling of whisky and he'd brought her roses for the first time ever. It was a good start. 'And I'm doing fine, thanks.'

'Bit of a shock when I woke up,' he began. 'I wish I'd known, but Brian couldn't wake me. Still, there's not a lot I could have done; it's women's work, giving birth.'

Alice smiled. 'It is.' She rang the bell at the side of her bed and a young nurse appeared, neat in her uniform. Alice's thoughts momentarily turned to Cathy and how one day she might be working as a nurse here at Clatterbridge Hospital, fingers crossed. 'Could we have our daughter, please?' Alice asked.

'Of course, Mrs Dawson. I'll go and get her.' She was back within seconds, clutching a little shawl-wrapped bundle. Jack had sat himself down on the armchair pulled up close to the bed and the look of panic on his face as the baby was placed in his arms made Alice smile.

'Just relax, Jack,' she said as the nurse hurried out of the room to answer a buzzer.

He looked up and then back down at the baby, who was staring at him with her big blue eyes wide open. 'She's not bad-looking,' he said. 'I can see me mam in her. Isn't that funny? Perhaps because she's got no teeth!'

'Can you? That's nice, but I think she looks like you,' Alice said, smiling.

'Do you? Poor little bugger,' he quipped. 'I have never before in my life held a baby,' he went on. 'This is the first time. And it feels quite nice.'

Alice breathed a sigh of relief. There was no way she was expecting Jack to win a father-of-the-year competition any time soon, but this was better than she'd hoped for. He looked quite relaxed and happy.

'Thanks, gel, for giving me a lovely kiddie,' he said. 'I promise I'll try and do my best for all of us. We're a proper family now. A daughter each, and our Brian, who's like a son to me. That'll do me.'

'I think we'll be okay, Jack, don't you?' Alice said as he nodded, not taking his eyes off his new daughter's face.

'We will, gel, we will.'

A Letter from Pam

I want to say a huge thank you for choosing to read *The Shop Girls of Lark Lane*. If you did enjoy it, and want to keep up to date with all my latest releases, just sign up at the following link. Your email address will never be shared and you can unsubscribe at any time.

www.bookouture.com/pam-howes

To my loyal band of regular readers who bought and reviewed *The Factory Girls of Lark Lane*, thank you for waiting patiently for the second in the series. I hope you'll enjoy catching up with Alice, Sadie and Millie. Your support is most welcome and very much appreciated. As always a big thank you to Beverley Ann Hopper and the Admins and members of her FB group Book Lovers, and Deryl Easton and the members of her FB group The NotRights. Love you all for the support you show me.

A huge thank you to team Bookouture, especially my lovely editor Abi for your support and guidance and always being there, you're the best, and thanks also to the rest of the fabulous editorial team.

And last, but most definitely not least, thank you to our wonderful media girls, Kim Nash and Noelle Holten, for everything you do for us. And thanks also to the gang in the Bookouture Authors' Lounge for always being there. As always, I'm so proud to be one of you.

I hope you loved *The Shop Girls of Lark Lane* and if you did I would be very grateful if you could write a review. I'd love to hear what you think, and it makes such a difference helping new readers to discover one of my books for the first time.

I love hearing from my readers – you can get in touch on my Facebook page, through Twitter, Goodreads or my website.

Thanks,
Pam Howes

 Pam Howes Books

@PamHowes1

Acknowledgements

As always, my man, daughters, son-in-law, grandchildren and their partners. Thank you for your support. I love you all very much. Xxx

Thanks once again to my lovely 60's Chicks friends for their friendship and support. And a big thanks to my friends and beta readers, Brenda Thomasson and Julie Simpson, whose feedback I welcome always.

Thank you once more to the band of awesome bloggers and reviewers who have given me such wonderful support for my Mersey Trilogy and again with the first two books in the Lark Lane series. It's truly appreciated and without you all an author's life would be a difficult one.

Lightning Source UK Ltd.
Milton Keynes UK
UKHW020617250119
336147UK00015B/302/P